MERCENARY

By the same author

Catalyst

MERCENARY

Paul Bennett

ROBERT HALE · LONDON

© Paul Bennett 2010
First published in Great Britain 2010

ISBN 978-0-7090-9153-0

Robert Hale Limited
Clerkenwell House
Clerkenwell Green
London EC1R 0HT

www.halebooks.com

2 4 6 8 10 9 7 5 3 1

Typeset in 11/14¼pt Sabon
by Derek Doyle & Associates, Shaw Heath
Printed in Great Britain by the MPG Books Group, Bodmin and King's Lynn

In roulette, because of the presence of a double zero, the bank has an advantage of 5.26%. The bets that pay off at higher odds have lower maximum limits to prevent the bank being hurt too badly in one spin. It's safer and easier for the bank to grind out its profits over time than to risk big wins and losses in one spin.'

(Adapted from) *The New Complete Hoyle*

In 1992, ten bank officials were assassinated by the European-established Moscow mafias for refusing to legitimize through their banks the criminal profits from phoney shell companies: forty of the Russian capital's 260 banks are controlled by organized crime.

PROLOGUE

Mbele Diamond Mine, Lunda Norte, Angola. Five years ago.

'Where are the diamonds?' the Russian said.

He was short and stocky, his upper body overly developed in relation to his legs and producing a simian appearance. His round face was topped by a mop of hair the colour of steel and dominated by cold grey eyes emphasized by a long scar pointing like an arrow from the corner of his mouth to just below his left eye. Like his tracksuited underlings, he looked like a common hood; if indeed they were mercenaries, then they were in the category of rabid dogs of war rather than that of soldiers of fortune. He repeated the question. His voice, heavily accented and with the typical deep and morose tone of a Muscovite, reverberated off the wooden walls of the hut.

Four men – a Texan, a South African, a Pole and a Jamaican – were hanging like pigs on a spit, their hands and feet tied around the beams supporting the low roof, their naked bodies, dotted with cigarette burns, dangling down towards the concrete floor. None of the men spoke. They had heard the question many times before and each time had given the only answer possible. 'What diamonds?'

The hut was quiet, the only sounds were the controlled breathing of the torturers, the low groans of the four prisoners, the drone of indecisive flies flitting from wound to wound and the soft plop of blood dripping from the leg of the Jamaican who had been hamstrung with a switchblade for spitting in the eye of the

Russian. The air was thick with the acrid smoke from black-tobacco cigarettes and the unmistakable odour of fear, sweat and burnt flesh.

The Russian sighed, waved his hand towards the flat iron sitting on top of the cast-iron stove and then pointed at the South African. An underling gave a twisted smile, picked up the iron, walked quickly across the room to preserve the heat and pressed it hard against the back of the tall blond man.

There was a long wailing scream. It filled the hut and travelled out in a seismic shock wave, causing the two guards outside the door to jump and the remainder of the invading force in the mess hall at the other end of the compound to pause momentarily in the lifting of beer bottles to lips.

Time seemed to pass in slow motion. Still the iron was held in place. Flesh sizzled, causing bile to rise in the throats of the other prisoners.

The South African, mercifully, lost consciousness.

'Now, I ask you again,' the Russian said to the other three, 'where are the diamonds?'

'If we knew,' the Texan drawled, his teeth gritted against the throbbing pain from the soles of his feet and his genitals where they had been repeatedly beaten by a thick flat stick, 'don't you think we would have told you by now?'

'Then where is Gordini?' the Russian said, changing tack. 'Where is your leader?'

'Dead under a bush somewhere,' the Pole grunted. 'Your men shot him when they attacked us. He was hit five times. Maybe more.'

'Yet he still managed to get away.' The Russian's thick eyebrows turned down in thought. 'Does Gordini have the diamonds?'

'Jesus Christ!' the Texan shouted. 'How many times do we have to tell you? We don't know nothing about no diamonds.'

The Russian held out a hand, pointing his index finger at the pile of Kalashnikovs leaning against the wall and snapping two fingers. One of the guns was snatched up and pressed into his hand. He turned it round and drove the butt hard into the Texan's ribs. The sharp crack was as audible as it was painful.

'The manager of the mine says otherwise,' the Russian said. 'Or, should I say, said otherwise. Five thousand carats missing from the safe, he told me. And I believe him. He was not as stubborn nor as strong as you. He squealed like a pig at the end.' He gave a deep bellowing laugh and shrugged his shoulders. 'If there are no diamonds, then I lose nothing by shooting you all. Think about that.'

He turned to his henchmen.

'I grow impatient,' he said. 'I am going to the mess hall for a drink. Fetch me when one of them decides to speak. Shoot them one by one. Start with the filthy Pole.'

He strode from the hut.

Eight men unenthusiastically picked up their Kalashnikov AKMs and watched him go. A debate ensued about whether they should all fire together or draw lots to select one of their number. After smoking a cigarette, they chose the former. The Pole made an effort to control his bowels and bladder – at this range, a volley of the steel-cored bullets would cut him in half. Eight pairs of eyes turned towards the Pole, raised their guns and took aim.

'Wait,' the Pole said quickly in Russian, 'I'll tell you where Gordini is.'

They laughed scornfully. They should have realized the Pole would be the first to break.

'Gordini is—' the Pole began.

'Behind you,' came a voice.

Gordini stood in the doorway. His shirt was covered in blood – most, but not all, of it his own. His left arm hung down uselessly, his right held a Uzi with a silencer. Aiming at bellies rather than chests so as not to hit any of his comrades, he swung the gun from left to right, spraying bullets all the time. Bodies fell to the floor, its surface quickly turning red as separate streams of blood coalesced first into rivers and then into a flood plain.

Gordini stepped over to his friends, kicking guns out of the reach of those who were still breathing as he made slow progress across the hut. Placing the Uzi on the floor, he took a long knife from the utility belt around his waist, sliced through the ropes holding the Texan's feet and, when they were safely on the floor, cut the bonds around the wrists. Together they freed the Pole, then the Jamaican and, lastly, the semi-conscious South African.

The four men found their clothes and dressed hurriedly, the Texan wincing from the stabbing pain from his ribs, the South African needing help and groaning as the rough material of his shirt touched his raw back. While they were doing this, Gordini issued orders in a low voice. He detailed the Jamaican and South African to the supply truck – they could lie on their bellies in the back and guard their rear. The Texan was firstly to hide the bodies of the two guards who had been on duty outside and then to collect passports, visas and as much of their kit as he could carry. The Pole was to find medical supplies and water, rations too, if possible, but they could live without food for a while. The four men gathered up the Kalashnikovs and magazines of spare ammunition.

'What about the others?' the Texan asked.

'There are no others,' Gordini said. 'All twenty are dead. It's just us five left out of the whole outfit.'

The Pole swore in his native language. 'Russians!' he said, spitting on the floor. 'What did we ever do to them?'

Gordini shrugged, his eyes narrowing from the resulting pain in his left shoulder. He didn't know whether the Pole's words were a comment on their current situation, or something that went back into the tragic history of his homeland. Now wasn't the time to find out which.

'On the count of three,' Gordini said, 'all fire one round.'

The loud co-ordinated gunfire was heard in the mess hall. One down, three to go, thought the Russian.

'OK,' Gordini said. 'From now on, not a sound. Meet me at the truck in five minutes.'

It was a sorry group that staggered and limped out of the hut to their respective destinations in the compound. Gordini headed for the armoury. He found some smoke grenades and stuffed as many as he could into the deep pockets of his combat trousers. Into the utility belt he slipped three spare magazines for the Uzi. He would have liked to have taken the Browning M2 heavy machine-gun to set up in the back of the truck, but he only had one useful arm and the silenced Uzi had to take priority – the Russian might have posted more guards by now.

From the armoury Gordini ran across the compound, keeping low to the ground. He stopped at the first of the fleet of jeeps the Russians had arrived in, lifted the hood and propped it open. With his knife he cut the lead that ran to the distributor cap. One by one he immobilized the other vehicles.

When he finally made it across the compound to the truck, Gordini passed the smoke grenades to the Jamaican and the South African. He wished them good luck and ran to the cab. The Texan was in the driving seat, taking short breaths and waiting for the order to start the ignition. The Pole took Gordini's Uzi and slid across the bench seat as he climbed awkwardly inside.

'Let's go,' Gordini said.

The truck's diesel engine coughed and spluttered geriatrically in the damp night air before eventually kicking into life. As they pulled away, the door of the mess hall opened. Armed men started to pour out. The Jamaican and the South African lobbed smoke grenades and immediately began firing. They didn't bother aiming: the effective range of the Kalashnikov may technically be 300 metres, but over forty it was pot luck if and what you hit. Added to that, the Texan was zigzagging the truck violently in an evasive manoeuvre to avoid the hail of bullets coming blindly through the thick blue smoke.

They smashed through the gates of the compound and headed along the dirt track from the mine. The Texan drove fast, avoiding potholes as best he could. Each time he hit one there was a chorus of painful groans as wounds were jolted against the hard surfaces of the truck. After three miles they reached the road that ran westward towards Malanje.

Gordini lifted the canvas flap that separated the cab from the back of the truck.

'What's happening back there?' he shouted, against the noise of the straining engine.

'Nothing,' the South African shouted back. 'No pursuit.'

'Then we have some breathing space,' Gordini said. 'Can you start patching us up?' he said to the Pole.

The Pole dug into his bergan and assembled a collection of different sized and shaped dressings, antiseptic, a roll of bandage for the Texan's ribs and a rubber tourniquet for the Jamaican's leg. 'Morphine, anyone?' he asked.

'Not yet,' said Gordini. 'We need to keep our wits about us. Adrenaline will numb the pain for a while. After that, try to hang on as best you can, lads.'

The Pole passed the tourniquet into the back of the truck and started to cut away at Gordini's jacket. 'This is not good,' he said, examining the wounds that had torn most of the left shoulder to pieces.

'Tell me something I don't know.'

'This is going to hurt,' the Pole said, taking the top off the plastic bottle of antiseptic.

'That's something I don't know?' Gordini gritted his teeth. 'What the hell was this all about?' he said. 'One moment we're celebrating the end of this lousy contract because the mine has been taken over, and – Jesus Christ!' the yellow liquid penetrated into the wounds with all the subtlety of a red-hot poker. '. . . And the next a bunch of Russians are spoiling our party by gunning down everyone in sight.'

He slumped back into the seat, breathing hard.

'And,' the Texan said, 'their leader kept asking us about diamonds missing from the safe. Five thousand carats.'

A whistle escaped from Gordini's lips. 'That's around two and a half million dollars. Three million, maybe, if they're the best quality.'

He fell silent.

'What are you thinking?' the Jamaican called from the back.

'Three things,' Gordini said. 'One, if there are three million dollars' worth of diamonds missing and they think we took them, which to them is the logical explanation, then they'll come looking for us. They'll hunt us down, sure as hell.'

'Shit,' said the Texan.

'Two follows from one,' Gordini said. 'It's time we got out of this damned country. Head for Zaire.'

'Out of the frying pan and into the fire,' the Texan said glumly.

Gordini shrugged. 'Quicker than going to the Congo.'

'Rock and a hard place,' the Texan said more glumly.

'Who cares?' the Pole asked. 'We need proper medical attention and blood. Our best chance is the UN aid station just over the border.' He turned to Gordini. 'You said there were three things. What's the third?

'It's time we got out of this damned business.'

1

The island of St Jude, Caribbean. The present.

My name is Johnny Silver. That or thereabouts. Not the best name in the world – too many mental pictures of one-legged pirates with parrots perched on their shoulders – but it suits its purpose. It has that Hispaniola ring about it that is appropriate to where I live and what I now do, and, misleadingly, is unlikely to be a name anyone in their right mind would choose of their own free will.

Paradise is a very personal concept. But St Jude, with its turquoise waters, iridescent green coral reefs and long-fringed palm trees rising at forty-five degrees over the platinum sand, would have coincided with most people's definition. My priority was haven rather than heaven, and in that respect St Jude was as near perfect as you could get. It is a tiny island, has one very expensive and very exclusive hotel, no airport, and is a two-hour boat trip from the nearest decent-sized centre of population. It is quiet, very quiet. And that is exactly how I like it. Just enough visitors to scratch a living from the beach bar, and little chance I would know any of them. Or, more to the point, that they would know me.

Just another day in paradise. That's how it started, Phil Collins fashion, but not how it ended – that was more Chris Rea, Road to Hell. It was a quarter to eleven on a typically hot sunny day. Bull Adams and I had completed our punishing daily routine of thirty minutes jogging along the beach and an hour-long swim back and were now sitting in cane chairs in the shade of the bar, sipping ice-cold beers and recuperating. I was in front of my laptop putting the finishing touches to my column of the Cyclops 'hot share tips of the week' page on *The Wall Street Journal* Internet site, Bull had his legs propped up on a chair and was gazing at his boat bobbing about lazily beside the jetty. There was the sweet smell of bougainvillaea in the air. All seemed right with the world. Then we heard the shouts.

Even from a distance the group looked like trouble. Six men doing all they could, and more, to impress six young women. I narrowed my eyes and assessed their erratic progress along the beach. The women were huddled together, walking with swaying hips: the men were circling around them, engaged in a mock free-for-all fight among themselves, legs sweeping and arms slicing through the air in a series of badly executed karate moves copied from some second-rate TV series or dubbed Hong Kong movie. They were emitting a mixture of battle cries and high-pitched oriental shrieks designed to strike fear in the hearts of ordinary mortals. I gave a small sigh and decided to reserve judgement – no one knew better than I that it was often impossible to tell the good guys from the bad. Nevertheless, I moved my chair slightly to one side, so that I could check the article on the screen and still see the men at the same time. Reserving judgement is one thing; taking risks is an entirely different matter.

'What do you reckon?' Bull said.

'It's obvious,' I said. 'The women will want to spend the day fishing on your boat while the men drink themselves insensible at my bar.'

'Yeah,' he said, nodding his shaven head. 'And what time does the Tequila Fairy arrive?'

Bull stood up. He was six foot six, his body heavily muscled and black as night. As he took a short step into the sun his skin seemed to glisten. There was a chorus of girlish giggles from the women and an ominous jealous silence from the men. Bull ignored both and walked across to his boat, his right leg dragging in the sand. Each month it dragged a fraction less, but, like my shoulder, it would never recover fully.

The group was twenty yards away by now. There was to be a wedding at the hotel tomorrow – it's hard to keep anything secret on a small island – so I guessed that two of the number were the lucky bride and groom and the rest were along for the ride. The men, who had broken off from their Ninja dance and moved protectively closer to the girls, were dressed in bathing trunks that reached past their bony knees, and multicoloured short-sleeved shirts that only served to emphasize the whiteness of their skin. From their pallor, demeanour and what would definitely be a gargantuan final bill from the hotel, I marked them down as new-breed, barrow-boy traders in options, futures or derivatives, driven by money and adrenaline in equal proportions – a familiar and dangerous mixture. The women – three blondes, two brunettes and one with dark hair, all just about wearing skimpy bikinis in eye-dazzling colours, designer sunglasses perched on their heads, gold chains around ankles, lips glossed like freshly picked, dew-covered strawberries – well, I hardly noticed them. They formed a single file to walk up the narrow wooden jetty. There followed a short conversation and an exchange of money. The men would be after marlin and Bull could take them to the exact point in the sea where they ran thickest and fastest. If he wanted to. But that would depend on his opinion of their ability to be discreet – too much word-of-mouth recommendation can have its drawbacks.

They walked back down the jetty, the women still wiggling their hips, the men in that bouncy gait and nodding-head style that is supposed to signal street cred, but looks, to an impartial observer like myself, more like a bad impression of a myopic wading bird checking the shallows for the next meal. They headed in my direction, intending to get a few drinks inside them while Bull was making the necessary preparations. Just as long as they didn't mind waiting.

As they approached I could see the men sizing up the bar – wooden shack, tall black-plastic stools at the counter, a few cane tables and chairs under an off-white canopy, the hand-painted sign saying 'Johnny Silver: Proprietor' in faded red letters – and wondering how many days', even hours', salary it would take to buy the lot.

Their leader, a man of around twenty-five years with a footballer's severely cropped hair and the beginnings of a beer belly, leaned over the bar.

'Six beers and six daiquiris,' he said in an East London accent.

Please would have been nice. And I could have done without the accompanying 'make it snappy, buster' click of the fingers, too.

'We open in just five minutes, gentlemen and ladies,' I said, pointing at the clock on the wall and smiling at him. I turned back to the screen of the laptop. 'Take a seat, please. Make yourselves comfortable. I'll bring your drinks over.'

He looked at me in exactly the same way he had sized up the bar. Took in my advanced age (over the hill at thirty-five), my long black hair, three days' growth of beard, bronzed skin, tattered, grey cotton T-shirt and sun-bleached denim jeans cut off above the knees. Couldn't hide the expression that told me he thought I was some kind of alien creature with no right to be on the same planet as him.

'Let's get this straight, mister,' he said. 'Just so as there's no misunderstanding, you know? We want six beers and six daiquiris, and we want them now.'

'You're on holiday, friend – be mellow, chill out for a while, take in the view, breathe in the cool fresh air, listen to the sound of the waves rippling over the sand and the beating wings of the humming birds as they sip nectar. I'll be with you in five minutes.'

I turned away from him and started on the last few paragraphs, hoping that he would cool down.

Maybe he would have done, if it hadn't been for the presence of the women. And if one of the blondes hadn't whimpered, 'I want my daiquiri, Wayne.'

Wayne leaned further over the bar.

'Rippling bloody waves! Humming bloody birds! Sod 'em. Who are *you* to tell *me* what to do?' he shouted.

'The name's on the sign, friend,' I said.

'Johnny Silver?' he said.

I thought I saw his lips move in time with the syllables.

'I suppose,' he grinned at his friends, 'he's one of the Silver family. He don't need our money, lads, because he's an eccentric millionaire.' He gave a mocking laugh. 'Is that right, Johnny Silver? Are you a merchant banker.'

The laughter spread among the group. One of the men made a gesture with his thumb and index finger, just in case someone had missed the joke. Two of the women blushed, three tittered and the daiquiri-thirsting blonde just stood there stone-faced, tapping one foot impatiently.

'Hardly seems likely,' I said, almost finished now despite the distractions. 'Just take a look around you. Are these the trappings of a banker?'

He walked across to one of the tables. Picked up a chair. Smashed it down on the table, breaking both to pieces and bringing forth gasps of surprise from the women and grunts of approval from the men.

'No,' he said. 'Don't think so. Not a banker. You're just a jerk.'

'You took the words right out of my mouth,' I said, logging off with a sense of self-satisfaction. I rubbed my left shoulder to increase the blood circulation, stood up slowly, gave an exaggerated sigh and shook my head reprovingly. 'That will be fifty bucks for the furniture.'

From the pocket of his shorts he took out a wad of money the thickness of *Webster's Dictionary*, peeled off a fifty-dollar bill, crumpled it up into a ball and tossed it down on the sand.

'If you want it, come and get it,' he challenged.

The men formed a horseshoe around the money, the intentional gap an invitation to step inside so that they could close ranks and surround me. The women retreated to one of the unbroken tables to take up ringside seats for the spectacle: the blonde gave Wayne's arm an encouraging squeeze as she drifted languidly past.

I came out from the shade of the bar and stood on the edge of the beach letting my eyes grow accustomed to the brightness of the sun. I saw Bull climb off his boat. So did Wayne.

'It ain't your fight,' he shouted. 'You keep out of this, gimpy.'

How to win friends and influence people!

I nodded at Bull. He sat down on the jetty, leaned back against a bollard, lit a cigarette and settled himself down to watch.

'Let me give you some advice,' I said. 'Pick up the money, give it to me, apologize nicely and shake my hand. I'll get you your beers and daiquiris and we can all have a relaxing drink together. That way no one gets hurt.'

The men made clucking noises and waggled their elbows up and down.

'There's six of us and only one of you,' Wayne said. 'We're relaxed already, Johnny Silver.'

'You got it wrong, my friend. There's one of me and only six of you. I'll ask you one last time. Pick up the money.'

Wayne looked at me hesitatingly. OK, I was taller, leaner and fitter than he had expected from my appearance seated at the chair in the shadows, hunched over the laptop. But he didn't want to back down in front of his friends, particularly the women and especially the Miss Daiquiri contestant. And, he was probably thinking, the odds were still heavily stacked in his favour.

Me, I don't gamble – it's one rule I haven't broken for years.

He shook his head at me and pointed at the fifty-dollar bill.

I closed my eyes and, while giving an exaggerated sigh, concentrated on producing a mental picture of the scene and its players. When focused, I opened my eyes and walked towards them.

They prepared themselves, legs apart and hands waving in the air. In their minds they were high and mighty samurai warriors about to teach a revolting peasant a lesson he would never forget. In reality. . . .

I singled out one of them, hoping that having dealt with him the others would quickly become disheartened. Took three steps so that I was inside the circle and a fourth that turned into a rapid sweeping movement with my left leg. The heel of my bare foot connected with the kneecap of the chosen victim. He went down on the sand, clutching his knee and whimpering loudly.

An arm flashed towards me, fingers rigid for a karate chop. I spun around, caught hold of the wrist with both my hands, made a fulcrum of my right shoulder, turned and simultaneously knocked the legs of my assailant from under him. He landed on top of his friend, who whimpered some more.

Someone grabbed my T-shirt from behind. I sent my elbow forcefully backwards, felt flabby flesh offer little resistance and heard an expletive uttered in an escape of breath. Another body sank to the sand, its hand still clamped on my T-shirt and ripping it off as he fell.

I turned around to face the remaining three. There was a collective catching of breath. They were staring wide-eyed at my left shoulder. Or, more accurately, at the collection of old star-shaped scars where the bullets had entered for split seconds before their momentum had carried them out the other side. If Russians could shoot straight, they wouldn't need Kalashnikovs. And I wouldn't be here to tell the tale, of course.

The ringleader gave a sheepish grin and nodded submissively at me. He bent down towards the money. Stretched out his fingers. And flung a handful of sand in my face.

It was one of the oldest tricks in the book. I should never have fallen for it. Being out of practice hadn't helped, but the big mistake had been in underestimating the opposition.

Eyes closed, I recalled the scene and backed away from where I pictured the danger might come. Nothing happened. Then I heard the sound of a bottle breaking. Forcing my stinging eyes into slits, I got a blurred watery glimpse of two men holding chair legs and Wayne wielding a broken bottle. A chair leg came down towards my neck. I caught the descending arm, whipped it down and then up again in a 360° sweep, and flipped the man over into a forward somersault.

The bottle was stabbed towards my face. I ducked, sent a straight left into Wayne's stomach. His body arched, but not as much as I had hoped. I clasped my fingers together and followed swiftly with a double-handed blow up into his groin. He went flying backwards, landed flat on the sand and let out a long painful wail. The last man dropped his chair leg, backed away and held his hands in the air.

It was over.

Or should have been. But I hadn't allowed for the stone-faced blonde. How many mistakes can you make in one day?

She was on me in a flash, a tigress leaping at her prey. Her lips were curled into a snarl, her teeth bared, her long fingernails stretching out to rake at my face.

I grabbed her hands and forced them back. She bit my arm, tearing out a strip of flesh. I spun her around, pinning her arms across her chest and against my body, picked her up and carried her to the jetty, her legs kicking helplessly in the air. At the end of the jetty I threw her in the water.

Bull gave a deep resonating laugh.

'Thanks for your help,' I said, turning back towards him.

'One of me and only six of you!' He smiled and shook his head. 'You really must stop watching those John Wayne films. Anyway, I knew you could do it, man. And you only had to ask. I would have taken care of the blonde, no problem.' He walked across to where the women were tending to the untidy pile of men spread-eagled on the sand. 'Well, who's for some marlin then?'

They didn't reply. Not in words as such. Plenty of moans and groans, though.

Bull took these as a negative response.

'Maybe tomorrow,' he said.

'It's the wedding tomorrow,' the dark-haired girl said.

'Which one is the lucky bridegroom?' I asked.

A fickle finger of fate pointed to Wayne. He was coiled up in the foetal position, holding his testicles tenderly.

'Wouldn't you just know it?' I said to Bull.

'Life can be a bitch,' he said philosophically.

'And the even luckier bride?' I asked the dark-haired girl.

The finger pointed to the blonde, her hair hanging in rats' tails as she emerged from the water.

'Gets bitchier by the minute,' said Bull.

The men started to drag themselves up from the sand. Three of the women took hold of the bridegroom and dragged him as near upright as was possible. Bull walked up and stuffed the wad of money for the fishing trip back into Wayne's shirt pocket. Slowly, the group moved off in the direction of the hotel. Funny, but there was no wiggling of hips or bounce in their walk now.

Bull and I stood there watching the retreat.

'Shoulder held up, then?' he said.

I nodded.

'And you finished checking the Cyclops column?'

I nodded again.

'Two good things in one day,' he said. 'Beers must be on the house.'

From a distance there came the sound of whirring rotor blades. A helicopter approached and circled above us. It moved a little along the beach and descended in a storm cloud of whirling sand.

'Shit,' said Bull, sprinting back to his boat as fast as his legs would carry him.

I ran to the bar. Felt around under the top of the counter. Found the two strips of sticking plaster. Tore them away and grabbed hold of the Browning High Power pistol.

Bull emerged from the depths of his cabin with a pump action shotgun in his hand.

It was the moment we had dreaded for five long years.

They had finally found us.

Running isn't always the answer to a problem.

2

The Netherlands. Ten years ago.

If you are dying, then this was as good a place as any. Better than some anonymous battlefield in a country few have heard of and even fewer care about.

The hospital was set in a large secluded wooded area ten miles south of Amsterdam, equidistant between the A4 and A2 motorways and, thus, conveniently placed for the city and Schipol Airport. It was modern, bright and clean, and equipped with all the facilities that private patients either need or simply demand. The staff were friendly, concerned and professional, and not only spoke more correct English than the English or Americans, but delivered it with a slight lisp that was soft and charming.

It was the days before I was Johnny. I was Gianni Gordini then. Middle son of three: one born out of love, one out of wedlock and one out of retribution. Guess which one was me.

I sat on a black leather sofa in a clinically white waiting-room, sipping espresso coffee and killing time while the three other members of my family sat pointlessly at the great Alfredo Gordini's bedside like the Magi worshipping around the crib. Alfredo had been in a coma for three days now and I could only imagine the scene inside the private room – drips going into the body, tubes coming out and feeding into plastic bags, monitors emitting regular loud beeps that belied the faintness of the beating heart. My role was peripheral, superfluous even: one more shoulder to cry on, one more arm to wrap around my mother and support her. I took it philosophically, which wasn't difficult since I had lived on the absolute fringes of this family for much of the last twenty-six years.

I placed the empty cup on top of the copies of *The Wall Street Journal* and *The Times* (read from cover to cover and back again) so as not to mark the highly polished surface of the black ash coffee table. I leaned back, put my hands behind my head and stared thoughtfully up at the ceiling. Why? That was the question. It made no sense.

Alfredo Gordini had been travelling in a grey Mercedes taxi from the recently opened Amsterdam branch of Silvers *en route* to the airport and back to New York. While waiting at a set of traffic lights on a quiet road on the outskirts of the city, a motor bike had pulled alongside. The pillion passenger slid up his visor, peered closely into the back of the cab and then stretched out his right arm. His hand held a gun. His finger pulled the trigger. The gun, set on automatic, began to pump bullets through the window of the Mercedes.

Maybe it was the taxi driver so typically pulling away sharply at the first twinkle of green from the lights. Maybe it was the thickness of the glass and the distortion it caused, bending the light rays between victim and assassin and the bullets likewise. Or maybe he was just a lousy shot. The bullets, intended for Alfredo's heart, hit him in the side, spread out on impact and sent fragments of shrapnel into lungs, kidney, spleen and spine. With anybody else, it would still have been enough to kill. But Alfredo had always been a stubborn man, and especially so, it seemed, when it came to dying.

Sure, Alfredo had made enemies: loans refused or called in, causing businesses to fold, shares to plummet, people to lose their jobs. But who could have hated him so much that they would take out a contract on his life?

The door to the waiting-room opened, cutting off my fruitless speculation. My mother walked in, her eldest and youngest sons, Roberto and Carlo respectively, following close behind. She was dressed in black, as if prepared for the worst, her long black hair scraped back and wound into a bun, the usual sparkle in her dark eyes replaced by a look of determination.

I stood up and went to my mother. Put my arm around her and led her to the sofa. Sitting down beside her, I held her close and looked up at Roberto and Carlo.

'What's the prognosis?' I asked.

Roberto leaned against the wall and crossed his arms, Carlo crossed the small room to sit in a chair opposite me. Roberto shrugged his shoulders and said, 'They don't know is the short answer. The doctor said that they've done all they can to repair the internal injuries. It's the shock to the system and the resulting coma that concerns them most now. It could last days; it could last months. All we can do is wait.'

'No,' said their mother. 'That may be all I can do, but while Alfredo lies in that room and the rest of you are here there's no one minding the shop. And neither Wall Street nor the City like that very much. Your father had become the personification of Silvers – he was the outward face, the captain of the ship. Silvers is left with a void, and we must fill it quickly before confidence is eroded.'

Carlo's brows furrowed. He felt in the pockets of his expensive silk suit for his cigarettes and flashy gold lighter and then remembered the no smoking rule in the hospital. He clasped his hands, as if to prevent them wandering of their own accord. 'What do you mean?' he asked. 'Fill the void?'

'Someone has to take Dad's place,' Roberto said, straightening himself up to his full height of five feet eight inches. 'I would have thought that was obvious, little brother.'

And, I thought, we all know who Roberto has in mind for the vacancy. But, I was forced to admit, it was the logical move: Roberto had worked in the New York office for nearly fifteen years now, Carlo had served only a couple of years with the bank, mostly in New York but the last few months in Amsterdam on the opening of the office. And myself, although the most academically qualified, had been tucked away for three years in the back rooms of London, working my way up a very long ladder. So Roberto would be the new captain of the ship and admiral of the fleet, and

I would have snakes to worry about as well as from where and when the next ladder would appear.

'I have decided on a plan of action,' my mother said calmly. 'Roberto, as the eldest son,' – his top lip curved in a smile – 'you will run New York.'

The smile faded.

'Carlo, dear little Carlo,' she continued, 'you will be the family's presence in Amsterdam.'

'Does that mean I run the show here?' he asked.

'Yes, Carlo,' my mother said. 'You run Amsterdam. With some conditions, but I will come to those in a moment.'

Carlo shrugged his shoulders as if to say that any conditions were unimportant in the overall scheme of things.

'Gianni,' my mother said, 'it is time for you take your rightful place. You, Gianni, will be head of the bank in London.'

'No,' said Roberto, 'that's not' – he pulled back just in time from saying fair and sounding like a petulant child – 'that's not a good idea. Gianni has always taken orders from others, he's never given any. London is the biggest of the three operations, it's the original Silvers and the most important. It needs someone with experience.'

'No one can deny, Roberto,' she said, 'that you have the most experience. But that experience is best utilized in New York where you gained it. Gianni has spent the last three years learning the London operation from the inside. He knows the system, he knows the people. My decision is made.'

Roberto scowled and looked across at me accusingly.

'Now for the conditions,' my mother continued. 'Although in charge of your own operations, you will work as a team: we will hold regular meetings to decide on any matters that relate to the bank as a whole.'

'Who will chair the meetings?' Roberto asked.

'As the major shareholder of the bank,' she said, locking eyes with Roberto, 'I will. I shall, of course, rely on your individual expertise, listen to your opinions and then help us come to a unanimous family decision.'

'Sounds fair,' said Carlo, shrugging again.

'The second condition is that you make best use of the resources at your disposal. There are good people in the bank. Listen to them and be guided by them. Lastly, each of you will work within strict limits on lending and investment. You will not exceed those limits unless we all agree at one of our meetings. Is that clear?'

The three of us nodded, Roberto grudgingly.

'I shall remain here for a while, the three of you will go to the Amsterdam branch and prepare a press release and a memorandum to all staff. You will bring them back for me to check and sign and take a last look at your father before you take up your new positions.'

'Let's go,' Roberto said, anxious to be the one to draft the documents and put his spin on the contents. He headed for the door, pausing only to turn and say, 'Come on, you two.'

'Thanks, Mom,' Carlo said, as he followed his eldest brother.

'And thanks from me, too,' I said.

My mother smiled at me.

'Watch over Carlo as best you can,' she said. 'He's young and impetuous. Be his steadying influence.'

'Haven't I always?' I said, walking towards the door. 'When I've been allowed to, that is. Don't worry, Mother. This could be the making of Carlo.'

'One last thing,' she said. 'I'm taking a big risk here. I am trying to put things right. But you know that this would not have been Alfredo's decision.'

I came back and kissed her on the cheek.

'Thanks for everything,' I said.

'This is your big chance, Gianni. Grasp it with both hands while Alfredo can do nothing to take it away from you. I hope this makes up a little for the past. Don't let me down, my son.'

'I wouldn't give Roberto the satisfaction,' I said.

'Roberto is like his father,' she said. 'He will never be fully satisfied.'

Not while I'm around, I thought. And that applies to both of them. Roberto was his father's son.

3

St Jude, Caribbean. The present.

One man jumped down from the helicopter, stooped low to pass under the slowly rotating blades and then walked across the beach directly towards me. He was wearing a cream-coloured lightweight suit, dark-brown shirt and tan loafers that were filling with sand with each step. If he was a professional assassin, it was a bloody good disguise. I tucked the gun into the waistband at the back of my shorts, took a spare T-shirt from the bag under the counter and slipped it on to hide both the scars and the gun. Only when he smiled did I recognize him. It was a smile that I had never trusted.

'Of all the bars in all the world. . . .' I said.

'Gianni,' he said, 'come give your big brother a hug.'

'Thanks, Roberto, but I'll pass. I'm too old for new experiences. And anyway, I'm not Gianni Gordini anymore. If I ever was, that is.'

'It's been a long time,' he said.

Not long enough, I thought.

In the nine years since I had seen him, Roberto had put on maybe forty pounds of weight. It didn't flatter him. He had lost a lot of hair at the temples and acquired grey in what was left – not a good trade. He was forty-five and, standing there mopping his lined and sweaty brow with a silk handkerchief, looked ten years older.

'How about a drink for old time's sake?' he said in a nasal New York accent that I would have had too, if I had ever been allowed to spend some time at home.

I placed two unopened bottles of beer on the counter.

'That should see you for the flight back,' I said. 'Goodbye, Roberto.'

'Use your head, Gianni,' he said, frowning. 'Would I come all this way if it wasn't serious?'

'Mother?'

'No, Mom's OK. She. . . . Look, let's sit down in the shade and talk. Surely you can spare me a few minutes of your time. It don't look like you got much else to do.'

I opened the two bottles of beer and led the way to a table under the large sun-bleached canvas shade. Roberto sat himself down heavily and took a long pull from the bottle. He looked around him, registered the faded bar sign and the broken table and chair lying on the sand.

'Business good?' he asked.

'Thinking of investing?'

He laughed. Always was shrewd.

'How did you find me?' I asked.

'Mom,' he said.

All through the years of exile I had written regular letters to my mother. She was usually good at keeping secrets – too damned good, in my opinion. Well, at least this wasn't a major breach of security.

'Mom knows she's breaking a confidence,' he said, 'but in the circumstances she didn't think there was any other alternative. Carlo's gone missing. We're worried.'

I bet you are, I thought.

'Does my little brother still run the European operations of the bank?' I said.

'Yes,' he said, shrugging his shoulders to dismiss the uncharitable implications of my question or his interpretation of it, 'but—'

'Is it profitable?' I interrupted.

It was a fair question. Roberto was the cool and calculating one of the family, the objective surgeon who would impassively cut out one organ if he felt there was any chance it might jeopardize the health of the body as a whole. Carlo, on the other hand, was the gambler, always searching for the big win, not satisfied with grinding out a profit on each deal – wasn't the best psychological profile for a banker.

'Sure,' he said. 'Carlo makes big profits.'

'As far as you are aware.'

Roberto avoided the implied question by taking another long swig of beer.

'Do you have anyone checking the books?' I followed up.

'I shipped our best compliance officer over from New York,' he said. 'Purely a precautionary measure, you understand.'

'Oh, I understand,' I said. 'What I don't get is what any of this has to do with me.'

'We – the family, Mom in particular – want you to find Carlo.'

It was my turn to laugh.

'What? Leave this thriving business and go to Amsterdam?' I said. 'Doesn't make economic sense, Brother. Go to the police, or get a private investigator on the case, if you're that worried.'

'We'd like to keep the police out of it,' he said. 'And we tried a private investigator. No luck.'

'How long has Carlo been missing?'

'Five days.'

'You really gave your private investigator a run at it, didn't you? Do I detect a whiff of panic in the air?'

'Carlo could be in trouble,' he said.

'That sounds very likely,' I replied.

'Find him for us. Tell him that whatever he's done, it's not a problem. As long as we know about it.'

'A cover up, huh?'

'The bank has to protect its interests and its image.'

'Don't I know it?' I said. 'So, just as long as you can keep everything quiet, whatever Carlo may have done you'll forgive and forget?'

'I wouldn't rule out having to make a few changes in procedures.'

'And personnel, too. Especially Carlo.'

'Just find him for us, Gianni.'

'Why me?'

'Because Carlo always looked up to you. He trusts you. If he hears you're looking for him, he won't hide from you like he would the police or a PI.'

'Finish your beer, Roberto,' I said. 'It's time you left.'

'And you'll come with me?'

I shook my head.

'It's your mess, Roberto. You clean it up.'

'But think of Mom. Think of the family.'

'It's your family, not mine. The ties were broken long ago, if they ever really existed. And if it's so important for the family, why did the big chief send you? Why didn't he come himself?'

'Father doesn't get around much anymore.'

'Not for me he doesn't, you mean.'

'What if we pay you for your time and trouble?' he said. 'Name your price.'

'You couldn't meet it, Roberto. Now, you've tried moral blackmail and money. Both have failed. It's time you took the hint. Get out of here, Roberto, and don't come back.'

He stood up, glared down at me.

'You'll regret this, Gianni,' he said.

'Threats won't work either. Goodbye. And give my love to Mother.'

He turned on the sandy heels of his loafers and stormed back to the helicopter. It took off immediately, heading in my direction and swooping low over the bar as it passed. The rotor blades whipped up a sandstorm and blew it over me, the bar and all its contents.

He'd always been petty minded.

Still, if that was the worst he could do, who cares?

'It's time you went home,' I said to Bull.

He avoided my gaze and refilled his tumbler with rum. His hand was unsteady as he picked up the glass and pressed it to his lips.

We were sitting opposite each other, slumped in two cushioned cane armchairs, in my cabin in the little shanty town that housed the few original inhabitants of the island and the many shipped in to work at the hotel. It was one o'clock in the morning and through the window behind Bull I could see a crescent moon hanging in a pitch-black sky. We'd both made a few bucks during the day – Bull from taking a couple from the hotel island-hopping, myself from stocking them up with booze and flying fish sandwiches for the trip and then servicing the regular trickle of tourists who were looking for something a little more native and a lot less sanitized than the bar and restaurant at the hotel. Bull should have gone home an hour ago, but he was putting it off. As usual.

Bull was married to a cappuccino-skinned Jamaican beauty: she was what Ian Fleming once indelicately termed a 'Chigro' – of mixed Chinese and black African descent – and she would have had most men rushing home the moment they had finished their day's work, and nipping back at lunchtime too. They had a son. But not for long, it seemed.

The boy, Michael, was three years old and would be lucky to make it to his fourth birthday. He had a congenital heart condition that had first manifested itself six months ago and that only a transplant could cure. That meant taking him to the States, finding a suitable donor – which was easier said than done, given the mixed bloodline – and paying a whole lot more money for the operation than Bull and I had stashed away. The boy was getting weaker by the day, and Bull could not bear to face him or the inevitable.

'I've been thinking about going back into the business,' he said.

'It's a young man's game,' I said. 'You're out of training, out of practice and couldn't run to save your life. Forget it.'

'I need money, Johnny,' he said. 'And I need it fast.'

I did the same mental calculations as the week before and the week before that. Cash the few investments, try to find a buyer for the bar, sell the boat. It didn't add up – it had never added up. Short of robbing a bank, there was no hope.

'Leave it with me,' I said. 'Go home, Bull. Mai Ling needs you. Little Michael needs you. I'll think of something. I promise. OK?'

He looked at me with big, brown, puppy-dog eyes, downed his rum and limped silently from the cabin.

I couldn't sleep that night. Too much had happened in the day. Letting my pride, and the stupid desire to test the uncertain capabilities of my left arm, had got the better of me and propelled me into a fight that could only be bad for business if the hotel happened to hear about it. Finally, there had been Bull, so little hope left inside him that he was contemplating doing the hopeless. And, sandwiched in between, the ghost from a past I thought I had successfully exorcized.

I climbed wearily out of bed, grabbed hold of the rum bottle, searched around until I found the pack of cigarettes that I had hidden away three years earlier and went to sit on the concrete steps outside the cabin. I drank a little rum, and then a little more, lit a cigarette which made my head swim as the unaccustomed nicotine hit my nervous system, and gazed up at the moon and stars.

I never knew my father. No, let's put that another way. I don't know who my biological father is or was, and never really knew the man who was supposed to be my father. Although it took a long while to work all that out.

I was born in New York. The birth certificate named my parents as Rebecca Silver and Alfredo Gordini. Funny, I started life as a lie and after thirty-five years was still living one.

My mother was heiress to the Silver fortunes, amassed over a couple of hundred years of, initially, money-lending, progressing to merchant banking and, in current terminology, investment banking. Alfredo Gordini was a third-generation Italian immigrant who, through a combination of ruthless ambition and simply being in the right place at the right time, had built up an insurance business, risen up the social ladder and ensnared my mother while she was on a shopping trip to New York. Despite initial opposition from the Jewish Silvers and the Catholic Gordinis, they married: not inconsequentially, I imagine, Roberto was born five months later.

Ten years after that, I came along. I spent my first four years in America, during which time I have only the vaguest memories of Alfredo and unhappy ones of a spiteful and teasing Roberto. Then began the years of exile. I was packed off to England to the first of a long succession of boarding-schools, most of the changes being of my own making: I was a serial rebel, committing some expulsion offence or other at each school as it failed to live up to what I sought most in life – to embrace me as part of a family.

When I came back to New York in the holidays, Alfredo was invariably and conveniently away on business – as well as the New York branch there was the main bank in London to look after – and I spent time with my mother, little Carlo and my Uncle Gus, short for Giuseppi. Those were the happy times, all too infrequent and all too short. As I got older I was 'encouraged' to spend the holidays with friends from school, which I duly did – no matter the long list of my shortcomings, never let it be said that I cannot take a hint.

Even after finishing my education (Cambridge, England, and Harvard Business School), I wasn't allowed to settle in the States. I was sent packing to London, installed on the bottom rung of the Silver's corporate ladder and told to cut my teeth when what was really meant was kick my heels. I might have been there now, if it hadn't been for two events that brought about a rapid rise and an even quicker descent. The former was the failed assassination attempt on Alfredo: the latter – my fall to earth with a thump – was as a result of an error of judgement on an investment that went seriously belly up. There were no excuses I could offer. For the good of the bank, I was told in no uncertain terms, I had to go. In the land of clichés and mixed metaphors, the sacrificial lamb was to fall on his sword and never darken their doors again.

There seemed only one logical course of action. The Italian side of the family didn't want me, so it was time to explore my Jewish roots. I went to Israel, where at last, I was welcomed with open arms. By the army. Who taught me how to kill. And gave me plenty of opportunities to practise the newly acquired skill. The army fed me and clothed me and stretched out an arm to wrap round my shoulder. Just as long as I did my job – killing.

4

Bull and I were still hung-over as we walked along the beach to the bar. Or what was left of it.

Someone had done a pretty effective job of trashing the place. The tables and chairs were scattered across the sand in more pieces than I could count; the sign had been broken in two, leaving the words *Johnny Silver* separated from *Proprietor*; the two heavy padlocks had been forced, the drop-down bar front now hanging by one hinge and the door, kicked in, lying on the floor; what was left inside hardly seemed worth the effort of salvaging. The refrigerator was on its side ten feet away from where it usually sat, its top half poking through the wooden wall against which it had been thrown with force. Every glass and every bottle had been smashed, the floor awash with a heady cocktail of mixed spirits and beer topped by a slick of vegetable oil from the fryer I used to cook the flying fish. They had missed the Browning, and it felt good in my hand as I took off the safety and scanned the beach and the horizon for culprits.

'You shouldn't have got into that fight yesterday,' Bull said. 'Hell hath no fury like a woman deprived of her daiquiri.'

'Or a bridegroom with swollen testicles? Is that what you're thinking?'

'Makes sense to me,' he said.

'Maybe you're right,' I agreed. 'On the other hand, maybe you're wrong.'

'You seem to have covered all the possibilities.'

'Always the best way,' I said.

I clicked the safety catch back on the Browning before tucking it into the waistband of my shorts – that was always the best way, too.

'They could have come by boat,' I said. 'Slipped in under the cover of darkness, trashed the place and slipped away again.'

'Who's they?' Bull asked.

I shrugged. 'Anyone who is short of a few bucks and doesn't mind what they do to earn them.'

'Rings a bell,' said Bull.

'We were never like that,' I protested. 'OK, we got paid – most of the time – for what we did, but we did it for the cause as well as the money. Until Angola, that is, and by then we were running out of options.'

'And causes.'

'What was it the Texan said when we quit Bosnia? "Never come across a cause yet that was worth dying for. But a fistful of dollars. . . ." Angola was the biggest mistake we made, no cause and no dollars in the end.'

'It wasn't your fault,' Bull said. 'We all agreed to take on the contract. Seemed like easy money at the time.'

'We should have known that there's no such thing as easy money.'

'Well,' Bull said, 'my hard-earned money is still on Wayne and Miss Daiquiri.'

'Reckon we'll know soon enough.'

'How?' he asked, running his hand over his shaved head in puzzlement.

'If no one shows up in the next couple of hours, you win your bet. But if you see a helicopter. . . .'

We were halfway through clearing up the mess when the helicopter flew into view. Bull had gone home and returned with Mai Ling, extra brooms and mops and little Michael. The boy sat on the sand propped up against a palm tree and watched us listlessly as we swept and scrubbed and stacked the cane furniture into a bonfire to be lit at a ceremonial beach party when and if the bar ever reopened. Even when the helicopter landed he could hardly summon up the energy to get excited.

I ushered Mai Ling and Michael into the relative safety inside the bar and Bull and I took up our positions from the previous day; Bull on the left flank with the pump-action shotgun and I at point with my hand on the butt of the Browning and itching like hell to use it.

Like yesterday, one man jumped down from the cabin and ducked under the rotor blades. Unlike yesterday, the man was wearing a broad-brimmed straw hat, long white collarless shirt, loose white trousers and brown leather sandals. He removed the hat so that I could see his face, and smiled. Warmly.

I ran across the sand to meet him.

'Uncle Gus,' I cried, throwing my arms about him.

'Gianni,' he said, hugging me back. 'Or should I say Johnny?'

'You've been fully briefed by Roberto then.'

'I'm here as peacemaker,' he said. He looked past me at the bar. 'And a little late, it seems.'

'I'd offer you a drink,' I said, 'but I'm fresh out of everything.'

'I suggest we go to the hotel and talk. But first, why don't you introduce me to your friends.' His brown eyes skimmed over Mai Ling and Michael and alighted on Bull with a twinkle. 'Especially the hunk,' he added.

'You haven't changed then?'

'It's in the genes.'

'And how are you spelling that?'

He laughed. 'Depends on the contents.'

Together we walked over to Mai Ling and Michael. Bull replaced the shotgun in the special compartment under the decking of his boat and joined us. I made the formal introductions. Uncle Gus complimented Mai Ling on her beauty and Bull on his physique. To Michael he did not speak; just gazed down sadly and ruffled the kid's hair. After a little small-talk, Mai Ling, realizing we needed to talk, shooed us away so that she and Bull could carry on with the clearing up. As we set off for the hotel I could hear Bull mumbling to himself.

'Should have known,' Bull said. 'Never bet with a man who doesn't gamble.'

We sat at an isolated table at the far end of the heart-shaped swimming pool overlooking the beach, where a canopy decorated with flowers was being set up for the wedding. Uncle Gus fanned himself with his hat while waiting for the drinks to arrive, his long silver hair fluttering with the movement. There were more lines on his face than when I had last seen him, but they could not conceal the kindness in his eyes nor the smile which generally played on his lips. Generally, but not always.

'What's wrong with the boy?' he asked, frowning.

Knowing Gus, it was an expression of genuine concern rather than simply a delaying tactic so that we would not be interrupted by the drinks when discussing serious business.

'Heart condition. He needs a transplant, and he needs it soon.'

'Sounds serious. And expensive.'

'Very. And that applies to both.'

A waiter, dressed in a uniform of bright yellow trousers, matching shirt and navy-blue sash around his waist, brilliant white napkin spread over one arm, arrived carrying a silver tray. He placed a long glass of rum punch on the table in front of Gus and a bottle of beer flecked with beads of condensation and a frosted glass in front of me. The check he slipped under the ashtray to stop it blowing in the breeze. I glanced at it and then stared enviously at the printed figures.

'Wouldn't take many rounds of drinks like this to rebuild and restock your bar,' Gus said.

'If I charged these prices, there wouldn't be any point in the guests coming. And anyway, bright yellow doesn't suit me.'

'You should be more adventurous, Johnny,' he said.

'I'm all adventured out, Gus.'

'Maybe,' he replied. 'But that's why I'm here. To change your mind.'

'Roberto tried bribery and threats yesterday. They didn't work. What makes him think that old loyalties and charm will do the trick? Unless he believes that I will be much more receptive after seeing my livelihood lying in ruins.'

'It does seem to be a bit of a coincidence, I must admit,' Gus said.

'And bears the hallmark of Roberto's petty spite.'

'How can brothers be so different?' he asked, shaking his head sadly.

'Half-brothers, Gus.'

'That's just speculation on your part,' he said.

'And that's just bullshit on your part,' I countered.

He removed the little umbrella from his glass, rolled it between his slim fingers, dropped it into the ashtray and took a long slow sip through the straw.

'Come on, Gus,' I said, 'you know Alfredo is not my father. Why else the treatment I had from him? Or the treatment I didn't have?'

'Let's get back to the subject, shall we? The identity of your father is not relevant.'

'To me it is.'

'Then forget about it for a while. Forget about your hatred for Alfredo and your loathing for Roberto. Think about Carlo for a moment.'

I was tempted to ask 'Am I my half-brother's keeper?', but knew it was a rhetorical question. There had been the promise to look after him. But hadn't that been made by Gianni Gordini, not Johnny Silver? And surely it hadn't been meant to last for ever. Or was I just splitting hairs?

'What do you think has happened to Carlo?' I said.

'Either he has done a disappearing act because he's embezzled a chunk of the bank's money, in which case Silvers is in trouble, or he's so scared of something that he's gone to ground, if which case Carlo is in trouble. Whichever view you take, it doesn't look good.'

It was my turn to indulge in some displacement activity. I raised my glass and drank some of the cold beer, lit a cigarette and slowly exhaled the smoke.

'And,' Gus added, 'your future doesn't look bright either.'

'I can cash my investments and fix up the bar,' I said, shrugging more casually than I felt. 'It'll hurt, but I'll get over it.'

Gus shook his head at me and frowned. 'You've changed your name and, short of camping out in a rain forest or encasing yourself in an igloo in the Arctic, you've chosen one of the remotest places on earth in which to live. How long do you think it will take Roberto to work out that you're hiding from someone or something? And then what do you think he will do?'

'Splash my photograph, biography and current address all over the front page of every newspaper in the world. That would have all the subtlety, not to mention the malice, of Roberto's style.'

Gus nodded.

Hell!

'I could pack my bags and move on somewhere else,' I said, although it was the last thing I wanted to do.

'And when Roberto tracks you down again, what then?'

I shrugged.

'You can't run for ever, Johnny,' he said.

It looked like I was backed into a corner. And when that happens, the only course of action is to come out fighting.

'I'll do it,' I said.

Gus smiled and raised his hand in the air to signal to the waiter that he wanted more drinks; the rings on his fingers and the silver identity bracelet around his wrist sparkling brightly in the reflected light from the water.

'But only on certain conditions,' I added.

'Are you going to drive a hard bargain?' Gus asked.

'They don't come any harder. First, I want you in Amsterdam as liaison between me and the family. I do not want any further dealings with Roberto, and none at all with Alfredo.'

Gus looked relieved. 'I don't see a problem with that.'

'Second, I want access to the compliance officer who is investigating the bank's dealings in Amsterdam. If there's a trail of embezzled money, I want to be hot on it until it leads me to Carlo.'

Gus nodded. 'Sounds reasonable.'

'Third, I want this treated as a professional contract. Arm's length, as we used to say in the bank. I'm not going to be taken advantage of just because of blood ties.'

'By contract, I assume you mean some kind of payment.'

'A quarter of a million,' I said. 'Fifty thousand up front in cash for expenses, the balance held by you to dispense when Carlo is found, or you're satisfied I've done all I can to find him.'

'Dollars or pounds?' he asked.

'I was thinking dollars.'

'I'm thinking pounds,' he said. 'Let's hit Roberto where it really hurts – his wallet.'

'Lastly,' I said, 'I want the name of my father.'

'You've forgotten the moon on a stick, Johnny. Don't you want to add that to the list as well?'

'Those are my terms, Gus. If the family doesn't like them, I disappear. And by the time Roberto finds me, it will almost certainly be too late for the bank and Carlo.'

'I need to make some phone calls,' he said. 'Your mother first, I think.'

'Give her my love.'

'Then Roberto.'

'Tell him I hope he rots in hell.'

'I might save that for a time when the negotiations are at a slightly less delicate stage, if it's all the same to you?'

'It's the thought that counts,' I said.

I walked back from the hotel on my own, deep in thought and unsure whether to be pleased or not. There was no sign of Mai Ling or Michael, but Bull was standing in front of the bar, smiling proudly.

'If you had some booze, you'd be back in business,' he said. 'If you had a fridge to keep it in and some glasses to serve it from, that is.'

'You've done a good job,' I said. The inside of the bar was clean and tidy, the floor dry and the bar front and door were back on their hinges. 'Now can you board it up?'

He stared at me.

'And then pack your bags,' I said. 'The helicopter leaves in two hours.'

He shook his head wildly as if to clear his brain. 'Did I black out for a while? I seem to have missed something of importance. Bags? Helicopter?'

'We have a contract,' I said.

'Oh yeah,' he said. 'What happened to all that stuff about out of practice, out of training and can't run to save your life?'

'None of that is relevant. This contract is different.'

'That's what they always say.'

'All we have to do is find my brother,' I said. 'For once there won't be people trying to kill us. This one will be sweet and easy.'

'Why me?' he asked.

Good question. And a delayed echo of my own thoughts the previous day.

'Because I need someone to guard my back.'

'On a sweet and easy job?'

'Why take risks?' I said.

'Uh huh,' he said, unconvinced. 'Anything else I should know?'

'Only what it pays,' I answered.

'So what does it pay?'

'Enough for Michael's operation.'

5

The other travellers in first class didn't quite know what to make of our unlikely trio. They alternated uneasily between the two extremes of staring fixedly at us and desperately trying to avoid our gaze. Even the steward found our appearance hard to take in his measured stride without the occasional raising of a perfectly plucked eyebrow. I didn't blame them: years ago – another time, another life – I would have done the same.

With only two hours before the helicopter took off, Bull and I had had just enough time to secure the bar and the boat, issue instructions to Mai Ling for the journey to America, say a brief and almost tearful goodbye to Michael and throw a few things into a bag. We had changed into khaki chinos and shirts, relics of our mercenary days and still stained with patches of pink where the blood hadn't entirely washed out. If I'd borrowed Gus's straw hat, Bull and I could have been mistaken for Robinson Crusoe and Man Friday.

'The first thing we have to do when we land,' Gus said, taking a glass of champagne from the steward's tray, 'is to get you both some new clothes. At the moment, the pair of you are about as inconspicuous as camels in the Kentucky Derby.'

'While *you* blend in perfectly,' I said, looking pointedly at his white shirt, trousers and sandals.

'I can get away with it,' he said. 'It's one of the few benefits of being an eccentric. I am a threat to no one.'

'And we are?' I said.

'There is something about your eyes,' he said. 'And I don't just mean the way they rove around, scanning everybody and each situation, alert for danger. There's a look about you both. It's not exactly a coldness, not exactly a hardness, it's. . . .' He sighed. 'I don't know. But whatever it is, it unnerves people.'

'Windows on the soul?' I said. 'Or just past images of death showing through?'

'Maybe a haircut will help,' he said, answering the questions by avoiding them.

'Nothing drastic,' I said, unwilling to return to the distinctive short crop of Bosnia and Angola where depriving the lice of a cosy home had been the sole factor in choice of hairstyle. The Russians hadn't got a good look at me during their raid on the camp, but if any photographs existed of me in my mercenary days I wanted to look as different from them as possible.

'Can we settle on more businesslike?' Gus said.

'Depends on what you define as my business. Like I said, nothing drastic.'

'No rebirth, then?' he asked.

'That comes when I find Carlo, and the family keep their side of the deal. You will see to it that they don't renege?'

'I have your mother's word.'

'And what about Alfredo the Great, is he in any position to countermand her?' I asked distrustingly.

'Your mother can handle him – being the main shareholder helps more than a little in that respect. Alfredo is still the titular head of the bank, although most of the day-to-day responsibility has devolved to Roberto, but he was never the same man again after the shooting incident.'

'Some good came from it, then.'

'They think it was the Russians, you know.'

'Russians?' I said, noticing Bull's head swivel towards us anxiously from across the aisle.

'There were ten heads of European investment banks assassinated that year – Alfredo was the only target to escape alive. There was a news embargo at the time – neither the governments involved nor any of the banks wanted to alarm investors or shareholders – and it's only been recently that some of the details have been emerging.'

'Why assassinate investment bankers?' I asked. 'Alfredo excepted, that is.'

'Because they wouldn't do what they were told – launder money for the Russian mafiya.'

'So Alfredo got shot because he had principles? Who would have thought it? Unbelievable!'

'See him in a new light, do you?'

'No, just one small bright spot on an otherwise black surface. Still, it's an improvement on Roberto, I suppose.'

'Roberto may be ruthless, but you can't say he isn't effective.'

'Too quick to judge, too prone to carrying a grudge,' I said. 'Was Alfredo the same when he was running the operation?'

'Pretty much.'

'And is that why you left the bank?'

'No,' he said, smiling. 'I just didn't fit in – you can understand that.'

'You were always the same, Gus. If that was the reason, then why take you into the bank in the first place?'

'You force me to admit,' he said, gazing down at the layer of wispy cloud, 'that I just wasn't cut out for it. Entirely unsuited. To be frank, I found banking a bore, and maybe that was why I wasn't any good at it.'

'That's not what Mother used to say. She described you as cautious but imaginative.'

'Like I said, entirely unsuited to be banker.'

'So what do you do now?' I asked, sensing his reticence to discuss the matter further.

'Live very nicely off the lump sum settlement and the pension that Alfredo gave me when I resigned. He was very generous.'

'This really is a day full of surprises. On an island with a zero crime rate, my bar is trashed. You show up out of the blue. And Alfredo is both principled and generous.'

'And don't forget the Russians,' Gus said.

'Don't worry, there's no chance of that.'

Gus and I continued to talk through what was either a late lunch or an early dinner, depending on what time zone the airline was operating on. This indeterminate meal – shrimp salad, dry chicken breast wrapped in spinach and soggy filo pastry, strawberry fool and cheese and crackers – was designed more for eating up time than eating up. Bull cleared his tray and, even from across the aisle, I could still hear his stomach rumbling. Before Gus reclined his seat and settled down under the thin blanket to snatch a little sleep I extracted enough from him to update me on little Carlo and the bank.

Carlo, contrary to the leopard and spots theory, must have changed his ways – maybe the lesson had been learned the easy way. In the eight years since I had last seen him there had been no disasters; no quick-buck investments in schemes too good to be true, no double-up gambling in what is always a vain attempt to turn persistent losses into instant gains. The branch in Amsterdam, ideally placed, as intended, to take advantage of the growth in the European economy and the expanding Community and its satellites eagerly waiting to join, had expanded rapidly. So much so that Carlo's operation now contributed a fifth of the bank's combined profits. With New York also playing an increasing role, the original Silvers in London now accounted for less than half the profits of the group as a whole. I wondered whether my mother was pleased about that or viewed it nostalgically, the old having to give way to the new.

The Amsterdam office, Gus told me, was unrecognizable to the one I had briefly known. It had moved twice since its set up and now occupied a large modern building in the heart of the city. Carlo still lived in the same apartment and it was here that Bull and I would stay – I hoped that this too would be unrecognizable.

As Gus's breathing slowed and became deeper, I moved over to sit next to Bull. From the narrowing of his big brown eyes I could tell there was much on his mind.

'What was Gus saying about Russians?' he asked, indicating

what was uppermost.

'Nothing to concern us,' I answered. 'Ancient history, that's all. Part of my dim and distant past. What we need to concentrate on is the future.'

'And it's thanks to you that Michael will have one,' he said.

'As soon as we find Carlo you can join Mai Ling and Michael in America. Gus has made all the arrangements. Once they arrive, the hospital will start on all the tests, and then it will simply be down to finding a suitable donor.'

'How long do you think it will take to find Carlo?' he said, anxious to wrap up the contract and be at Mai Ling's side to help her through what might be a long wait.

'A week, maybe,' I said. 'Any longer than that and I don't think we will find him at all. Amsterdam is not that big a place. There can't be that many places to hide away. And Carlo, unless he has changed radically, is not the type of person to blend in easily. He'll have left a trail – all we have to do is get on to it.'

'You make it sound so easy,' he said.

That was the intention, I thought.

'A week, two at the outset,' I said, 'and you'll be in the lap of luxury in the good old US of A, courtesy of Silvers, bankers to the gentry.'

'I wonder what the Texan is doing right now?' he said. 'Maybe I could meet up with him when I'm in the States.'

'You forget our agreement,' I said. No contact. It was for the common good. If the Russians found any one of us, he could not lead them to the others. We had our fall-back position in case of dire emergency – placing messages in the personal columns of favourite newspapers and *Soldier of Fortune* magazine – but none of us hoped that such a situation would arise. 'Better – safer – that we stay separate.'

'Do you miss them?' he asked.

'What, the Texan? Red? That frustrated cowboy? With his driving?' I laughed. 'If you got out of a mission alive, then Red would do his damnedest to kill you on the way back. And the Pole? Stanislav? Silent, brooding, with that kind of manic depression that is so infectious you could easily end up slitting your own wrists.' I shook my head. 'Not to mention the South African. Pieter? Tall, blond, good-looking. A magnet for every female, which meant as often as not married. Do you remember the fights he landed us in with cuckolded husbands out seeking revenge? As if life wasn't dangerous enough fighting the enemy. And you ask me if I miss them?' I sucked air in through my teeth. 'Of course I bloody do.'

'They were good times,' Bull said wistfully. 'We were a good team.'

'No, Bull,' I corrected. 'We were a great team. The mere fact that we survived proves that.'

'It seems like so long ago now.'

'We were different people then. Different lifestyles, different needs, different names even. You can't go back. Life is like water-skiing – if you don't keep on going forward, you sink.'

He nodded. Unconvincingly.

The plane, stacked up over Schipol, banked and circled around one more time. It was the price you paid for flying into Europe's second biggest hub: from here it was possible to fly long haul to anywhere in the world, or be in half-a-dozen capital cities within an hour or so. The other drawback was a route march along one of the four seemingly endless corridors from landing stage to baggage retrieval, immigration and customs. After fifteen minutes of jumping on and off moving walkways I felt as if I should have already been in Brussels, Paris or London.

'What does it feel like to be back?' Gus asked.

'When I have so many happy memories of the place?' I said. 'What do you think?'

'What exactly was the problem?' he said. 'I mean, why did you have to leave Silvers? Your mother won't talk about it.'

'Too ashamed, I shouldn't wonder,' I replied.

'I can't believe that,' he said.

'Silvers lost a lot of money because of a poor decision. End of story.'

'What was it? A loan without sufficient collateral? Badly timed investment?'

'I prefer to think of it as simply putting too much in a trust fund,' I said. 'An error of judgement that neither Alfredo nor Roberto would ever have made. Maybe I should have seen that the payback would always be zero.'

'You can't win them all,' Gus shrugged.

'With this family,' I said, 'you can't win *at* all.'

6

Amsterdam. Ten years ago.

Despite the unpromising historical precedents of triumvirates in Rome and King Lear's splitting of his kingdom in three, the system worked well. Monetary limits on individual actions were set according to age and experience – Roberto with the highest, then myself and lastly young and impetuous Carlo: they were strictly adhered to. Regular meetings were held each Friday evening in Amsterdam and under my mother's chairmanship were reasonably civilized, considering the sibling rivalry and Roberto's animosity. Wall Street and the City were reassured that the business was in the stewardship of safe hands and that the bank would continue to grind out its profits. Alfredo's condition got neither better nor worse, the unchanging state of coma forcing upon him a period of non-interference that would have driven him mad under normal circumstances. Life couldn't have been much better for Gianni Gordini. And that, Fate decrees, is always the most dangerous time.

I had fallen into the habit of spending Friday afternoons in the Amsterdam office. While my mother, Roberto and Carlo were visiting Alfredo, I had taken it upon myself to look over the dealings for the week, fulfilling my promise to keep a watching brief. As soon as Carlo had left for the hospital, I would take the bulky printout from the wide middle drawer of Carlo's desk and run an eye over the figures. I hadn't made it past Tuesday when the alarm bells started to ring.

At first I tried to tell himself that I was wrong – it could easily have been that I had read about the company recently – the press, an analyst's report, maybe even heard it mentioned on the radio or TV – and that was why the name seemed so familiar. But I was uneasy, and had to check. I scanned the printed list of personnel on Carlo's desk, dialled a number and called for the company file.

I read it once; then, disbelieving the evidence of my own eyes, read it again. Carlo, I thought, shaking my head, you've been a naughty boy.

The meeting lasted only half an hour, there being nothing exceptional to report. Or nothing anyone was prepared to admit to.

Twice, I had asked, 'Anything else we should know about?' Carlo had shaken his head on both occasions. Twice, I had been tempted to take the file from my briefcase and pass it across the table to my mother. And twice, I had said nothing and done nothing. Now I sat uncomfortably in Carlo's apartment, drinking watery coffee and staring at an unwanted brandy, waiting for an opportune moment which I knew would never naturally arise.

'Nice place,' I said, purely for something to say.

The apartment was on the top floor of a four-storey house overlooking one of Amsterdam's many canals. The main room, dissonant with the age and character of the building, was furnished in an ultra-modem style that was more eye-catching than eye-pleasing: lots of brushed steel and odd-shaped semi-reclining white leather chairs more suitable to a clinical psychiatrist's consulting-room than someone's home; spotlights recessed into the ceiling directed harsh concentrated beams of light on to technicolor abstract paintings that made no sense at all to me.

'Do you see the paintings?' Carlo asked.

See them, hear them screaming, feel the pain in my optic nerves, I felt like replying, but that would hardly create the right atmosphere for what I had to say.

I nodded.

Carlo puffed out his chest and made a minute adjustment to the sleeves of his silk shirt so that the gold cufflinks were completely on show. 'I picked them up for just a few thousand bucks,' he said. 'One day that artist is going to hit the big time, and I'm going to make a killing.'

I forced a smile. This was getting harder with every minute.

'You've not touched your brandy,' Carlo said anxiously. 'It's the real stuff – cognac extra vielle, you know? Don't you like it? Can I get you something different?'

He walked across the room to a tall mirrored cupboard and opened the doors to reveal a hi-tech equivalent of an old-fashioned bureau. Papers were strewn about inside, even though there seemed to be storage slots and holes for every conceivable purpose. Carlo pushed the top edge of the central compartment and it slid out on a spring. He produced a small package from the hidden drawer. 'How about something to smoke?' he said, smiling proudly. 'Believe me, Brother, this is pure gold.'

'If that's what I think it is,' I said angrily, 'get rid of it right now.'

'Cool down, Gianni. This is Amsterdam. You can buy this stuff in any café or bar. It's easily available to anyone.'

'You're not anyone, Carlo. You're a member of the Gordini family – a member of the Silver banking dynasty – and that carries responsibilities. Think of the harm it would do if someone got hold of the story that you smoked dope.'

'I only smoke in the privacy of my home. And, let's face it, if you were searching the place, would you have found it? Relax, Brother.'

I sprang out of the chair, strode across the room and snatched the package from his hand. I left the room and flushed it down the john.

'Sit down,' I said, on returning. 'You and I need to have a serious talk.'

'Spare me the lectures. You don't have to treat me like a kid any more.'

'Really?' I said. 'Then let's have a full and frank adult conversation. Tell me about Majestix.'

'What's to tell?' Carlo said. 'Majestix is an emergent technology company.'

'Cut the crap, Carlo.'

'They design software. They're working on a couple of very interesting projects. Once they get the bugs ironed out and launch the products on the market, it's my bet that Microsoft will make a bid.'

'Is that why you loaned them five million dollars last week?'

'You been spying on me, Gianni?'

'Answer the question.'

'Yes, that's why I loaned them five million dollars. It's a good investment – big fat profits for the bank. And what's the problem? Five million is within my agreed limit.'

'Not when you add it to the fifteen million you've already lent them, or taken as share capital, it's not.'

Carlo's face went white. He sat down, picked up his brandy glass and downed the contents in one large gulp.

'They've got a bit of a temporary cash-flow problem,' he said.

'A cash injection of twenty million in the last three months is *not* "a bit of a temporary cash-flow problem". It's a bloody great black hole sucking in money.'

'What could I do?' Carlo whimpered. 'I had to keep pumping in more money or they would have gone bust. And then I would have lost the original five million. Think what Roberto would have said about that. And what he would have done. It'll be OK, Gianni. All they need is a little time. I know these guys, Gianni. They're on the brink. A few weeks, month or two, maybe, and we'll get our loans repaid and double our investment on the shares. Trust me.'

I sighed heavily. Ran my hand thoughtfully across my mouth. Looked over at my brother. Shook my head sadly.

'What are you going to do?' Carlo asked.

'I don't know. I know what I should do, and that's tell Mother and Roberto.'

'And they'll crucify me.'

'What choice do I have? If either of them asks to see your books, they'll spot the loans as easily as I did. And if they kick you out, can you blame them? There were conditions, remember? You exceeded your limit, Carlo.'

'But not your limit,' Carlo said.

'What the hell does that mean?'

'Transfer the loan and share purchase to the London books. That way nobody has exceeded their limit. All I ask is that when the bank makes a big fat profit, you give me the credit for the original tip on Majestix.'

'You're that confident about them?' I asked.

'It's a sure-fire bet,' Carlo said casually, sensing me wavering. 'Why don't I set up a meeting with them? Once you've spoken to them, heard their ideas, seen the potential, I guarantee you'll feel the same way as I do. Come on, Gianni. Do it for little brother. Get me off the hook.'

'If I do it, you have to promise to stick to the rules from now on. And no drugs. OK?'

'Sure, Gianni. I promise.'

'Very well. I'll transfer the loan and the shares across to the London books. But you better be right about this, Carlo.'

'Thanks, Gianni. You won't regret this.'

But I did. I had already made the arrangements to transfer the loan and shares into the London books when I found out that the proposed meeting with the emergent technology *wunderkind* had run into 'logistical difficulties'. When I finally met them the following Friday, my heart dropped straight through the floor of Carlo's fourth-storey apartment and didn't stop until it landed beating rapidly in the basement.

It wasn't that the two principals of the company were stereotypical long-haired boffins just out of short pants, or that I could understand very little of the acronym-rich terminology they used, or that I felt unconvinced about their tenuous hypothesis that the whole basis of the computing industry was making people crave for something that not only did they not need but up to that moment did not want either. Although none of that had inspired confidence. It was that they did not have a single clue about business, their idea of solving a problem being to throw more resources at it: where they should have been standing back and taking a critical overview, they were digging themselves deeper and deeper into the complexities until completely buried by them.

Two weeks later, the expected happened – they asked for another loan or for the bank to buy more shares, the latter betraying their own pessimistic view on the future of the company. I refused; how could I sanction throwing more good money after all the bad? I gave them a little breathing space, generating some cash by tweaking the finances – selling the computer equipment, office furniture and cars and leasing them all back.

Four weeks later, the inevitable happened. Every last penny had run out and the software still had more bugs than a rotting corpse. It was time to cut the losses and put Majestix out of its misery. And it was time to face the music at the Friday evening meeting.

'How much?' Roberto shouted, his face having gone past the white of shock into the red of anger. Purple veins throbbed visibly on his forehead. 'How much did you say?'

'Twenty million dollars,' I said, looking at Roberto and avoiding eye contact with my mother. 'We may salvage something if we can sell the copyright on the software to another developer.'

'If we can find as big a fool as you,' Roberto said. 'So the London office has lost us a cool twenty million dollars?'

It was a rhetorical question, asked solely for the purposes of public humiliation.

'Yes, but. . . .' I began.

'Don't bother with any buts,' Roberto said. 'There are no excuses worth twenty million dollars. The rest of us sweat blood to add every single dollar to the bank's profits and you drop twenty million in one go. Not only that, you do it at the precise time when we have all worked hard to restore confidence in the bank functioning normally without Father.'

My mother buried her face in her hands.

I turned to Carlo.

Carlo turned his face to the table. Studied his glass of water. Made a slow but slight alteration to the geometric positioning of his pen on the pad of paper.

'Let me explain,' I said.

'This isn't the time for explanation,' Roberto said. 'It's the time for resignation. Are you going to do the honourable thing? Or do you have as much honour as business acumen? And by that I mean zero.'

'Look,' I began.

'I'll look all right, Brother,' Roberto said, spitting out the last word. 'I'll look at the balance sheet for the London office. And I'll see red.'

'Here's the file,' I said, passing the bulging folder across the table. 'Read it before you pass judgement.'

Roberto picked up the file and tossed it into the bin.

'I haven't got time to read dead files,' Roberto said. 'Someone here has to concentrate on getting this bank back on track. Now, are you going to make us vote on it?'

I looked at the faces in the room. Roberto, the twisted smile of a gloating winner on his lips – to him, the twenty million was value for money; Carlo, sweet and innocent, and silent; my mother, biting her lower lip as if to stop herself saying, 'You let me down, Gianni. I can't save you now'.

'Get out, Gianni,' Roberto said with contempt. 'Get out of this room. Get out of our bank while it's still solvent. And get out of our lives, you bastard.'

I got up slowly from the table, waiting for Carlo or my mother to have a change of heart and call me back. No chance. I walked to the door. Shrugged my shoulders at my mother. And took one last look at Roberto and Carlo.

'At least I'm a bastard by birth,' I said to them. 'And not by my own making.'

7

Amsterdam. The present.

Dutch customs welcomed us with open arms. The trouble was the hands had plastic gloves on.

The three of us made an unlikely trio and, as Gus had said, there was an air about Bull and I that said we were going to be trouble. We were yanked out of the line of people filtering through the nothing-to-declare channel as if we were wearing suits with little arrows on them. We filed up to a low counter. Behind it stood a large man in what looked like a brand-new dark-blue uniform. He had a round face and a short moustache which, along with his bulk, made him look like Oliver Hardy or an overweight Hitler. By the scowl on his face I guessed at the latter. He pointed a pudgy finger at the counter and indicated that we should open our bags.

He delved into Bull's rucksack, removed items of clothing piece by piece with a thumb and forefinger as if handling toxic waste and dumped them in an untidy heap on the counter. Next he turned to mine and went through the same overdramatic pantomime so that there were now two untidy heaps on the counter. Dissatisfied that he had found no contraband, he turned to Gus's finely tooled leather bag. As he was about to reach inside a man dressed in the same dark-blue uniform but with lots of gold braid on his arm and epaulettes came into the customs hall. He glanced at Gus, did a double-take and hurried over to us.

'What is the meaning of this?' he said to Hitler.

'Routine check, sir,' was the tremulous reply.

'And is this how you conduct all your searches?' he asked. Hitler remained silent, anxious not to get in any more trouble.

'Mr Gordini,' the superior officer said to Gus. 'Allow me to apologize for the treatment you have been subjected to. This man is new here and doesn't know who you are, otherwise he would not have stopped you and your companions. Please let me make amends by offering you some coffee while your belongings are packed for you.'

Gus accepted and the man led us along a corridor. He walked ahead in a manner which suggested that every last move had been practised to perfection in front of a mirror. As we walked behind, I turned to Gus and whispered, 'How do you know him?'

Gus just gave me a shrug and a wicked smile.

The office was large and equipped not only with a desk, but a table and chairs set out for a meeting. We were ushered to the table. He pressed an intercom button on his desk and asked for a jug of coffee to be brought in.

'While we are waiting,' he said, still trying to work out why two such unlikely characters should be accompanying Gus, 'may I introduce myself? Peder van Eisen, head of Customs.' He turned to Bull and me and said, 'Now, may I have a look at your passports.'

We handed them over. He flicked through the pages and lingered over the stamps inside.

'So you are a Gordini too,' he said to me.

'Rebecca's son,' I said.

'And you seem to have travelled around a lot.'

'Call it a sabbatical,' I said.

'Why were you in Israel?'

'Going back to my Jewish roots.'

'And Bosnia, Crotia, Serbia, Angola.' He made a waving gesture with his hand to indicate that he couldn't be bothered with all the other countries.'

'Bull and I were in what you might call law enforcement.'

'You were in the police?' he said, sounding surprised.

'More like the army,' I said.

'Ah,' he said, as if it had all begun to make sense. 'Would that be a private army?'

'Very private,' I said.

The coffee arrived, relieving me of the need to explain further, but he had got the picture.

He poured coffee and passed it around the table.

'You know why you were stopped?' he said.

'Because we look like easy targets,' I said.

'Exactly. I would advise you in future to look – how can I put this – less conspicuous.'

'Wouldn't a professional drug smuggler take the trouble to blend in with the background?'

'Oh, they take the trouble, all right.' He got up from the table and went across to his desk. He picked up a folder and looked inside.

'Look at this,' he said, handing the file to me.

There was a picture inside that made no sense.

'A baby,' I said. 'What has that got to do with smuggling dope?'

'Look at the next picture,' he said.

I turned over the first picture and studied the second. It was the same baby, but this time without all the swaddling clothes. Now it was clear. The pallor, the posture like a broken doll. The baby was dead. And on its chest was a pattern of stitches running in a T-shape. I felt the bile rise in my throat. I showed the picture to Bull, who took one look and averted his eyes.

'This is the trouble they take. The baby's dead – might be natural causes, might not, it doesn't matter to them, it's just a vehicle – and they cut into the body, remove the internal organs and fill the void with heroin. This is the sort of people we are dealing with. Nothing – no life – is sacred to them. They are the scum of the earth and we are forever playing catch up with their new and ingenious ways to get past us.'

'Why not hit them at source rather than going for the couriers?' I asked.

'Because for that we need co-operation, and the governments in the source countries don't give a damn. All they care about is their own economy and the payoffs in their own pockets. Getting rid of the drug barons would cost them dear, both as a nation and as individuals.'

'There must be ways,' I said.

'If you think of one, let me know.' He took out his wallet and slid a card across the table. 'Here's my number. Ring for me if you have any problems here in the future. And take my advice, try to look more' – he searched for the right word that wouldn't cause too much offence – 'more normal.' He took one last look at me and Bull, six foot six, shaved head, muscular body, black as night. 'Forget it,' he said.

Forgetting his advice was easy. But there could be no forgetting the sickening vision of the stitched-up baby.

8

Carlo's apartment was pretty much the same as my last ill-fated visit. The only difference was that the paintings had gone and, judging by the clean rectangles where they had hung, had not been replaced with whatever was the latest fashion trend in the art world. Had he made the killing he'd expected, or simply sold them for what he could get?

Bull gazed around the room with a critical eye. Took in the brushed steel and white leather chairs, the sparkling glass coffee table, the harsh lighting, the whole minimal look.

'Don't reckon he spent much time here,' he said. 'Either that or he's got even worse taste than you. Which would be difficult.'

'My interior designer walked out on me,' I said. 'I wonder what Carlo's excuse is.'

I went through to the kitchen to make some coffee. It was clean and tidy, nothing out of place. While the coffee was brewing, I checked out the two bedrooms. Both beds were made up with fresh, neatly ironed sheets. Carlo must have a cleaner. Would be good to talk to her. Find out if anything, apart from Carlo, was missing.

I poured brandy into the coffee and passed a cup to Bull, who was perched on one of the chairs as if it might break at any moment. He shivered. 'Be good to get some warm clothes in the morning,' he said.

'And some food,' I said. 'Let's drink our coffee and call it a day.'

*

Later we would argue over who heard the noise first, whose senses were the sharpest, whose reactions were quickest. I suspect both of us thought it was a draw but were too proud to admit that.

It was Bull's coffee cup that did it. He'd placed it on the floor so as not to mark the table. We awoke to the sound of a curse as someone tripped over it. I opened the door of my bedroom a crack and peered through. The intruder was dressed all in black and was wearing a watch cap. The bureau door was open and the figure was rifling through the papers inside by the light of a torch.

I gestured to Bull, black as night right down to his boxer shorts, who was peering out of his bedroom, and signalled towards the intruder. As I came out of the bedroom into full view, the intruder turned and ran. Straight into the arms of Bull. He pinned his arms to his sides.

'Let's see what we've got,' I said to Bull.

I grabbed the watch cap and pulled it off. A cascade of long blonde hair flowed to the intruder's shoulders.

'Get off me,' she said, struggling against Bull's hold.

Bull raised her arms above her head and said, 'Frisk her, Johnny.'

She was clean. No gun. Just some car keys and a set of pick-locks.

'Bull's going to let you go. When he does, you move slowly and carefully to that chair. Any quick movements and you'll realize how Bull got his name.'

Bull let go. She shook herself and walked slowly to the chair. As she turned I got my first real look at her. She was five ten, maybe eleven. Hundred pounds or so. Filled her black jeans and sweater in all the right places. Her face, framed by the blonde hair, was lightly made up, although it didn't seem to me as if she needed any. Her eyes were deep blue and shone like beacons. Her lips were full and red. If you're going to have intruders, then you'd pick this one.

'I'm going to ask you some questions,' I said. 'If you duck any, I'll call the police. Is that clear?'

She nodded.

'What are you doing here?' I asked.

'I might ask the same about you,' she replied.

It's hard to be taken seriously when you're only wearing boxer shorts.

'Let's start again,' I said, sighing. 'What's your name?'

'Verkenner,' she said. 'In English that means Scout.'

'Scout,' Bull and I echoed simultaneously.

'You got a problem with that? she said.

'Why Scout?' I asked.

'It's a name my dad gave me because I'm good at tracking down people.'

'Useful talent to have,' I said. 'And what are you doing here, Scout? Who are you trying to track down?'

'My father,' she said. 'He went missing three days ago.'

'And what does that have to do with my brother Carlo, the guy who owns this place?'

'My father is a private investigator. He was hired to find your brother. After just one day he went missing. No phone calls to tell me what he was doing. Not a word. Zero. Zilch. *Nada*. I've been to all his usual haunts when he's on a case and drawn a blank. I thought I might find a clue here.'

'And did you?'

'Not yet,' she said. She looked at me sternly. 'You should be more careful where you put your coffee cups. I could have broken my ankle. Slapped a law suit on you for compensation. How about that, buster?'

'My name's not Buster. I'm Johnny and this is Bull.'

I pondered for a moment. I could turn her over to the police, but that seemed a bit harsh. I could let her go, but I had the feeling she would dog our feet and maybe mess something up. Did I want her inside the tent or outside? No contest. I liked her style.

'We're looking for my brother. It could be we share a common cause. Seems too much of a coincidence that your father goes missing as soon as he starts investigating Carlo's disappearance. We need someone with local knowledge – mine is out of date. Maybe we can join forces. What do you say?'

'As long as you don't slow me down,' she said grudgingly.

Scout made coffee while Bull and I put on some clothes. Then we all gathered round the bureau and examined its contents.

The neatness of the apartment didn't extend to the bureau. It had every semblance of bills thrown on a heap without much attention to referring to them later. Some were still in unopened envelopes. This seemed to be the ostrich school of filing, or an example of the impulse control disorder that Carlo was prone to and which could lead him into rash decisions.

Scout and I scrutinized each bill and then passed them to Bull for putting into date order. A pattern rapidly emerged. Carlo was in deep trouble. Every credit card was up to its limit – and they were big – through a series of cash transactions, and his bank account was in the red, consisting of a succession of withdrawals way above his monthly salary. I started to get an ache in the pit of my stomach about what we might find at Silvers.

'Get me the latest bill for his credit cards, his mobile phone and the last bank statement.'

'What are you going to do?' I said.

'I've got contacts working in the credit-card companies, the phone company and the bank.'

'You've got a contact in Silvers?' I would have to address the security there when I paid my first visit.

'I told you I was a good tracker. How do you think I do it?'

Bull got the bills in order.

'Jeez,' he said, looking at them one last time as he passed them to Scout. 'I haven't earned this much money in my whole life, let alone spent it.'

'But what was he spending it on?' I said. 'That's the key question.'

'Drugs,' said Scout. 'It's got all the hallmarks of drugs. A habit he can't kick.'

That ache in my stomach got worse. I remembered back to the last time I was in this apartment. I pressed the catch on the secret compartment and watched as it slid open.

No drugs, thankfully. It was empty apart from one item. A golden gambling chip marked with the logo of a casino – El Dorado.

'Where is this place?' I asked.

'Leidseplein,' she said. 'Where all the nightlife is. If you want to enjoy yourself in Amsterdam, you go to Leidseplein. Restaurants, bars, nightclubs, casinos. El Dorado isn't the only one.'

'OK,' I said. 'Meet you there at eight. We'll go somewhere for dinner and, when the action has hotted up go on to the casino.'

She nodded, frowned and then shook her head.

'Take a tip from someone who's used to working undercover. You guys are going to have to smarten up if you don't want to attract a heap of attention.'

'We can do that,' I said.

'OK, then. See you there. And,' she said, still not convinced, 'don't let me down.'

Who the hell was supposed to be running this show?

9

Amsterdam is a dangerous place. If the trams don't get you the trucks will. If the trucks don't get you the cars will. If the cars don't get you the cyclists will. Even the pedestrians have sharp elbows. We'd had breakfast with Gus at his hotel, picked up some cash as an advance on expenses, a couple of mobile phones, got the name of the compliance officer and then diced with death by walking around the city getting a haircut, picking up new outfits and some food for the apartment. After dropping everything off at the apartment, Bull went to do a more thorough reconnaissance of the city and I changed into a new suit and headed off to Silvers.

Business must have been good. The bank was now housed on the top two floors of a brand new tower block overlooking the canals. Didn't have much soul, but then banking never did. Nor a heart, come to think of it.

The offices were mainly open-plan with two rooms screened off by smoked glass, one for client meetings, the other the office of Carlo. Which was where I was sitting waiting for the arrival of Ms Oakley, the compliance officer. It was an odd office seemingly furnished by whim. Nothing matched – an antique partners' desk behind which Carlo would sit, a Scandinavian pine table and chairs for formal meetings, an odd sculpture made of bronze in the representation of a stylized horse grazing, several paintings consisting of wide bands of colour and nothing else – and everything appeared as if purchased without any thought as to what would fit together.

She came in like an extra from *Conan the Librarian*. Dark-grey trouser suit, low heels, white blouse, dark hair scraped back and held by a lethal-looking grip and a pair of black, heavy-rimmed spectacles. She sat down in Carlo's seat and gave me a forced smile.

'What can I do for you, Mr Gordini?' she said.

No introduction, no handshake, nothing. I got the distinct impression that she regarded me as something lower than an amoeba in the evolutionary chain. 'You have instructions from my brother Roberto?' I said.

'That is correct.'

'So you are authorized, indeed ordered, to talk to me about the state of the bank's finances and anything that might relate to Carlo's absence?'

'That is correct.'

'So what have you found out?'

She opened a folder on the desk and consulted it. A stray wisp of hair dropped across her forehead and she flicked it away in annoyance. Her nails were not like I was expecting – didn't match the rest of the look – they were long and varnished a deep brown. She saw me looking and clenched her fists.

'It would appear,' she said, 'that there are ten million euros in bearer bonds that we can't locate. They were in the safe when they were last checked a few days ago, but now seem to have gone missing.'

This was bad. A bearer bond is just what it says – it's like a blank cheque – all you have to do is have the bonds in your possession and they can be cashed at any bank. You don't have to present any ID. Possession of the bonds – bearing them – is all that counts.

'None of the bonds has been encashed to date. While they are missing, I've put them down to a loan account in your brother's name – we don't want anyone to get the wrong impression.'

'Or, more importantly, the right one,' I said. 'What else have you dug up?'

'I would have thought that was enough.'

'How long have you been going through the books?'

'Three days.'

'And that's all you've got?'

She nodded.

'So you've stopped digging?'

'I am thorough, Mr Gordini,' she said, with a lot more condescension than was necessary. 'I am acknowledged to be the best at my job that there is – and not just within Silvers. I continue to dig.'

'Maybe I could help,' I said.

'You?' she said, suppressing a smile but unable to hide a look of contempt.

'I used to run the London operation, you know.'

'So I heard,' she said, as if I'd fallen into a trap and proved her point. 'I think you can leave everything in my capable hands.'

So my reputation had preceded me.

'Do you read the Cyclops column in the *Wall Street Journal*?' I asked innocently.

'Hot share tips of the week? Of course I read it. Doesn't everybody?'

'I write it.'

'What? You?' she said, her voice an octave higher.

I smiled at her and nodded. How's that for your Darwinian theory?

'But Roberto said. . . .'

'I imagine he did. The point is that I have some skills that might help you speed up your investigation. I'm used to digging around and sniffing out things.'

She regained her composure.

'Thank you for the kind offer,' she said, 'but I think I can manage without calling on your services.' She focused on the folder again and took out a silver plastic card. She passed it across the desk to me. 'That's to help with your expenses – it's a debit card on an account I was instructed to set up for you.'

She closed the folder and stood up.

'Rest assured I will be in contact should I uncover anything else. Thank you, Mr Gordini.'

'You catch more flies with honey than you do vinegar,' I said to her back, as she walked to the door.

'Excuse me?' she said. 'I don't understand.'

'Apparently not,' I said, walking past her. 'Don't worry, Ms Oakley. I'll find my own way out.' At the doorway I turned around and added, 'Nice nails by the way.'

She looked down and then put her hands behind her back.

'*Ciao,*' I said.

10

'You guys scrub up well,' Scout said.

'I could say the same thing about you,' I replied.

Scout, Bull and I were sitting at a pavement café in the main square in Leidseplein eating steak and *frites* and watching the world go by. Every big city has a place where locals and tourists mix to eat, drink, to promenade, to see and be seen. Leidseplein was Amsterdam's version and at eight o'clock it was already busy, bright and colourful from the women's dresses. From our table we could look across the square to the two casinos, the Lido and the El Dorado, and left and right to the surrounding cafés and bars. Every so often someone would walk by smoking and leave a hint of cannabis in the air – this was Holland after all.

Bull and I, sitting with our backs to the wall – old habits die hard – were wearing dark suits and crisp white shirts and Scout, blonde hair caressing her shoulders, had on a little black dress that would be perfect in the casino later on when the action got started. You had to look at her twice to recognize that this was the same girl as the intruder of the night before.

I poured some red wine, leaned back in my chair and looked at her in a new light. This more feminine version carried an air of vulnerability and at the back of her mind, I guessed, was anxiety over her father's disappearance.

'We'll compare notes later, but first tell us about yourself,' I said.

'Mother English, Father Dutch – so I'm bilingual.' Her fingers ran up and down the glass distractedly as she cast her mind back.

71

'My mother died when I was about ten so I was pretty much brought up by my father with a little help from my grandparents. Dad is an ex-cop – inspector in the Amsterdam police. When he retired he set himself up as a private detective – missed the investigations, I suppose. Or maybe it was all he knew how to do. Anyway, I studied law at the university in Den Haag and bored myself silly. After I graduated I joined Dad in what now became the family business. Dad taught me all I know.'

'Sounds like he did a great job. You've turned out a bit sassy, but—'

'Are you being funny?'

'Apparently not.'

I sipped my wine and looked at her over the rim of the glass. She was truly beautiful and I found it hard not to stare at her.

'What sort of business did the agency specialize in?' Bull asked, filling the silence when I was lost for words.

'A lot of divorce work. You know, catch the spouse *in flagrante delicto*. That's how I learnt to track people. It worked well. If you suspect you might be followed, the last thing you're expecting is a girl.'

I nodded. It made sense. A great indictment of adulterers.

'So,' I said, 'this was more exciting than the law?'

'There was other stuff as well. Teenagers going missing, or parents wanting to see what they were up to and whether it involved drugs. A bit of corporate work too – industrial espionage, I guess. Referrals from Dad's friends in the force – cases that were considered dead, but the victim wanted some resolution. We made a good living.'

I noticed the use of the past tense, but let it slide for the moment.

'What did your father tell you about the Case of the Missing Carlo?'

'Not a lot. I was working on another case – errant husband, wife wants a divorce and to take him for all she can. Our paths didn't cross for the couple of days he'd been working on finding Carlo. There was the usual file, but very little of any worth in it. That was when I started to get really worried.'

'Why?'

'There were two things. Firstly, Dad was a stickler for keeping detailed records. It was out of character of him not to leave some record of what he had been doing.'

'And secondly?'

'The door of the agency was kicked in.'

'Nothing like good detective work to turn up the clues.'

'I'm worried, Johnny. Don't make fun of me.'

'I'm sorry, Scout,' I said, feeling a heel for trying to lighten the mood by making a dumb joke. 'Once we're on the trail of Carlo, I'm sure your father will turn up – the disappearances can't be coincidental, so maybe we'll find them both in the same place. But where to look? That is the question.'

'Start with the casino and keep our fingers crossed?' Bull said.

'Not much of a plan,' I said, 'but it's all we've got.'

'How did you get on at Silvers?' Scout asked.

'Not good. Carlo, it appears, has taken ten million euros in bearer bonds, so now he could be anywhere, living it up. But that wasn't all. Either their compliance officer wasn't as good as she says, or Ms Oakley – Ms Straight Lace, more like it – is hiding something, or at least not telling me all she knows. She must have dug up something else that could have been useful in the three days she's been working on the case.'

'Why would she hide something that might lead us to Carlo?' Scout asked.

'That's the problem.' I pondered for a moment and couldn't think of a good answer. But there was something nagging at my brain. 'You say you have a contact inside Silvers?'

She nodded.

'Can you arrange a meeting for me?'

'No problem. I haven't learnt a lot today either,' she said. 'Carlo hasn't used any of his credit cards recently – not surprising as he's up to the limit. I've got feelers out at the airport, but no luck so far. I won't get detailed telephone or mobile bills until tomorrow, so there's still hope there. My contacts are trying to trace my father's usage of credit cards and mobile too. Better luck tomorrow, hopefully.'

I leaned back in my chair and stared up the street hoping for inspiration to come. That's when I saw her. I didn't recognize her at first. Only the nails were the same – either she'd forgotten earlier to change them to librarian mode, or vanity had got the better of her. Everything else about her was different. Dark hair no longer scraped back but flowing loosely over bare shoulders and the gossamer straps of her midnight-blue dress. Strappy, impractical shoes with high heels. And no glasses. She was walking along the street accompanied by a dark-haired, swarthy man – so swarthy that even two shaves a day won't remove the permanent black tattoo on his face. I whispered to Scout and Bull and pointed in Ms Oakley's direction.

'I can't believe the transformation,' I said. 'You should have seen her this afternoon. The type you wouldn't look twice at. And now look at her.'

'She's OK, I suppose,' said Scout grudgingly.

'Can you follow her?'

'Better than anyone else.'

'See what you can find out and meet us back at the apartment.'

She grabbed her coat and set off about twenty paces behind the pair. A man at a table in the corner took out his wallet, threw some notes on the table and left. Twenty paces behind Scout. What the hell was going on?

'See that man?' I said to Bull. 'Grey hair, trench coat with collar turned up?'

'Yep.'

'Follow him and find up why he's tracking Scout. Watch over her. See you later.'

Bull set off in pursuit. Now, if someone got up and followed Bull, I was in trouble. I'd run out of people for the caucus race. Still, this was a good sign – something was happening at last. I might not know what it was, but there was a chance that it could lead somewhere.

I sat there for a while, but no one suspicious got up. I fingered the golden chip in my pocket. Time to visit the casino and stake it on a turn of a wheel. I had a feeling our luck was changing.

The casino was on the ground floor of a modern eight-storey block. In the basement there was a theatre-restaurant where diners could watch a risqué cabaret while eating. The casino itself was on the ground floor and above that was a hotel. I was ushered inside the building by a squat man in a dinner jacket who looked more bouncer than concierge and through maroon-velvet brass-studded doors by someone who could have been his clone. I stood for a while inside the door and surveyed the scene. Because old habits die hard, I made a special point of noting the exits.

With my back to the cashiers' cages there was a highly polished wooden bar at the far end of the room. In the middle were tables for roulette, blackjack, baccarat, poker and, for our American friends, craps. Surrounding these were rows of slot machines. Waitresses circulated with trays of drinks and each of the gambling tables was manned by a stunning woman in a short black skirt, black jacket and waistcoat, white blouse, black bow tie and red high heels. They all seemed to have blonde hair and been chosen from the Croupier Barbie range.

I used my Silvers card to get €500 of red ten-euro chips and went across to the roulette table and watched the action for a while, familiarizing myself with the table and the four other players. In a casino the odds are always stacked in favour of the house. Your best chance of not losing too much was the even-money options on the roulette table – black or red, odd or even and 18 or less (manqué) or more than 18 (passé). I noted the wheel here had two zeros, doubling the odds in favour of the house. The croupier was efficient in her task: spinning the wheel clockwise, rolling the ball anticlockwise, announcing the winning bets and raking the chips to her end of the table. I sat down next to her.

I played red and black for about a quarter of an hour with no great losses or gains, simply transferring chips to the croupier and back again and vice versa. Frankly, it was rather boring. Maybe if I was playing with hundred-euro chips there might have been more of an adrenaline rush – or maybe I'd seen so much in the past and put my life on the line too many times that this was always going to be pretty tame.

I saw black chips and silver chips being wagered by others round the table but there was not a gold chip in sight. The only way to find its worth – and its secret – was to play it. I took it from my pocket and laid it before me while I deliberated what colour to place it on. The croupier saw the gold chip and deftly pulled it toward her and even more deftly palmed it. What was going on? If she was trying to steal my chip, then no matter how deftly she did it, it was still too blatant to get away with it.

There was a pause in the proceedings.

The croupier pushed a button at the side of the table and a light came on.

'Change of croupier, ladies and gentlemen,' she announced in a heavy accent which, by its moroseness, was probably Russian or Eastern European – some oppressed nation that hadn't got used to enjoying itself after many years of Soviet rule. She turned to me and whispered, 'Follow me, sir.' Another blonde-haired croupier seamlessly took her place.

She led me back through the doors to the lobby, nodded at the bouncer and pressed the button for the lift. Curiouser and curiouser. We travelled to the third floor and I followed her along the corridor. We entered a room. It had been done out in black and white and kept minimalist. White walls and carpet, black wardrobe, black dresser set up as a bar with a selection of alcoholic and soft drinks, and a huge bed with black satin sheets.

'Vodka with ice for me,' she said, looking at me slightly puzzled. 'Help yourself.'

As I poured her a stiff vodka she took off the jacket. And, as I got the same for myself, she unbuttoned the waistcoat.

'Well,' she said, letting her skirt drop to the floor. 'What is your pleasure? There's some outfits in the wardrobe if you'd like something special.'

She took the drink from me and sipped it and then put the glass down while she took off the bow tie and unbuttoned the shirt.

When the shirt came off to reveal a black basque, black stockings and suspenders I finally got the picture.

She was in good shape. Slim, but well endowed, helped, admittedly, by the upward and outward thrust of the basque. Her skin was clear and milky white as if intentionally to contrast the black of the bed. I guessed her age as twenty-five or so, although I didn't know how much toll this kind of work took on a girl.

'I'd like to talk,' I said.

She shrugged at me. 'Whatever,' she said. 'It's all the same price.'

'And the price is?' I asked.

'One golden chip, of course,' she said, looking puzzled again.

'And,' I said, 'humour me. How much is the golden chip worth?'

'One thousand euros,' she said. 'For that you get a whole hour.'

'Then let's talk first and see how much time we've got left.'

'As you wish. I'm here to serve you.'

I went to the wardrobe and found a black silk wrap and handed it to her so I could concentrate better. At €1,000 per hour I didn't want any distractions.

'What's your name?' I asked.

'Anna.'

'OK, Anna,' I said. 'I'm looking for my brother, Carlo Gordini.'

'Oh, Carlo,' she said with a hint of a smile. 'Dear sweet Carlo.'

'Tell me about him, Anna.'

'He is one of our regulars. We have a few men who work in Amsterdam and come once a week or so – the tourists, we only ever see once. Carlo, he would come every night.'

'Did you, er. . . ?'

'No, he only had eyes for Natasha.'

'Tell me about her,' I said, sipping the vodka. It was good, Russian and high strength.

She gave a loud laugh which echoed around the almost bare room. Drained her vodka and held out the glass for a refill.

'Poor sweet Carlo. He was a naughty boy.'

'Why? What did he do?'

'He fell in love.' She laughed louder this time. 'It sometimes happens. The girls are pretty here. They do exactly what a man wants. It can cloud a man's head. But none had it as bad as Carlo.'

I was beginning to dread the worst. If he had fallen in love and followed some impulse there was nothing he might not do.

'There is a private room here – for poker. High stakes. Carlo was not very good. Lost heavily. He should have stopped, but he fell in love with Natasha. She was one of the dealers. Natasha said it was love at first sight for both of them. His money must have helped too, though.'

'How did she know he had money?'

'Because of the poker and because of the golden chips.'

It was my turn to look puzzled. I nodded at her to continue.

'Carlo couldn't bear the thought of Natasha being with another man,' she explained. 'We work a six-hour shift here. Every night Carlo would buy six golden chips and spend all of Natasha's time with her.'

At €6,000 a night, even discounting the losses at poker, it was no wonder he had no money.

'Carlo's gone missing,' I said.

'That is good for Carlo,' she said.

'I don't understand,' I said.

'Five nights ago Natasha didn't show up for work. The boss thinks Carlo is responsible. He has men out looking for him. Bad men. It is better if they don't find him.' She made a throat-slitting gesture with her hand.

'Have you heard anything from Natasha? Do you have any idea where they might have gone?'

'Far away, I hope. For their sake.'

'And no contact from her?'

She shook her head.

'Tell me about Natasha. Where is she from? How did she finish up here?'

'The same way we all finish up here. We seek a better life and the men say they can give that to us. And they have been good to us.'

Turning them into prostitutes – albeit high class ones – didn't fit my definition of being good to someone.

'We come from Chechnya. Life is bad there. Either we are fighting a war against Russia or we're plotting one during a ceasefire. Much of the country's money goes on arms and armies. We are poor. There are food shortages – when food comes you spend all day queuing up and hoping there will be some left when it's your turn. Can anyone blame us for wanting a better life?'

She gulped down the second vodka and shook her head as I offered a refill.

'The men come. They are Russians, but they say they are good Russians. They will help us escape poverty. Smuggle us into a new country. They charge us little and treat us well. Everyone is sent to a hospital and is checked out to make sure they are fit for whatever work they find us in the new country. Then they give us the chance of a new life.'

'Not much of a life,' I said.

'I have plenty food, good vodka to drink, good clothes to wear and I get to keep twenty per cent of the money I earn. And in two years I am free to leave and go my own way.'

I was sceptical about the Russians keeping their side of the bargain. 'How many girls,' I asked, 'have you known who have left?'

'Plenty. Soon I will leave too. I have three months to go and plenty money saved.'

'So where do the girls go when they leave?'

'I do not know. None has ever made contact after they leave – maybe they don't like to be reminded of this life. But wherever they go, it must be a better place than Chechnya.'

'Look,' I said, writing on a napkin next to the drinks, 'here's my mobile number. If you hear anything from Natasha, let me know. There will be a reward.'

I stood up to go.

She let the robe slip and looked up at me.

'I could tell when I first met you that here was a man who would not need to pay. You are handsome, big and strong. You have no need for the likes of Anna. It would make you feel bad. But what if you consider the gold chip for the information and have the rest for free? We still have ten minutes.'

'Another time, maybe,' I said.

She shrugged. 'Ten minutes would not be enough, anyway,' she said. 'When I'm free of here I phone you and we meet up, yes?'

'I'd like that,' I said. I drained my vodka glass. 'Here's to freedom,' I said.

'No, wait,' she said.

The killer charm always works. She'll be foregoing her twenty per cent, I reckoned.

'She's in Holland.'

'What?'

'Natasha. She's in Holland. She doesn't have a passport. None of us has. The boss man, he keeps all our passports. So Natasha must still be in Holland.'

Bingo. Sometimes being wrong can be better than being right.

11

'Have you got a pencil?' I asked Scout.

It was midnight and she had just arrived back at the apartment. I was on my mobile phone talking to Bull.

'What do you mean, have I got a pencil?' she said. 'I've been schlepping around half of Amsterdam for the last three hours and all you do is ask me for a pencil. Hell, Johnny, where are you coming from?'

'Just trust me, OK? I need a pencil. A pen would do. Otherwise any instrument with a narrow barrel.'

She stared at me and heaved a sigh, dug into her handbag and produced a cheap ballpoint. It would serve its purpose. She handed it to me and I was out the door.

'Stay here,' I said, looking back.

I came out of the front entrance to the house, crossed the street, turned left, left, left and left again. Which brought me directly behind the guy in the trench coat. I wrapped my left hand around his mouth and dug the ballpoint into the small of his back with my right.

'Do you know,' I said, 'what damage a bullet from a Browning High Power can do to a man's spine at point-blank range?'

He gave a gurgle. I took it as a yes.

'So, we're going to walk across the street, into the building and up the stairs. If you give me any problems you'll be walking on your hands for the rest of your life.'

He did as I said. Up the three floors to Carlo's apartment. Bull joined us.

Scout looked puzzled as we entered.

'Who. . . ?' she started to say.

'That's what we're going to find out,' I said.

I turned to the man in the trench coat. He had a pale complexion like he didn't get out much, small eyes and was short and stocky. He was also sweating, despite the chill of the evening. Must have been the presence of the ballpoint. I nodded to Bull and he started to frisk the man. He was carrying. Glock 9mm – in that case, probably a professional. Bull handed me the gun and said, 'Wallet has cash but no ID.' He turned the man around so he was facing me. The man noticed the ballpoint for the first time and gave a scowl that told me he didn't seem pleased that he had been suckered.

'Now I'm going to ask you some questions,' I said, placing the nose of the Glock against his temple. 'If I don't get an answer, then my trigger finger is going to get twitchy, and you don't want that to happen, do you? What's your name?'

'No speak English.'

'Ask him in Dutch,' I said to Scout.

She did.

'No understand,' he said.

This was going to be a long night.

'Scout, could you get me a couple of dishcloths.'

She gave me a strange look, but trusted the bizarre request this time. I took one of the dishcloths and tied the man's hands together in front of him. The other cloth I stuffed in his mouth.

'Maybe some fresh air will loosen your tongue,' I said to the man. 'What do you reckon, Bull? Shall we open a window?'

Bull opened the window on the canal side of the apartment and I led the man towards it. Bull and I took a leg each and threw him out the window, catching him at the last moment and leaving him dangling. It was three floors up and below him the water gleamed like polished stone in the moonlight. He didn't like it one bit. Craned his neck to look up at us and gave stifled noises that would have been cries of panic without the cloth in his mouth.

'Listen carefully,' I said. 'If you're prepared to talk, nod your head.'

He nodded his head vigorously and we hauled him in slowly to spin out the suspense, if you pardon the pun. We dumped him in a chair facing the window and I removed the gag.

'We're losing our touch,' Bull said.

'What?'

'A few years ago he would have looked into our eyes and talked. He would have seen that we meant business, and that business was death. Now he stalled. Didn't believe us.'

'Maybe you're right,' I said.

'We're gonna have to toughen up,' he said. 'Starting now.'

'OK,' I said to Bull and the stalker. 'Let's start again. What's your name?'

'Bronski,' he said, glancing at the still-open window. That one word was enough to set alarm bells ringing in my head. Or rather the way he said it. Deep-toned, bored intonation.

'Well, Mr Bronski, what are you doing following my friend Scout?'

'Orders.'

I sighed.

'Let's not make this too lengthy, Bronski. Be specific. Whose orders?'

'Almas?'

'Yes.'

I looked across at Scout. She shrugged her shoulders.

'Tell me about him, or it, or whatever.'

'Big company here in Amsterdam. Much money. Much power. I protect people. I had call from the chief executive at Almas saying would I do this little job for them. The pay was good, so I said yes.'

'What does this Almas do?'

'Everything.'

God, this was like pulling teeth.

'OK, what were you supposed to do after trailing Scout?'

'Grab her when she was alone. Take her to a house.'

'Why?'

'I don't ask questions from Almas. Just do my job.'

'What's the address of this house?'

He gave it to me. I looked at Scout again.

'Run-down area to the south of the city. The sort of place you don't go unless you have to.'

'Which is a shame,' I said, 'because that is exactly what we're going to have to do tomorrow.'

'It is tomorrow,' said Scout, yawning.

'What are we going to do with Bronski?' Bull asked.

'Have you got a car, Scout?'

She nodded.

'Then let's all go for a ride.'

Her car was an anonymous black VW Beetle, ideal for trailing someone inconspicuously, but not accommodating four adults, two the size of Bull and Bronski. Bull had his knees round his ears and Bronski was stuffed into one corner.

We drove to the west of the city to a place called Erasmusparkand. Scout's driving was in the *Italian Job* mode – she seemed to know every back alley in Amsterdam and intended to use every one at the maximum possible speed. No one spoke – none of us dared to break her concentration. We dumped Bronski, bound hand and foot and gagged, in a group of trees. I kept the Glock. I was getting the feeling that it might come in useful.

On the way back we stopped at Scout's apartment and collected some things – we all agreed that it wasn't safe for her to be alone. By the time we got back it was three in the morning and we were all feeling the pace. There was still a debriefing to do before hitting the sack.

I made a huge pot of coffee and we sat together as comfortably as we could in the impractical chairs.

'I'll start, shall I?' I said. 'The gold chip isn't for betting. It's worth a thousand euros and pays for an hour of whatever is your pleasure with your pick of the dealers, who are all stunning, by the way.' Scout gave a feminist grunt. 'Carlo's been buying them like there's no tomorrow so that he gets all the time of his new love, Natasha. And so she's all his. He's also been losing big time at the tables. The girl has disappeared too. Good motive for stealing a bunch of bearer bonds. If my source' – another grunt from Scout – 'is to be believed, then they're still in Holland – the girl doesn't have a passport.'

'You can buy a lot of passports with ten million euros,' Scout said.

'If you've got the sources,' I said. 'I'm hoping that Carlo doesn't know that kind of people. If he gets outside Holland, our chances of finding him and the money get a whole lot slimmer.' I was beginning to wonder whether this haystack actually had a needle in it. 'What did the previous Ms Librarian get up to?'

'They walked round the Leidseplein soaking up the atmosphere and then went to El Dorado. They toured the tables like they were casing the joint, placing small bets here and there and taking everything in – they acted like it was more a job than a bit of fun. After that they went to The Bulldog, one of the coffee shops, and watched people rolling up joints – they just had coffee. Then it was back to the square and brandys at a table outside. I sat behind them and listened to what they were talking about.'

'Learn anything useful?' I asked.

'Only that I should have studied Italian. They were talking nineteen to the dozen and I couldn't understand a word of it. Strange though, the guy seems to speak perfect English – ordered the brandy with an American accent.'

'They didn't spot you?'

'No way.'

'Then I presume they were being very careful to speak Italian to each other. Damn. I wished I'd been there. Can't be helped. And after the brandy?'

'Proper gentleman. He walks her back to her hotel – she's staying at the Schiller, just about the most chic hotel in the city – and then he gets a taxi. She goes straight to her room. Exit Scout, straight back here.'

'Seems like there's more to this that we have to find out. We need that meeting with your contact inside Silvers. Tomorrow would be good.'

'No problem, as long as I'm there – I'm the draw.'

I nodded. Then thought for a while, weighing up options and possibilities.

'We need to get out of here, find somewhere anonymous where we can hide away and they won't think of looking for us.'

'Who's they?' Bull said.

'That's the problem. Let's start by following up on our friend Bronski and this Almas company. See if we can find out why they're interested in Scout.'

'I don't know about you guys,' Scout said yawning, 'but I need some sleep. It's been a long night and it sounds like tomorrow won't get any easier. Where can I sleep?'

I indicated the room that Bull had been using.

'Goodnight and sleep tight,' she said.

'Yeah,' we said.

We watched her go into the bedroom and then looked at each other.

'First or second?' Bull asked.

'I'll take second.' I put the Glock on the coffee table. 'Wake me in two hours.'

12

Whatever they did at Almas there were a lot of people doing it. Their offices were on the top three floors of a modem building on a business estate so close to the airport you could see the colour of the lipstick the cabin crew were wearing. Bull and I approached the reception area where a large purpose-built desk was ruled by a hard-looking lady of about forty. She had large, black-rimmed glasses that she peered over to examine us. The glasses accentuated the lightness of her eyes. Her hair, judging by the eye colour, was artificially jet black and it did nothing for her except to make her look more formidable. She wasn't fazed by Bull, which was always a bad sign. Our chances of getting past her seemed as remote as sneaking a giraffe into a rabbit hutch.

'We'd like to see your chief executive, please,' I said, with what I imagined was wasted politeness.

'Do you have an appointment?' she said.

'Not exactly,' I said.

'Mr Garanov doesn't see anyone without an appointment.'

'He'll see us,' I said, trying to think of a good reason why.

'Mr Garanov doesn't see anyone without an appointment.'

This was looking like a stalemate.

'Perhaps if I give you my calling card.'

I reached inside my jacket and took out the Glock from its place inside the waistband at the small of my back. I ejected the clip and placed the unloaded gun on her desk. She looked at it in horror, got up quickly and, carrying the gun between finger and thumb, scuttled off to an office in the corner of the building, looking back at us as she did so.

'You didn't say it,' Bull said.

'I'm saving it for our exit.'

'Can't wait,' Bull said with a grin.

The receptionist reappeared flanked by two gorillas in tight-fitting dark suits.

'If you would follow these gentlemen,' she said, her composure returning to normal aided by the presence of the heavies, 'Mr Garanov will see you now.'

It's wonderful how the presence of a Glock can make even the busiest man find a time window in his diary.

One of the gorillas moved behind us and the other set off in front. Bull made a point of walking backward so that he could keep an eye on the trailing gorilla. We reached the corner office and the first gorilla knocked and, when summoned, we all trooped in and the gorillas took up station at each side of the door.

Garanov did not offer us a seat. He sat behind a large black desk, the muscles of his upper body straining against sleeves of the pale-blue shirt. He had a thick neck and close-cropped hair which was probably black and streaked with grey if you used your imagination or grey and streaked with black if you didn't.

'Do you know it is illegal to carry guns in this country?' he said. 'You can only own a gun if you belong to a registered gun club; you must keep it at that club and can only fire it at that club. You could be in big trouble.'

'You should have told that to Bronski,' I said.

'Who?' he replied.

'You sent Bronski to tail one of our friends and snatch her if he got the chance. Only Bronski wasn't good enough. And that will be the same for anyone else you send, so don't waste your time thinking about it.' I moved closer to the desk and leaned over towards him. 'What does this company do, Mr Garanov, that it has to rely on muscle like Bronski?'

'We do a multitude of things. We're an investment company with a finger in – how do you say it? – many pies.'

He smiled at me. It didn't suit him. Came out all lop-sided. It was hard to get those underused muscles to work.

'If you do anything to harass or harm Scout in any way, we will be back. Only next time we won't hand in the gun.'

We made our way towards the door and stopped at the entrance. Bull looked me. 'Time to say it,' he said.

I nodded and faced Garanov.

'Remember,' I said, 'we deal in lead, friend.'

'So what did we accomplish there?' Bull asked as he sipped his espresso.

We were in one of the brown cafés, the fourth we had tried so that the smell of skunk wouldn't get to us – this one sold cannabis cake instead.

'Well,' I said, 'we had the first laugh since we got here.'

'Gotta count for something,' Bull said, nodding his head.

'And we know that these Almas guys are up to something. We can check them out and it might give us a clue. Garanov didn't strike me as the sort of guy who would pussy-foot around. We've shaken his tree so let's see what lands on the ground.'

'This is escalating, isn't it?' Bull said.

I nodded.

'Do you get the feeling we might be outgunned?' he said.

I nodded again, knowing what was coming.

'What happens to the money if we call in reinforcements?' he asked.

'Michael gets his operation and we all split the rest.'

'That seems unfair,' he said.

'We stick together and look after our own. That was the philosophy that kept us alive in Bosnia, Serbia, Angola and all points north, south, east and west. We're not going to change it now.'

It was his turn to nod, only he did it with sadness in his eyes.

'I'll make the arrangements,' I said.

13

While I went to an internet café, Bull and Scout were off finding a place where all of us, current and future, could hit the mattresses. I ordered a double shot of espresso, logged on and entered the bible of the mercenary, the *Soldier of Fortune* website. From there it was through to the bulletin board and posting the coded message that we had agreed upon when we left Africa. Now it was down to when the three of them would get round to checking the bulletin board and noticing the message. After that I could make the necessary arrangements to wire them funds if they were needed. I hoped it wouldn't be long. I had a feeling that the search for Carlo was spiralling out of control and, the worst thing was, I felt naked and exposed without a gun in my hand.

I finished the coffee, ate the little gingery biscuit that came with it, letting it dissolve on my tongue to make the pleasurable taste last longer, and leaned back in the chair, staring at the screen. Would they respond? Would they then come? How had the years affected them? Had they grown soft? Lost that survival instinct? It didn't bear thinking about.

I hunched back over the keyboard and emailed my editor at the *Wall Street Journal* and made grovelling excuses why there wouldn't be a 'Hot Tips' column this week and maybe the next too. I told him I was working on a big story and the result would be worth it in the end. I hoped Lady Luck would be on my side and I could deliver on my promises.

It took me three attempts to get a cab, drivers not being

interested for some reason. The third driver seemed to agree to take me with much reluctance. When we got to the address I saw why. The area was run down: blocks of flats where the concrete had long since been blackened by the everyday pollution, turn-of-the-century houses with neglected façades, communal rubbish bins spilling over, stinking and unsightly, the odd abandoned stripped and burnt-out car, a group of down-and-outs sitting on the floor drinking cheap booze. It was the side of Amsterdam the tourist board didn't want you to see, but that existed in most major cities. I paid the driver, who heaved a sigh of relief.

The address we had was a three-storey house with peeling paint and roof in need of repair. While waiting for Scout and Bull I decided to circle the block and take a look at the back. There was an alley way leading to a small paved area and an entrance to each of the houses.

Arriving back at the front of the house, Scout's Beetle turned into the street and pulled up alongside me. Bull prised himself out of the confines of the front passenger street and stretched. Scout got out with more style. Her blonde hair was swept back today and held in place by a large tortoiseshell clip. She was wearing denim jeans with a cutaway T-shirt which showed an inch of trim waist and on her feet were hi-top trainers.

'We need to get on,' she said. 'Your meeting with my source in Silvers is set for one o'clock. He's on a tight time schedule so you can't afford to be late.'

'What are we going to do?' asked Bull.

'There's a quiet alley behind these houses. I'll stay here and watch the front, you go round the back and kick the door in. Keep in touch via the cell phone.'

Bull nodded. Rang me, waited till I had answered and set off.

A minute later I heard his voice.

'I'm in,' he said. 'All quiet so far. I'll unlock the front door so we can search together.'

I heard the sliding of bolts and the turning of keys. Whoever lived here valued security and who could blame him considering the neighbourhood. Bull swung the door open.

'Bet you wish you still had that Glock now,' he said.

'Whoever was here will be long gone by now. Once Bronski didn't report in the alarms would have been going off. I'll look around upstairs, if you'll check down here with Scout.'

'You don't have to babysit me all the time,' Scout said. 'I've done karate, you know.'

'No offence, Scout, but there's a whole world of difference between the amateur – albeit a gifted one – and a professional. This is our realm we're moving in now. It's a place where *we* take the risks, not you.'

I started at the top and worked down. The rooms were largely bare, but some bore evidence of the house being used as a squat – paintings drawn on walls, some incense sticks on the floors, bare mattresses probably crawling with some form of verminous wildlife, the odd article of clothing and one shoe. The only point of interest was some bloodstains on the floor of one of the rooms on the first storey: they looked pretty fresh to me – bright red rather than dark brown.

We met in the kitchen. There was the remains of a meal on the big, wooden table. Like the blood it looked fresh.

'Someone left in a hurry,' Scout said.

'There's a cellar,' Bull said, pointing to a panel in the floor. He heaved it up to reveal a set of stairs. 'Let me borrow your lighter.'

I passed it to him and he flicked it on inside the top of the stairs.

'There's a pull cord.' A light came on inside. 'That's better,' he said, disappearing from view. A moment later, 'You might want to see this.'

Scout started down and I followed close behind. The light wasn't good – just a bare low-wattage bulb – but it was bright enough to make out the three chairs. Two chairs sat facing the third, but it was what was on the two chairs that set my mind racing: three sets of leather straps – one big enough to go round the chest and secure to a chair, the other two the size to bind hands and feet. And one large pad to act as a gag.

'At least that's good news,' I said. 'I think your father is still alive.'

'How do you make that out,' asked Scout.

'Two people were supposed to be bound to the chairs, but there's only one gag. They wanted one person to talk and the other to act as pressure. Here's what I think was the plan. Bronski is supposed to kidnap you and bring you here. You're bound to the chair and gagged. Your father is bound to the other and threatened with something nasty happening to you unless he talks. Is your father stubborn?'

'Runs in the family,' she said.

'Let's hope he can hold out. Once he's told them what they want to know, he's of no further use.'

'And what do they want,' Scout said.

'The same thing as us – the whereabouts of Carlo and the missing ten million euros.'

14

It was close to the time when we were due to meet the source inside Silvers, but first Scout wanted to change! We went back to the hotel that she and Bull had found. It was tucked into a narrow street behind the Waterlooplein station and close to the university and botanical gardens. The hotel only had six rooms and we had booked the lot: the proprietor must have thought that Christmas had come early. Each room was pretty rudimentary with not much more than a bed and a wardrobe with shared toilet and washing facilities on each of the three floors. Scout disappeared to her room while Bull and I walked around outside, circling the hotel and theorizing about from where any dangers might come. As long as we were all careful that we were not followed then we were safe enough – it wasn't the sort of establishment or location where anyone would expect us to be.

A large woman with long lank hair appeared from the front door of the hotel. She was short and could have done with losing a lot of weight and resembled a hospital matron who had fallen on hard times. She was dressed in a voluminous dress in a grey colour that probably started out as white many years before and a grubby apron. She had on slippers and stockings which were baggy round the ankles. I didn't fall in love at first sight.

'Who pays the bill?' she said.

'That would be me.'

She produced a small notepad from the pocket of her apron and scribbled some figures.

'You pay now,' she said. 'Advance. Next pay at the end of the week.'

I checked her scribble. She'd probably bumped up the price, sensing we were desperate – anyone who stayed here was probably desperate – but it would hardly make a dent in our expenses allowance. I counted out the cash and peeled off an extra hundred euros. 'Clean up the place,' I said. 'New sheets, pillowcases and towels. OK?'

She nodded, put the cash in her apron and bustled off, probably already planning where she could get the best discount on linen or disinfectant – I hoped it was the latter.

Half an hour later Scout reappeared, although I had to do a double-take to recognize her. She had been through another transformation. Gone was the tomboy in jeans and trainers and in its place was a beautiful young woman. She was wearing a white, floaty, floral print skirt, which ended a couple inches above her knee, a close-fitting suede bomber jacket and dark brown knee-high cowboy boots with low heels. I tried not to stare.

We boarded the glass-topped boat, as arranged, at the Waterlooplein station. The three of us went to the back and Scout and I took up seats in the last row on the right. Bull sat in the row in front and got up and stretched every time it looked like someone was heading to take up the seats on the left at the back. Six and a half foot of toned muscle put them off, preserving our privacy.

The boat chugged along past the Portuguese synagogue and, after a few minutes, made the first of its scheduled stops by Anne Frank's house. The three of us remained in our seats while the other passengers disembarked. When the gangway was clear Scout's source boarded. He was tall and gangly, his limbs seeming uncoordinated, like a badly controlled puppet. I put his age at twenty-two or three, although his fresh faced appearance probably took a couple of years off. He was wearing steel-framed glasses which made him look more of a geek than he probably was, to give him the benefit of the doubt. He had on a regulation dark-blue business suit, white shirt and sober tie and carried a plastic bag on which was the logo of a sandwich shop.

Scout rose and met him halfway down the boat. She kissed him on both cheeks, lingering, I thought, a little longer than was necessary for pure politeness. The young lad blushed. Scout led him by the hand to the back of the boat and made the introductions, although I'm not sure that Bull or I registered. I could have been juggling flaming axes for all the notice he took of me – his doe-eyes were locked firmly on Scout.

His name was Arnie, which was as far away a likeness as you could get. From what Scout had told me he was a clerk at the bank, one of the back-room staff who saw a lot of what was going on and knew more than management assumed. He'd been there for three years. Joined straight from university with a first-class degree in economics.

'Tell me what you know about Carlo?' I asked, dragging him back from his dream world. 'And don't hold back to spare my feelings.'

Arnie looked at Bull and me and seemed nervous. A bead of perspiration ran down his forehead and settled on the end of his nose. Scout gave him an encouraging pat on his knee. He took a deep breath and let it out.

'He's not like what you would expect from someone who is running a bank,' Arnie said.

'In what way?'

'He likes to get involved in his clients' businesses. I'd assumed when I'd joined that he would be more distant – you know, taking more of an objective overview – but you can't knock it, his approach seems to be paying off. His first two years were nothing out of the ordinary, but in his third year there was a big leap in profits and growth has been pretty spectacular since then.'

'Any reason for that pattern?' I asked.

'Well, it was not until his third year that he made his first investment in Almas. . . .'

'Almas?' I echoed. 'Silvers has invested in Almas?'

'We hold a thirty per cent stake in it.'

'Tell me about Almas.'

'Almas is a privately owned holding company not listed on any stock exchange and it has a range of subsidiaries, heavily diversified.'

'Such as?'

'They started out as diamond traders – that's where the name comes from. Almas.' He paused as if it should be obvious. '*Almas* is the Russian word for diamond. Then there's—'

'Whoa, whoa,' I said. This was getting interesting, like in the Chinese curse – may you live in interesting times. I had a sinking feeling in the pit of my stomach. 'So Almas is owned by Russians?'

'Nothing unusual about that,' Arnie said. 'The Russians are the *nouveau riche*; they have more money than anybody else nowadays. Perhaps not the Chinese, I suppose. Or maybe the Arab sheiks, you know UAE and such. And maybe—'

'OK, Arnie, I get the picture. So, apart from diamonds, what else is Almas into?'

'They own a casino—'

'Wouldn't happen to be the El Dorado?'

'Yes, how did you know?'

'Just a lucky guess. Go on.'

'They have a distribution company – trucks shipping stuff all around Europe. Oh, and there's a big private hospital south of the city near the airport.'

It didn't make much sense to me. Usually there's some logical link for ownership of various companies, some good reason to expect synergies between the different arms of a group, but this seemed too diversified, too unconnected – diamond trading, a casino, a hospital, no pattern was emerging. I decided to park the problem until I got a flash of inspiration.

Scout gave Arnie another pat on the knee – I wished she'd stop doing that.

Bull looked at me, shrugged his shoulders and said, 'I suppose there are a lot of Russians. It doesn't have to be the same one.'

'The same one as what?' Scout asked.

'We had a run in with a Russian in Angola,' I said. 'A little dispute over the ownership of some diamonds. We were lucky to get out alive. That's why we decided it should be our last job – didn't want to push our luck.' I turned to Arnie. 'Anything else you can find out about Almas would be useful.'

'No problem,' he said. 'I'll be in touch just as soon as I've got the file back from Ms Oakley.'

So we were following the same route, Ms Oakley and I. Didn't necessarily mean that there was something fishy going on. Didn't mean you could rule it out, either. Two trained bloodhounds following the same scent could just be coincidence, but deep inside I doubted it.

Arnie looked at his watch. The first passengers started to arrive back from their visit to Anne Frank's house.

'I need to go,' he said.

'Anything else you can tell us about Carlo? I asked.

He shook his head and then his eyebrows narrowed as a thought must have struck him.

'I'll run a check on his Silvers card, shall I?'

'Carlo has a Silvers card?'

'Of course. All the senior people have.'

'Does Ms Oakley know about this?'

'She hasn't asked, no.'

'Well, best not to mention it, Arnie. For once we have a chance of being ahead of the game, let's not give away that advantage.'

'I'll be in touch then,' Arnie said.

'Thanks so much, Arnie,' Scout said, kissing him on the cheek. He blushed. 'Get back to us as soon as you can.'

He walked along the aisle of the boat, gave one last puppy-dog backward look at Scout and, still clutching his sandwich bag, got off.

Bull came and sat down next to Scout and me.

'We could just give up and go home,' he said. 'No one would blame us. We were sold a pup.'

'We took a contract,' I said. 'If we renege on a contract, then we have no honour. We can't look ourselves in the eye when we're shaving each day. We've started so we must finish, wherever that might end up.'

'And there's still my father to find,' Scout said. 'I can't do that on my own.'

'I knew it was a waste of breath,' Bull said.

'But you were right to question,' I said.

'Not difficult,' he said. 'That's all we seem to have. Questions. When are we going to find answers?'

'Good question,' I said.

15

And then we got the breakthrough.

Scout's mobile sounded just as the boat was about to depart on its next leg of the trip. She answered it and said 'yes' a few times with a puzzled look before her expression became earnest.

'That was the hospital,' she said. 'They have my father. He's in a pretty bad way. They searched through his phone memory and my number came up as the most frequent that he had called.' She suddenly looked very vulnerable – a side of her that I had never seen before. 'We need to leave right now, Johnny.'

The three of us pushed our way through the last few straggling passengers to board and stepped on to the pavement. Scout hailed a taxi and, after we had climbed inside, spoke to the driver in Dutch. He lost no time in pulling away and speeding up the road. We headed south-west in the general direction of the airport before turning south. Soon a hospital complex came into view. I had been here before. It was the place that Alfredo had spent so much time in recovering from the gunshot wound.

The place had changed over the years. And so had the ownership. A large sign outside proudly proclaimed that the hospital was part of the Almas group – them again, I was beginning to feel haunted by Almas. In addition to the main H-shaped building of yesteryear there were now three others, all in pale-coloured bricks: a one-storey rectangular building, a second H and what looked like a smaller version of the Coliseum in Rome. Signs directed us to the visitors' reception in the rotunda.

As we walked alongside the green lawns, Bull hung back. Too

close to home for him, I suspected.

'Mind if I give this a miss?' he said.

'Save it for another time,' I said. 'Do a reconnaissance. See what you can find out.'

He nodded, grateful to be let off the hook. His time would come – hopefully.

Scout and I went through the automatic doors into a land of plenty – plenty of black leather chairs, white marble coffee tables and chintzy curtains around the wide windows. A woman, dark-brown hair scraped back off her expertly made-up face, tailored light-blue uniform of skirt and jacket with a crisp white blouse, looked up from behind the reception desk and smiled a practised smile. Scout introduced herself and stated our business. The woman dialled a number and spoke in Dutch. She waved, more instruction than invitation, at the chairs where we should wait.

Scout sat on the edge of a chair, looking nervous and concerned. I wondered how long her patience would last. Not long, I guessed, as an unmistakable administrator trip-trapped on high heels towards us. She was wearing the same light-blue uniform and carrying a clipboard. What Scout wanted to see was someone in a white coat with a stethoscope around his neck. The woman introduced herself as Sondra and sat down opposite Scout. Her skirt rose up a little too far on legs that didn't justify it.

'Most unusual,' she said, looking at the clipboard. 'We are a private hospital and not used to this.'

'To what?' Scout asked with a hint of irritation.

'Your father,' the woman said, 'if indeed he is your father, was found outside our gates early this morning. He was unconscious and, according to the doctor who examined him, was in a bad way. We couldn't just leave him there so he was admitted. You realize we will have to call the police and report the incident?'

Scout nodded. 'Can we see him now?'

'I don't like to have to talk about money,' the woman said, 'but . . . you must understand that there will be charges to pay. It would set a bad precedent if we catered for anyone who turns up on our doorstep.'

101

I took my Silvers card from my wallet and handed it to her before Scout could explode at the lack of sensitivity. 'Debit that,' I said. 'Now can we see him?'

The woman was more used to dishing out brusque rather than receiving it. She blinked at me and then looked down at the card and noted its number on the top sheet on her clipboard.

'Follow me,' she said, rising out of the chair like she was climbing out of a Ferrari.

She led us out of the building and across to the nearer of the two H-shaped blocks. Once inside, she led us off to the wing on the right and down a long corridor painted a pastel yellow and with deep-pile blue carpet on the floor. She stopped outside a set of double doors and punched in a code on the keypad. On the other side of the doors was a nurses' station, behind which stood two nurses in starched white uniforms and a doctor, in answer to Scout's prayers, in a white coat with a stethoscope in his top pocket. The doctor refrained from shaking our hands and gestured that we should follow him. We went past a number of rooms with clear glass panels in their doors until the doctor stopped at one, peered through the glass and turned the handle.

'You should prepare yourself,' he said. 'He's in pretty bad shape.'

We followed him inside. The room was more five-star hotel than hospital, nothing having been spared on the decor or furnishings – deeply upholstered chairs in light brown, a rosewood dressing table-cum-desk, a matching wardrobe with mirrored doors and subtle lighting from spots on the ceiling. There was even a tall vase of flowers on the bedside cabinet. No trouser press though: probably an army of support staff to handle all the domestic necessities. And on the adjustable bed up against an apple-white wall was Scout's father. That was obvious the way she rushed to his side and cradled him in her arms. He didn't stir.

What I could see of him didn't look good. His face was badly bruised, one eye closed tight by swelling, one arm encased in plaster, one leg, the same, sticking out of the bed. There was a drip feeding into his left arm and one feeding out to a bag hung on the bedside.

'It is your father then,' the doctor said.

Scout nodded, her eyes fixed on her father.

'He's not in pain,' the doctor said. 'From what we can tell he seems to have been given a large dose of sedatives, accounting for his unconscious state, and that's probably for the best. He's taken a very bad beating. There's heavy bruising all over his body, including the soles of his feet and there's a large burn on his back. The police will want some sort of explanation, but that can wait – his recovery is our first priority. We've patched him up the best we can so far. Once he regains consciousness we'll know more about any other problems.'

'What can you tell us about the burn?' I asked, knowing the answer.

'It looks like it was made with an old-fashioned flat iron, but I can't be sure.'

If he wasn't sure, I was. Russians. Can't resist playing with a flat iron when they're after answers.

'How long before he regains consciousness?' Scout said.

'Could be as much as a day,' the doctor answered. 'Hard to tell when we don't know what drug he was given and how long ago that was. It's best that he sleeps though. Sleep is a great healer. If you'll excuse me, I need to be making my rounds. Press the red button' – he handed her a remote device – 'if you need anything.'

Scout watched him leave and then pulled up a chair and settled herself so that she was close enough to still hold her father's hand. I felt without function – apart from an arm around her, there didn't seem much I could do. For something to do I stepped across to the window and looked out over the manicured lawns. That took up about ten seconds. I bent down to the vase of the flowers and smelt a white flower that looked like it might be an orchid – but, bearing in mind how little I know about flowers, it could have been virtually anything. It had no smell, hot-housed until it was only good for decoration. There was a black mark on its stem. I put out my right hand to remove it and then stopped.

'Scout,' I said. 'Let's go find some coffee before you settle down for your vigil. It'll do you good.'

'I could just press the button,' she replied. 'I'm sure in this place they would send some.'

'I need some air,' I said. 'And to stretch my legs. Come on. You won't be missing anything.'

Reluctantly she followed me from the room and through the maze of corridors until we were outside. Bull was sitting on a bench, smiling.

'You look a changed man,' I said, as Scout and I sat down.

'Just been talking to an old lady catching a few rays in a wheelchair. Had a liver transplant two weeks ago. Two weeks ago! You should have seen her. You'd never have guessed. Maybe it will go like that for Michael once we've found a donor. Kind of gives you hope. This lady said she couldn't wait to get back on the booze – got the liver of a twenty-year-old and she was gonna show it a good time. What a character.' He came out of his optimistic reverie and said to Scout. 'Sorry. Should have asked before. How's your father?'

'Hard to tell,' she said. 'Still unconscious. But he's in the best place, I suppose.'

'I'm not sure about that,' I said.

'What do you mean?' she asked. 'It seems to have every facility he could wish for.'

'Every modern gadget,' I said. 'Including a bug in the vase of flowers.'

'That's nature for you,' Bull said.

'Not that kind of bug, Bull. A listening device.'

'Are you sure?' Scout asked. I nodded. 'But why?'

'Whoever is behind this – and my money is on Almas – tried to beat some information out of your father and that didn't work. They tried to kidnap you to put some pressure on him to talk and that didn't work either. So now they try the sneaky approach. Wait for your father to tell you whatever it is they want to know and bingo, they know it too.'

'And what do they want to know?' Scout said.

'It's got to be connected with Carlo, so it's either where's Carlo, or where are the bearer bonds, or both. I'll settle for both. Your father must have got further than we thought on Carlo's trail.'

'So what do we do?' Bull asked.

'Wait,' I said, 'and whisper.'

16

Stanislav – Stan the Pole, Stan the Man, Steady Stan, Stan the Rock – was the first to answer the summons. He was calling from Warsaw. I got the details of his bank, asked him to rent a large car and then gave him a shopping list. If he was surprised, he hid it well. But he said he had the necessary connections and would see us in three days.

Next came Red. The Texan was in his home state and would fly out in a couple of days. Last of the three was Pieter. He was in Cape Town and needed a day to sort out things at his end – women to placate, I guessed – and then would fly out.

I'd left Scout at the hospital with Bull standing guard over her and was now back at the hotel, lounging in a moth-eaten armchair, thinking. Nothing was adding up. We'd missed something. It seemed logical to assume that Scout's father had located the whereabouts of Carlo – that must be the information that Almas was after – and yet he had taken matters no further. What could have made him take that course of action? A hard luck story that touched his heart? Maybe. Money? A share of €10 million in bearer bonds could be a big incentive to turn your back on a contract. I settled on money.

But how had Scout's father located Carlo? He'd started out with the same information as us, probably even less since he hadn't found the gold chip. Yet he had solved the puzzle and we had not. What had we missed?

It was then that my mobile rang. It was Anna. She had some

news and wanted me to come to the casino at nine o'clock. I was to buy a golden chip and seek her out. She was due to deal at the blackjack table. I was to act cool. Hey, what else did I do?

By a quarter to eight there was still no sign of Scout and Bull. I changed into the smart suit and set off in search of a taxi. Scout had told me that she was one of the few people in Amsterdam who had cars. They were officially discouraged and only a small number of car-parking facilities were provided – parking, Scout had told me, was a nightmare that the majority of the citizens of Amsterdam avoided like the plague. The argument of the authorities was that cars would snarl up the city and pollute it, and that they had an excellent public transport system of trams, buses and trains. No one should need a car.

Once I had arrived at El Dorado I bought the necessary chips – the precious gold one and a few ten-euro chips to make it look like I was going to gamble – and headed straight for the blackjack table. I didn't want anyone beating me to Anna. She had looked so sophisticated, so beautiful that I didn't want that image spoiled by thoughts of what she might have just been doing. And then it struck me. What right had I to get moralistic or judgemental? There wasn't any difference between Anna and me. We both prostituted ourselves by selling our talents, Anna in the conventional sense and with me it was fighting and killing. We were professional soulmates.

Anna was wearing the standard black and white uniform, but this time with a black choker with a large diamond set in the middle. Her long blonde hair had been scooped back at the sides to reveal a pair of diamond ear-rings. As soon as she saw me she must have pressed the button to call the next dealer for a brunette was walking to the blackjack table as I was arriving there. Anna led me to her room and pointed at the bar with its assortment of bottles.

'Vodka and ice?' I checked.

She nodded. I fixed her a vodka and one for myself. I handed her the drink and she downed it in one. 'Another,' she said.

She sat down on the bed and kicked off those red heels as if it had been a long day rather than her session just starting.

'I'm getting too old for this,' she said, watching me pour the refill.

I picked up the two glasses and the bottle for good measure and joined her on the bed.

'Thank you,' she said. 'You're a gentleman. Not like some of the men I meet. They treat me like dirt. It's a job, that's all. It doesn't mean I'm not human.'

'If anyone mistreats you in the future, you get hold of me. They won't do it again. I'll teach them some manners.'

'Thank you. You're sweet. I will remember that.'

She reached out and held my hand. Squeezed it. Leaned over and kissed me on the cheek. I hoped she didn't need my help, but if she called I'd come running.

'I don't know if I should be telling you this,' she said. 'Can I trust you to be discreet with the information?'

'My lips are sealed,' I said. 'I have only the best interests of Carlo, and now it seems Natasha too, at heart.' I sipped the vodka while she pondered.

'Natasha phoned me,' she said, still with an air of reluctance.

I was going to have to tease this from her. 'When was this?' I said.

'A few hours ago.'

'And what did she want, Anna?'

'She wanted to know if any new girls had arrived. I told her just one – a replacement for her named Martina. Then she said I was to get in touch if a young girl called Irina showed up. She said it was important. I should ring her straightaway. I told her I would do what I could while I'm still here.'

'How were you to get in touch?'

'She gave me a mobile number. I suppose you want it.'

She didn't wait for an answer. I nodded in any case. She padded across the room to a chair where her handbag sat. Took out a small notepad and pen.

'This is where I keep my accounts of how much I have earned,' she said. 'So they can't cheat me.'

'The choker,' I asked, unable to hold back my curiosity, 'gift from a grateful client?'

'And the ear-rings too. There are some times when the job is good to me. Not all men are bad. I can tell the good from the bad. You, Johnny, you are a good man. I trust you with the information.'

She tore off a sheet of paper, took out her mobile and pressed some buttons. Finding what she wanted she wrote down the number and passed it to me. I glanced at it – it wasn't going to tell me anything, not yet at any rate – and put it away safely in my jacket pocket.

'Did Natasha say where she was phoning from?'

'She said she was close to the German border. That Carlo was trying to get her a false passport. He hadn't had much luck so far. But they were happy to be together.'

'Just close to the German border? Nothing more definite than that?' If Carlo was smart, and I wasn't sure of that, he would move around, not staying in a place for longer than a day.

'Nothing more,' said Anna, shaking her head. She seemed tired tonight, maybe if she napped for a while she could more easily get through the evening.

'How did you get here? How did you get into this position? You know, doing the job you're doing, illegal alien and all?'

'We come in trucks, people from all over Chechnya. The trucks have a secret compartment – it can take ten people at a time. Then we gather at – how do you say? – a transit camp. Here they check us out. Full medical. They will not take anyone who is sick and cannot work. And the girls like me, have to be clean, you understand?'

I nodded. I understood too well. Let's not go there.

'Then from the camp it is back in trucks to Holland. After we have earned enough money for them they let us go. They look after us good. Get us false papers, help us find work and a place to stay. Then it's up to us. We disappear in the system. We are free.'

'When did the last girl go?'

'A month or two back. She had served three years.'

'And how is she now? Has life turned out good for her?'

'I haven't heard from her. They say that we should not be in contact. It is dangerous for the ones who have left. They must break the links with their friends.'

Could be a lonely time for them, I thought. Still, freedom comes with a price. I checked my watch – enough time had passed so that it wouldn't look suspicious if I left.

'I'll go now, Anna. Take care of yourself.'

I rose from the bed, kissing her on the cheek this time. I was at the door when the thought struck me.

'You said you'd help Natasha while you can. What did you mean by that?'

'I am being allowed to leave soon. Next week or the week after. Will you come and see me when I have gone, Johnny?'

'I would like that very much, Anna.'

'I would like that very much too. I will give you my mobile number. Please give me a ring. And don't worry, I will get a proper job. Not this. You understand?'

I smiled at her. 'That would be good.'

She read out the number and I wrote it on the back of the piece of paper she had given me.

It was then that another thought struck me.

'You said that Natasha's passport is here. Where exactly?'

'There's an office on the fourth floor. Room 417. What are you thinking of doing?'

'I want to get Natasha's passport back. If we find her and Carlo, I don't want any ties back here. I want her to be free to choose her life wherever she wants to spend it.'

'The room is guarded. Big man. It won't be easy.'

'Nothing worthwhile in life is easy. Let's go back inside.'

I checked my watch. Not much time left of my hour.

'Let's have the pillowcases,' I said.

'Why, Johnny?'

'I need something to tie you up with to convince them that you're not involved in what I'm going to do.'

110

She laughed. 'You don't need pillowcases. Look in the wardrobe.'

I did as she asked and saw why she had laughed. Their was a full bondage kit inside – handcuffs, straps, gag.

'You had better strip off and put the gear on,' I said.

'My pleasure,' she said.

She slid off her dress. I turned my back. She giggled at my discretion. I heard the soft swish of silk as her underwear floated to the floor and the padding of her bare feet as she went across to the wardrobe.

'OK,' she said, a couple of minutes later. 'You can look now.'

I turned around and nearly hit the floor. Her outfit was basically a very small leather bikini edged with mink – no more than three triangles. Her shoes had the highest pair of heels I'd ever seen. They had flimsy straps across the top and two-inch wide straps around the ankles so that they resembled manacles.

'Do you approve, Johnny?' she laughed.

She handed me the cuffs and the gag – both in mink. I led her swaying on the heels to the corridor.

'Are there stairs so we don't have to use the lift?'

'End of the corridor,' she said.

'And can you cut out the giggling. You're supposed to be my prisoner.'

'Yes, Johnny,' she said, smirking now.

We went to the end of the corridor and opened the door to the stairs. I looked up and down and saw no one in sight. We started up the stairs with me supporting Anna to stop her falling over. At the fourth floor I peered round the door and saw that the coast was clear. We made our way to room 417. I knocked on the door.

'Tell him you need help,' I whispered.

'Don't forget he's big.'

'Yeah, yeah,'

She called out something in what I presumed was Russian. The door began to open, slightly at first but then fully when the person must have seen that it was Anna and that no threat was present. He stepped outside.

Big wasn't the word for him. I'd seen barns smaller than this guy. He was around six foot and so wide that I reckoned he had to turn sideways to get through the door. Not trusting my left arm, I threw him a right hook, making sure that all the weight came from as far back as my shoulder. I even turned my fist as I connected to increase the impact of the blow.

I heard the crunch as his nose broke, not for the first time judging by his appearance. He staggered back a few feet, shook his head and looked at me, grinning.

Hell.

I closed in and hit him again, this time on the chin. His head went back and he shook it again. Then stepped forward. He didn't bother dodging the next blow, just stood there and rocked a little before stepping closer. He grabbed me in a two-arm bear hug, pinning my arms, and began to squeeze. I gave him a Glasgow kiss, the dome of my head connecting with his forehead. He squeezed harder. It was going to take a tank to stop him and I didn't have one of those. He was squeezing so tightly it was becoming hard to breathe, my lungs compressed by the force he was applying. I tried to knee him in the groin, but he was too near and I couldn't get any power behind it. He was so close that I could smell garlic on his breath. He squeezed ever tighter – all the time with that stupid grin on his face. Sooner or later my ribs were going to break.

Then suddenly the pressure stopped. His body leaned into mine and he sagged at the knees. I let him drop to the floor and saw Anna behind him with a large, heavy alabaster table lamp in her hand.

'I told you he was big,' she said.

'And you weren't exaggerating. Let's get him inside.'

I dragged his body through the doorway and set him down on the floor. Anna closed the door behind me and we were safe for a while.

'Any idea where the passports are kept?'

'The filing cabinet on the left.'

I slid open the top drawer and looked inside. There were piles of passports. I opened the first one and groaned. They were in

Russian and I had no idea what the Cyrillic script represented.

'You better do this,' I said to Anna. I moved aside and let her hobble over.

She looked at the first few.

'You're in luck,' she said. 'They're in alphabetical order. Natasha's name begins with a z so it shouldn't be hard to find.'

I watched her hands move to the back of the drawer and pull out half-a-dozen passports. She flicked through them and found the one we wanted. She handed it to me.

'OK,' I said. 'Lie on the floor and I'll cuff and gag you. You'd better say that there were two men and one of them hit the guy from behind.'

I fitted the cuffs and rolled up the gag.

'Wait,' she said. 'You're fun, Johnny Silver. I like you.'

'And I like you, Anna. We may not meet again after this. The guards at the main door will be watching out for me. It'll be too dangerous for me to come back. I'll phone you and maybe we can meet up when your time here is done.'

'No maybes, Johnny.'

I nodded my head and kissed her on the cheek. Pushed the gag in her mouth and laid her gently on the floor.

'Good luck,' I said.

She mumbled something through the gag. Good luck to you too, I interpreted. I bent down and kissed her again in case we didn't meet up in the future.

'Thanks, Anna,' I said, ready to walk through the door. 'I couldn't have done it without you.'

She nodded her head and her eyes lit up with a smile that couldn't come from the gagged mouth.

It was a lovely smile that I would miss if our paths did not cross again. I walked through the door without looking back. Doesn't do to make friends in our business.

'*Ciao*,' I said.

Ciao. Hallo and goodbye in Italian. I hoped for the former.

17

The three of us sat round the breakfast table planning the day. Scout and Bull hadn't arrived back from the hospital till nearly midnight. Scout looked drained, but was determined to go there again this morning. Didn't seem that we had anything better to do. We might be getting closer to Carlo's trail, but only because we had narrowed his whereabouts down a bit. A hundred-mile stretch of border, that's as close as we had got. Needless to say, Natasha didn't answer her mobile when I tried calling so there was no lead coming on that front.

Bull poured coffee while Scout and I looked at an unappetizing platter of meat and cheese that from its colour and texture seemed like it had been standing on the table for the last week. The coffee wasn't much better – had that bitter taste that came with standing on a stove keeping warm too long. The hotel owner said it was fresh. I should have asked her, 'Fresh when?' We were going to have to establish some ground rules, and probably cross her palm with silver – or the Silvers credit card.

'What was the latest on your father when you left last night?' I asked.

'Whatever drugs he had been given should be out of the bloodstream sometime today. Then he will be in a lot of pain. The burn on his back might be the worst. Probably give him a morphine drip. All in all I don't think we'll get much out of him today. I'd still like to go though, if that's all right with you guys?'

'Sure,' I said. 'Bull will go with you again.' I looked at him to check that was OK. He nodded.

I took them through my conversation with Anna and asked Scout where she would try to get a passport and cross the border.

'I'd go south,' she said. 'The northern border is too close to Amsterdam that they might be seen while they're hanging around waiting for a passport. That leaves anywhere on a stretch between Arnhem and Maastricht. Getting a false passport is tricky. My guess would be for Carlo to park Natasha somewhere and hop into one of the big towns in Germany or Belgium. Pick up a passport at some port – air, rail or sea. Trouble is you can't just walk into a bar and tap the first person on the shoulder and ask for one. He'd need to gradually build up a chain of contacts. The only thing in his favour is that he has bags of money. That can buy a lot of useful contacts.'

Her mobile rang. She looked at the screen and said, 'Arnie.'

'Don't tell him where we are,' I said.

She gave me a withering look. As if I would, it said. She stood up from the table and walked to the window so that we wouldn't be a distraction. There followed a lot of yeahs and OKs from Scout before the conversation was finally over.

'Arnie wants to talk to us – he's made some progress.'

'Why couldn't he tell you over the phone?' I asked.

'He's gone nuts about security. Says it's too easy to tap into a mobile. We're to meet him at the zoo at half past four.'

'Hell,' said Bull. 'We could be wasting a whole day. Doesn't he realize the urgency of the situation?'

'Maybe he just wants to see Scout again.'

Scout blushed.

'He said we would understand when we meet him and he explains what's going on.'

'Nothing to do but wait,' I said. 'I'll go and do a recce on the zoo. If Arnie's so freaked out about security it might pay to get the lie of the land. Find the best place to meet where we can't be observed.' I peeled off some high-value euro notes from my roll and gave them to Bull. 'Work your charm on the matron and get things sorted out here. We need to make it liveable – we could be here some time. Then you guys go off to the hospital and I'll meet you at the zoo at four o'clock. Ring me if you need to change plans.'

I decided to walk to the zoo. It was only a couple of miles from the back streets of central Amsterdam where our hotel was located and I would have preferred longer, for I missed the daily run and swim. The walk took me to the busy junction of Visserplein, past a synagogue and over the canal before leading to the botanical gardens and Wertheim park. From there it was just a few hundred yards to the zoo.

The Artis Zoo was a Victorian concoction, a throwback to the times when society was unsure how to relate to zoos in general. Was their purpose to exploit the animals and crank up the fear factor of getting up close to savage beasts – being just a wire away from staring into a lion's mouth? Or was their function to educate people to appreciate and preserve the natural world? The upshot was a place of stunning Victorian architecture and little space for the animals to live and roam. The larger animals, unused to being kept in such confined spaces, did a lot of pacing around and scratching and other forms of displacement activity. Granted there was a recently refurbished aquarium and a planetarium, but overall I just felt sad for the poor cramped animals – not a life one would choose. Freedom can not be valued too lightly.

I started by doing a circuit round the perimeter and then worked in a spiral to the centre. Choosing the best place to meet was difficult. Should I be looking for a crowd-free area where the chances of being disturbed or observed were low, but if seen would look suspicious, or would the better alternative be the most crowded – the get-lost-in a-crowd principle? If going for the latter then the restaurant was the best bet: if the former, then it seemed the camel enclosure was the least favoured by the public. Still pondering, I headed for the restaurant and a decent cup of coffee.

I sat outside at the restaurant and shivered. It wasn't the coffee – that was good, double espresso, thick and strong; it was the place itself. I'd seen locations like it before – Bosnia, Montenegro,

Serbia, Sinai Desert. It was the perfect killing ground, overlooked high from each of the four corners, great shooting positions. You could lay down fire here and the targets were sitting ducks. It was going to have to be camels – ugly, smelly, flatulent, foul-mouthed creatures that they were, they were preferable to being so exposed to attack. I shivered again, finished my coffee and rang Bull to tell them where to meet me.

When they arrived I saw that Scout had changed from this morning's jeans and T-shirt. Back in siren mode for Arnie, she had come as Tomb Raider, khaki shirt and matching trousers tucked into high brown suede boots. Her blonde hair was loose and unstructured – free and easy. If it had the same effect on Arnie as it did on me, he'd do anything she asked.

Scout and I were looking at the camels, Bull had his back to the fence and was surveying the horizon.

'How was your father today?' I asked her.

'Groggy,' she said, sounding disappointed. 'Didn't recognize me.'

'It'll come,' I said. 'They must have used some pretty powerful stuff on him.'

'The doctors reckon it was probably some form of truth serum – sodium amytal was their guess.'

'If they used truth serum,' said Bull, 'then why would they need to plant a bug in the vase of flowers?'

'The doctors said that there are a lot of misconceptions about truth serums. The latest thinking is that all they do is make the person talk more rather than talk without lying. Some people mix fact and fiction because all they want to do is talk. Any information obtained is at best unreliable.'

'I can't help but think we're missing something obvious,' I said. 'That there's an elephant in the room.'

'Or a camel,' said Bull.

'No,' I said, 'we'd smell the camel.'

Arnie arrived looking nervous. He and Scout went through the kissing ritual and that seemed to make him more nervous. He looked at the camel and talked to me while doing so, avoiding eye contact. Maybe there was still that something in my eyes.

'Two of the million-euro bearer bonds have been cashed,' he said, the words exploding out of his mouth in a fast-running stream.

'Where?' I asked, thinking that at last we might get a lead.

'Switzerland, Zurich.'

'Do we have a name or an account number – anything we can trace back to Carlo?'

'That's the interesting bit. The Swiss won't divulge any account information – you know what they're like, anonymity above all else. But they have told us the bonds were cashed in two transactions.'

'Are you thinking what I'm thinking?' Bull said.

I nodded. Looked at Scout and said, 'I think we know at least some of the information they were trying to get out of your father.'

Scout shook her head. 'It would be out of character,' she said. 'I don't think my father has done a dishonest thing in his life.'

'There's always a first time. A million euros can make any man dishonest. Set him up for life. Make him forget the mission he started with. If you're going to take a bribe, it might as well be a big one.'

'So your theory,' said Scout, 'is that my father found Carlo and took a bribe to let him go?'

'Turn a blind eye,' I said.

'There's more,' said Arnie. 'Carlo has been using his Silvers card. Several transactions at petrol stations – enough to get him to Switzerland and back and beyond. Lots of petrol.'

'But I've checked all the hire car companies,' said Scout. 'My informants can't find any record of him hiring a car.'

And then it hit us all at the same time.

Scout went white, all colour draining from her face. 'Crap,' she said. 'Crap, crap, crap.'

'We made a blunder,' I said. 'We missed the elephant in the room. Carlo didn't have to hire a car.'

Scout finished the sentence, 'Because he has a car of his own.

Sorry, Johnny. It's so unusual for Amsterdammers to own a car, I overlooked it.'

'Any way of checking for the details of the car?'

Scout took out her mobile and walked a few paces away so that we couldn't hear the name of her informant. Arnie looked pleased with himself, although he must have guessed that the information he had provided wasn't exactly what we wanted to hear. After a few minutes Scout put away her phone and walked back to us.

'This is one big elephant,' she said. 'Guess what car Carlo has. No, I'll put you out of your misery. It's a bright red Lamborghini. He might as well have painted his name on the roof in big bold letters.'

'Or taken out an ad in every national newspaper,' I said.

'Or booked a slot on primetime television,' said Arnie, getting in on the act.

'Don't tell me he's got a personalized number plate too?'

Scout nodded.

'No wonder your father found him so quickly,' said Bull.

'My informant said that my father had phoned him last week. God, I'm so embarrassed. We've been wasting our time.'

'OK, no more recriminations,' I said. 'Let's make a plan.' I turned to Arnie. 'Can you keep a permanent watch on Carlo's Silvers card and relay information to us as soon as you find it?'

He nodded. 'There'll be a time delay, but nothing more than a few hours.'

'We'll need to split up and cover the major roads along the German border,' I said. 'Good job we've got reinforcements arriving.' I looked at Scout and smiled. 'Don't beat yourself up about it. It's as much my fault as yours. I should have guessed that Carlo would do something impulsive and dangerous. I thought he might have changed – matured – over the years, but I gave him too much credit. People like Carlo don't change.'

Arnie gave a polite cough. We all looked at him.

'There's more,' he said. 'I was taking some printouts to Ms Oakley's office. She was at the coffee machine and well . . . her handbag was on the desk, open. I didn't open it, I swear.'

As if we were going to tell on him if he had.

'Her passport was in the bag.'

'And?' I said.

'Ms Oakley isn't Ms Oakley. At least she is Ms Oakley, but she isn't.'

'Take your time, Arnie,' Scout said.

'Ms Oakley must be her maiden name. The name in her passport is Bellini.'

'Like in the drink?' Scout asked.

Arnie didn't have a clue what she was talking about. He spelt it out for her and she nodded.

'Bellini is a big client of the American bank,' Arnie continued. 'Powerful man. No wonder she throws her weight around. There are rumours about Bellini.'

'OK, spit it out, Arnie,' I said.

'Mafia,' he said.

18

I had a call from Gus, wanting a progress report. We agreed to meet at his hotel for dinner. That gave me some time to prepare – how to make little progress sound like a major achievement.

Gus was staying at the American Hotel and I knew why. It wasn't that it was situated in the Leidesplein, among the hustle and bustle of the nightlife; it was because the place oozed style – apparently, so the hotel notice proudly proclaimed, it's a monument protected by the city for its art nouveau architecture right down to the stained-glass windows. The dining-room was adorned with hand-made flowery wallpaper and chair covers and there were several pictures of naked girls with long flowing tresses à la Beardsley. Gus was admiring one as I was being shown to his table. He welcomed me warmly, throwing his big arms around me and raising a smile at my changed appearance – the short hair, the shave, the dark suit. He was wearing a beige suit with a black collarless shirt and black suede loafers. We ordered drinks – dry white wine for Gus and a cold beer in a frosted glass for me. He took a long sip of his wine and looked at me.

'Well,' Gus said, 'how have you been getting on?'

'It's got a little complicated.' I said. 'It's a long story.'

'We'll order first then.'

He summoned an attentive waiter with a slight flick of his hand and we negotiated the complex menu before settling on rack of lamb. Gus selected a red wine from the expensive list and then the waiter left us.

'Let's start with the detective that Roberto hired,' I said. 'We found him, but haven't got anything out of him so far – he's up to the eyeballs in drugs and luxuriating in a private hospital to the south-west of the city. What we do have is his daughter who is called Scout.'

'Scout? What sort of name is that?'

'Nickname. Supposed to be good at tracking people. Got some pretty good contacts too – cops, hire car companies, flight check-in people.' I didn't mention Arnie in case Gus let something slip – information was on a need-to-know basis. 'What we do know is that a big company called Almas kidnapped him and tried to extract information about where Carlo was and the whereabouts of the ten million euros. Did I mention the ten million euros?'

Gus shook his head, drained his drink and gestured to the waiter to bring refills. He was preparing for the long story I had promised.

'It seems that Carlo absconded with ten million euros in bearer bonds, two million of which have subsequently been cashed.'

Gus gave a soft whistle at the amount. 'So what is he using this money for? Didn't he have enough of his own?'

'Carlo has been gambling at El Dorado – lost big – and he seems to be involved with one of the' – I hesitated – 'croupiers. Russian girl called Natasha. Apparently he's head over heels in love.'

Our racks of lamb arrived, giving me a chance to draw breath. They were accompanied by a salad that was so artistically arranged it could have been made into an exhibit to accompany the paintings on the wall. Neither of us wanted to disturb it, but in the end we weakened and started by stabbing a tomato.

'We now know that Carlo was, or is, somewhere on the German border trying to get a forged passport for his girlfriend. Starting tomorrow we're going to cover the main roads along that border and hope that we spot him. I have two problems. One is Almas and what their involvement is' – Gus shook his head to signify that the name meant nothing to him – 'and the other is someone called Bellini.'

'Bellini?' Gus said, almost choking on his wine. 'What has

Bellini got to do with it?'

'That's what I'd like to know. His daughter, I guess, is the compliance officer investigating Carlo and the bank's funds.'

'Bellini,' Gus said, shaking his head pensively.

'You seem to recognize the name. I think it's your turn to talk.'

'Bellini is a bad man. The rumour – which he denies vociferously – is that he is the leader of one of the mafia families in New York. Some say he's legitimate now, but I wouldn't believe them. Once a man like Bellini has enjoyed power it's almost impossible for him to give it up.'

'He's a big customer of the New York office, so my source says.'

'Bellini has a finger in many pies, most of them illegal. Drugs, prostitution, gambling, the usual list that takes advantage of men's follies.'

'Sounds like the American equivalent of Almas. I did tell you it was complicated.'

'You better watch your step if Bellini is involved.' He pushed his plate away. 'Somehow I don't feel very hungry anymore.'

19

Pieter arrived on the red eye, meaning he was just in time for breakfast. Which was bad luck for him. I swear it was the same plate of cold meat and cheese that we had rejected the previous day. He was dressed in white jeans, slightly grubby, a dark-blue sweatshirt and desert boots. As he leaned back in his chair and crossed his feet I saw that the desert boots had holes in the soles. He had put on some weight, but he still had those boyish good looks that the women went for. He surveyed the dining-room with its collection of furniture so old that it looked like it would collapse if you breathed on it and said, 'Nice place you've got here.'

'We've lived in worse,' Bull said. 'Remember Bosnia?'

'The only thing keeping the cockroaches in check,' he said, 'were the rats.' He gave a shudder and shook his head. His long blond hair moved across his forehead with the shake, revealing that he was receding at the temples.

Pieter swept his hair back into place, turned his green eyes on Scout and said, 'And who is this lovely lady?'

'This is Scout,' I said.

Pieter looked blank.

'It's because she's good at tracking,' I explained. If I was Scout, considering the number of times she must have been asked the question, I'd have had a T-shirt printed up with the answer on.

'I think I'll call you Blue Eyes,' Pieter said.

'Scout will do,' she said, resisting the temptation to stick two fingers down her throat.

'But it doesn't do you justice. So, Blue Eyes it is.' He turned to me. 'What's going down, Johnny?' he asked. 'Something big or did you just get nostalgic for a reunion?'

'We have a contract.'

'With money, or is it one of your pro bono jobs?'

'Money – plenty for all.'

'Lead me to it.' He looked across at Scout. 'And where does Blue Eyes fit into the picture? I'm all for eye candy, but I just want to know the score. Are you and she an item?'

Scout blushed.

'No,' I said. 'We're not an item.'

'So the coast's clear?'

Scout looked horrified. Pieter's charm, in the intervening years, seemed to have worn as thin as the soles of his boots.

'I think you'd better start at the beginning,' she said to me. 'And speak slowly for your South African friend.'

I started at the very beginning with my initial reluctance to take the contract, Michael's need for a transplant and on from there, getting ever more complicated as the story unfolded. At times Pieter interrupted to clarify a point or ask the significance of a seemingly minor detail. He was as sharp as he had been all those years ago. My confidence in him returned. Even Scout seemed to warm to him a little.

'What's the worst-case scenario?' he asked when I was finished.

'That we get caught in the middle between Almas and the Bellinis.'

'Tools of the trade?'

'Stan is bringing them. He's coming overland.'

'Excuse me,' said Scout. 'Are you talking about what I think you're talking about?'

'Smart too, eh, Blue Eyes,' said Pieter.

'I'm not putting any of my people at risk without a few safeguards,' I said.

'You realize what will happen if you get caught carrying a weapon? We're talking prison, and a long stretch too.'

I nodded. 'Better than being dead because you can't fire back. This is a professional contract and we have to approach it professionally in all ways. This is what we were all trained to do. If it makes you feel better, I promise we won't shoot unless we have to.'

'Not a good defence in law,' Scout said.

'I'm interested in justice not the law.'

'He talks sense, Blue Eyes,' said Pieter.

Bull nodded his agreement.

Scout looked at the three of us in turn and said, 'Men!'

'You better believe it,' said Pieter.

She gave him a withering look and said, 'I'm off to get a fresh pot of coffee. Try to be grown up, boys, while I'm away.'

The three of us destroyed our macho image by giggling.

'What have you been up to over the years?' I asked Pieter.

'A bit of everything. When I got back after Angola I spent some time doing security jobs, worked my way up the ladder so I run my own company. Security consultant – anytime, anyplace, anywhere. You know, maybe the gold mines, maybe guarding some tourists while they're on safari – I handle most anything.' He changed the subject. 'What about you guys? Prospering?'

'We make a living. I run a bar and Bull has a yacht charter. We're the mainstays of the tourist industry on St Jude. Bull stills limps, I can't throw a left hook, but apart from that it's a good life.'

'And then you had to get involved in this?'

'We're regarding it as a means to an end.'

'Let's hope it's not a means to our end.'

Scout returned with a fresh pot of coffee and poured some into our cups. Pieter went across to his baggage and produced a bottle of Scotch. 'Anyone for a sharpener?' he said.

'Ain't it kind of early?' Bull said.

'Just to get the blood circulating – you know, medicinal like.'

'We've got some driving to do later,' I said. 'Better save it for now. We might even be celebrating by night-time.'

'OK,' said Scout. 'Down to business.' She moved the plate of cheese and ham and spread out a map of Holland and its boundaries over the table. 'This is the border – runs from Groningen in the north to Maastricht in the south, by way of Enschede and Arnhem. These are the main roads and major intersections. Our best plan is to split the roads up into sections and take one each.' She pointed at the map and checked with each of us in turn so that we were all sure exactly which stretch we were covering. 'Sit and watch the traffic by day and do a tour of the hotels and motels *en route* in the evening. It can't be too difficult to spot a bright red Lamborghini. Yes, we might miss him, or might not be able to catch up with him during the day, but they have to have somewhere to sleep at night. We need some hire cars, so I suggest we spend the rest of the morning making arrangements and then head off in the afternoon. Any questions?'

'Very thorough, Blue Eyes.'

'One last thing,' she said, turning to Pieter. 'If you call me Blue Eyes one more time I'll show just what damage someone with a black belt in Karate can do to a guy's private parts.'

'I love a girl with spirit,' he said.

Scout screamed, tore at her hair and stormed out the room.

'I think she likes me,' he said.

Pieter went off to catch a few hours' sleep before taking up duty on the road. Bull and I sat around the table finishing our coffee.

'What do you reckon?' Bull said.

'About what?' I said.

'Do you ever get the feeling we're like dinosaurs? You know, that our time has been and gone?'

'Not until we arrived here,' I said.

Bull became thoughtful. 'And what do you reckon?' he said.

'About what?'

'Pieter.' He made a waving motion with the fingers of his right hand. 'Flaky?'

'He'll need watching. Can't have him drinking this early in the morning. Let's give him the benefit of the doubt and put it down to jet lag. Once he gets down to work maybe all the old habits will come back.'

'Maybe,' Bull said.

'Let's hope so,' I said. 'Can't afford any weak links in the chain. I don't want a man who might be drunk watching my back.'

The thought made Bull shiver.

'Wonder how Red has turned out,' Bull said. 'Weathered the years better, I hope.'

I was beginning to wonder if this was such a good idea after all.

We all travelled to the airport by taxi and the others went off to pick up their hire cars and head towards their designated points along the Holland/Germany border. I stayed behind to meet Red, brief him and then send him on his way to join the troops. We were almost a complete set. I called Stan and diverted him to hold fire on the German side of the border and await further instructions.

It wasn't hard to spot Red. He was wearing cowboy boots, blue jeans, sweatshirt, Ray-Bans and a Stetson. So much for keeping a low profile. He strode across the concourse like John Wayne, dumped his huge rucksack at his feet and gave me a manly hug. 'It's been too long,' he said.

'Or not long enough,' I said. 'Sorry to have to call you when we're in trouble, but I need the old team together.'

'Not so much of the old,' he said.

'None of us are any the younger.'

'But we're wiser,' he countered. 'Hey, let's grab a coffee and talk over old times.'

We found a coffee shop and took two double espressos over to a table at the back in the corner. We faced outwards. Old habits die hard. A few other customers stared at us – whether it was Red's dark glasses or that indefinable glint in my eyes, I didn't know, but it kept everyone at a distance. Red took off his Stetson to reveal jet-black hair. That, the brown eyes and the dark complexion he owed to being half Comanche, which in lighter moments he would play up by doing the full kee-mo sah-bee routine. There was going to be some contest between Scout and Red as to who was the best tracker. I wondered who was going to be first to put their ear to the ground.

'What have you been up to over the years?' I asked.

'This and that,' he said.

'Come on, Red. Level with me.'

'I've mostly been doing the rodeo circuit.'

'Hard way to earn a living,' I said.

'Keeps me fit and in the open air. So what's going down?' Red asked.

I went through the story with all its complications. He listened attentively and nodded in all the right places. He seemed as sharp as ever.

'So you want someone to chase a Lamborghini? Well, you certainly came to the right guy. Ain't no one faster on four wheels. And when we find this Carlo, what do we do then?'

'Call me and I'll come running. He will trust me and relax. Then we find out what all this mess is about.'

'Hope the story's got a happy ending.'

'The best stories have a happy ending for the good guys and an unhappy one for the bad guys.'

'But that's fiction, not life. Remember the Alamo?'

20

I watched Red drive off in a blur of burning rubber and climbed into my rental car. I hadn't driven for a good few years and it took me a while to get acclimatized, especially to the Amsterdam traffic. I was armed with a road map and a list of accommodation courtesy of the tourist office at the airport. I headed east on the A9 before picking up the A1 for Arnhem. Once there, I zigzagged to Nijmegen and halfway down to Venlo so as not to overlap with Bull's territory. I stopped at each service area *en route* and checked out the parked cars. Later I would detour to the nearest towns and villages and scan the car-parks around the hotels, motels and guest-houses. It got monotonous very quickly and I had to concentrate hard so as not to overlook anything. I gave up at ten o'clock and booked into a motel in a small town on the Rhine called Emmerich, grabbed a burger and a beer at the motel café and settled down with the map to see if I could introduce any variety into tomorrow's vigil.

I thought about Carlo driving around in his Lamborghini, maybe with Natasha in the passenger seat, maybe not if he was entering Germany. I tried to second-guess him. Looked at the long list of hotels, motels and boarding-houses and knew we had underestimated the size of the task. There had to be a better way. If it was too laborious and slow to get us to Carlo, maybe we could get Carlo to come to us.

I was up early the following morning and went on a small shopping expedition. I bought a leather wallet from a gift shop, a pair of scissors from the local general store and a copy of that day's newspaper. Back in my room I cut up the sheets of the newspaper into euro-sized pieces and stuffed the wallet so it was bulging. I took the tourist office list of accommodation and marked all those with either four or five stars – I was reckoning on Carlo not settling for anything less – and planned a route. Then I checked in with the others, told them of my idea and that they should copy it.

At the first hotel I came to I walked up to reception and gave my spiel – I had seen a man driving a red Lamborghini and had noticed him drop the wallet. Show bulging wallet for verification. Did they have anyone here who would fit the bill? If not I gave them my mobile number and asked them to phone me if someone in a red Lamborghini turned up. I would then come and hand over the wallet in person as a pleasant surprise for the owner. I emphasized that there was a lot of money and there might be a reward which I was willing to split with the receptionist. That did the trick. It was then a simple case of moving to the next high-class hotel and repeating the story.

The call came through around six o'clock. It was Bull. The wallet story had borne fruit at a classy hotel in Maastricht. I told him I'd meet him there in around an hour and that he should stop Carlo from leaving until I got there. Let down his tyres, take Natasha as a hostage, anything so that he wouldn't slip through our net. You're six foot six with muscles like Samson, he's not going to argue and, sure as hell, he's not going to phone the police. I called the others and told them to meet me there as soon as they could. Then I set off, feeling elated – no, make that smug.

When I got there Bull opened the door to the room. It was a good size for a modern bedroom. In addition to the bed there were two armchairs and a table and two chairs for dining. All the fabrics were in a pastel pink to complement the darker pink walls. The bed was huge – queen size, or whatever the brochures like to call them. It looked like the interior designer had been asked to recreate a brothel and hadn't quite got it right. Carlo and Natasha were sitting on the bed looking frightened. There were suitcases opened and clothes scattered around. Carlo stared at me and his face brightened. He came across to me and pumped my hand. 'Gianni,' he said. 'I knew you'd come. I prayed you'd come.'

'Receptionist couldn't keep her mouth shut,' Bull said. 'I just got here in time. They were packing to leave.'

'We thought they'd found us,' Carlo said.

'It wasn't difficult,' I said. 'You really do need to learn to be anonymous, part of the crowd, if you're hoping to disappear. Why didn't you ditch the Lamborghini?'

'It's a great car,' he said. 'Once driven, it spoils you for anything else.'

I sighed. He'd never learn to be practical or not to follow his impulses.

There was a knock on the door. I opened it and Pieter stood there.

'This room's not going to be big enough,' I said to him. 'Can you see if they've got a conference room free – sufficiently large for eight people? And book us all some rooms for the night, please.'

Pieter nodded and left.

I took my first real look at the two of them. Natasha was wearing a simple shift dress in dark blue which did nothing to flatter her, but she didn't need that. She had, I presumed because of the preponderance of blondes at El Dorado, dyed her hair chestnut in some attempt to confound their searchers. She was undeniably pretty – good bone structure, pert nose, clear blue eyes – with a slender figure and long legs. I could see the attraction.

Carlo was wearing a pair of designer blue jeans with a shiny rivet decoration on the pockets and a white T-shirt that had Armani emblazoned on it in large letters, just in case someone might miss it. He had put on weight, his slim frame now run to a layer of fat that bulged around the middle and gave him a double chin. His hair was thinner too. Time had not been kind to him, or maybe he just hadn't been kind to himself. He still had that Italian charm though – black hair, dark complexion, mischievous and flirtatious glint in his eyes.

The phone rang. Bull answered it, listened for a moment and turned to me. 'Room C, ground floor.'

We trooped down: I stuck close to Carlo, Bull to Natasha.

The room was more sympathetically decorated than the bedroom upstairs. It was functional, bordering on the utilitarian – a rectangular table laid for twelve people with pads and pens. A long sideboard currently being set up as a bar while Pieter looked on impatiently. It might not have been a good move to have him make the arrangements. But it had been a long couple of days and we deserved some reward for our effort.

Carlo made to speak, but I silenced him.

'Don't say anything until the others arrive.'

'Others?'

'We come cheaper by the bunch,' I said. 'In the meantime help yourselves to a drink.'

Red arrived next. He asked no questions, just walked over to the drinks. He saw that Scout wasn't drinking. 'What will you have?' he said to her.

'Mineral water, still, please.'

He picked up a bottle, poured a glass, added some ice and took it over to her. She took a sip.

'This is sparkling,' she said.

'Sorry,' Red said. 'I'll get you another.'

'It doesn't matter,' Scout said. 'I'm only drinking so I won't be the odd one out. Maybe later I'll have something stronger.'

Stan was the last to arrive. He looked as meticulous as ever – Stan was our detail man. He had on sand-coloured trousers with a sharp crease, khaki shirt and dark-blue tie and a sports jacket in a colour that matched the tie. He was clean shaven as ever – even in the field he seemed to be able to find time for a shave and shower.

'Sorry I'm late,' he said in that humourless tone common to Eastern Europeans. 'I left the car the other side of the border and had to get a taxi here.'

'What sort of car did you get?' Red asked.

'Some sort of people carrier.'

'A people carrier?' Red wrinkled his nose in disgust. 'Why the hell did you get a people carrier?'

Stan shrugged. 'I assumed you'd be driving, so I went for the one with the most airbags.'

Red chuckled. 'You make fun of Comanche brave?' he said, lowering his voice an octave. 'Heap big politically incorrect. We Comanches more used to riding bareback than driving car.'

'Probably safer,' Stan said.

I made the introductions while everybody poured drinks and then settled in their seats. Carlo and Natasha sat at one end, I was at the other and the rest spread themselves around.

'OK, Carlo,' I said, 'start at the beginning and tell us what this is all about.'

He thought for a while, swirled the ice round in his glass, sipped his drink, thought a bit more, took a deep breath while fingers were tapping impatiently on the table and eventually said, 'It started around five years ago. You know that Dad was the subject of a Russian mafiya hit?' I nodded. 'Well, they didn't give up. Laid low for a while and then tried again. They came to the apartment – boss man called Garanov and two heavies. They had guns – big ones like you see in the movies. They sat me down with a heavy on each side and put forward their proposition. Either I helped them launder money or they killed me there and then. What could I do, Gianni?'

'String them along and go to the police?'

'They said that they had the police in their pocket. It would only make matters worse for me. Although what could be worse than getting killed I don't know.'

'A flat iron on your back,' said Pieter.

'Being hamstrung first,' said Bull.

'Being beaten on the balls with a big stick,' said Red. 'Pardon my French, ma'am,' he said for Scout's benefit – offending Natasha's sensibilities didn't seem to bother him. Must have reckoned she'd be used to it. 'We've been there, Carlo, but they still didn't get what they wanted.'

'Maybe I'm not as courageous as you. Never had the experience.'

'So you agreed to their terms?' I said, to move the conversation back on track.

'I did better than that,' Carlo said. 'If the bank was going to be involved in money laundering, I thought it should get some benefit from it. So, I said I'd help if Silvers took a share in their holding company and, therefore, a share in their profits.' Carlo looked at me and read the message in my eyes. 'Hell,' he said, 'if I didn't do it, someone else would.'

I put my head in my hands and looked across at him disbelievingly. 'Can't you see what you've done? You made yourself fully complicit to their illegal acts. If caught, you would have had the defence of being pressurized into laundering their money, but now you're as guilty as they are.'

'But I'm not involved in how they make their money; all I do is wash it through the system.'

'How they make their money *is* the problem. It comes from drugs, prostitution, people-trafficking, God knows what else. You're tacitly going along with what they do and all the suffering it causes. How could you be so stupid?'

'It's not stupid. Silvers get their share of the profits. I bet Alfredo or Roberto would see the sense in it. You've been out of the business for too long. You need to adjust your values to the real world.'

'Shall I slap him till he sees sense?' said Bull.

'No. It would take too long.' I paused to try to cool down a bit. 'So we're talking Almas here, I take it?'

'Wow, you've really been doing your homework. You figured out the Almas thing?'

'Let's just say we had a run in with them.'

'They – well it's all down to Garanov really – started off small with some diamond trading, then acquired the casino, then the hospital – what a brainwave that was, big profit earner – until it had a whole raft of companies.'

'I take it the diamond trading was legal – all declared for the tax authorities and the police?'

'Yes,' Carlo said. 'Well, some of it, I imagine.'

135

'So we have the position that Silvers is now up to its neck in drugs, prostitution, diamond smuggling, people-trafficking too and whatever else we haven't uncovered as yet.'

'You could put it that way, yes.'

I wondered what other way there was to put it.

'OK. So Almas is flourishing and you are making huge profits for the bank – that is why you have been so successful over the past few years?' I didn't wait for the inevitable confirmation. 'What changed?'

'I met Natasha,' he said. 'Fell in love.' He took hold of Natasha's hand and squeezed it. 'We wanted to get married. But Garanov wouldn't allow it. Said he had big plans for her.'

Natasha spoke for the first time. Her English and her accent were not as good as Anna's. Probably added to the exotic charm as far as Carlo was concerned. 'I should allow to leave the casino soon. I do my time. Other girls go, but not me. I no understand why.'

'I offered to pay for Natasha's release—'

'Pay with what? You were broke. Spent it all on gambling and golden chips.'

'I thought I could take a sort of unofficial advance on my bonus.'

'*Take* being the operative word. And a bonus built almost entirely on criminal acts.'

'Anyway,' he said, ignoring the implications of his actions, 'Garanov wouldn't have it. Said it wouldn't do Silvers – and therefore Almas's – reputation any good if people heard about me marrying a prostitute. He told me to drop the idea. Enjoy her while I could, that there were plenty of others like Natasha. Why get married when you could have your pick?'

'So you decided to jump ship?'

'Not at that stage, no. I still thought I might be able to win Garanov over. Maybe if I offered that Silvers would take a bigger stake in Almas – provide money for more takeovers. But Garanov was unmovable. Then came the final straw.'

Natasha chipped in again at this stage. 'I send money home each month from my earnings. To help the family. I had letter two weeks ago to say that my little sister Irina was going to follow me. She had already spoken to the men who arrange for the people to come here. I could not let that happen.'

'Irina is only sixteen,' Carlo said. 'Show them the photo,' he said to Natasha. She dug around in her handbag and passed a picture to me. It showed a younger version of Natasha with all her attributes, but with a fresh-faced youthful appearance. I put the picture in my pocket for later reference.

'You can see,' Carlo said, 'that's she's too young for that sort of life. We couldn't let it happen. We thought we'd go to the holding camp and buy Irina from the men.'

'And all live happily ever after,' I said.

'It was a good plan,' he said defensively. 'We just had a few problems to sort out, that's all.'

'Like getting hold of the money and a passport. How the hell did you expect to get a false passport? You don't have any contacts, I presume?'

'I reckoned that if I stole enough money I could let it be known that I was in the market for a false passport and would pay over the odds for one.'

'More likely to get mugged,' said Red.

'I see what you mean about knocking sense into him,' Stan said. 'This man does not know the Russians. You do what they want or else. To double-cross them is to sign your own death warrant.'

'Is it the same Russians?' Pieter asked.

'Sounds like it,' I said. 'Bull couldn't be totally sure when we met him, but I reckon the diamond trading seals it. You know what I reckon? This Garanov is the same man as Angola and he started his business off with the diamonds he accused us of stealing. He must have been some sort of underling at that stage – didn't have the funds to be running his own show. Told his boss that we were to blame, got himself off the hook and made a pile in the process.'

'We have a score to settle,' said Bull.

Pieter, Red and Stan all nodded.

'OK, Carlo. We're up to the stage where you steal the bearer bonds. What then?'

'We took off for the border and prepared to wait until someone took the bait on the false passport. And then this PI turns up. Your father,' he said, turning to Scout. 'He'd traced us the same way as you – through the Lamborghini.'

I shook my head in disbelief again. Found once, but he didn't change his plan. Just hire a car, that was all he had to do!

'I bought him off with one of the bearer bonds – would set him up for life, he'd said.'

'Must have thought stealing from a thief was fair game,' Scout said. 'Don't blame him. Wouldn't have troubled my conscience much, either.'

There was a general nod of agreement from around the table. It didn't surprise me – Carlo's stupidity made it difficult to side with him.

'Where do we go from here?' Scout said.

They all looked at me. I got up from the table to give myself time to think. Walked over to the bar. Filled my glass with ice and splashed in some vodka. Took a large pull.

'Well,' I said, still playing for time, 'we could take Carlo back to Amsterdam and get him to hand over what's left of the bearer bonds. But then he's back in the arms of Almas. That doesn't seem to get us anywhere. On the other hand if we help Carlo pull off his plan, we start to sever the link with Almas.'

'I don't know about anybody else,' said Bull, 'but I don't like the idea of a sixteen-year-old kid being sold as a sex slave.'

'I agree,' I said. 'Then the only thing to do is to go to this holding camp and get her out.'

'We've got the machinery,' Stan said.

'The least we could do,' said Red, 'is make a reconnaissance of the place and come up with a plan from there.'

'If we do this,' I said to Carlo, 'will you hand back the bulk of the money and disappear for good?'

'Of course,' said Carlo. 'As long as you leave us with enough to start a new life.'

'It depends what you mean by enough.'

'Say two million,' he said.

'Say half a million,' I countered. 'Economize for a change. It'll do you good to come somewhere close to reality.' I downed the rest of the vodka in my glass. 'We start tomorrow,' I said. 'Pieter, get rid of the damn car. Red, take one of the hire cars and go with him. Then it's two-hour shifts outside Carlo's room tonight. Bull, can you organize that?'

'Consider it done. I'll take first shift.'

'There's no need,' Carlo said.

'There's every need,' I said. 'I'm not having you run for cover with the rest of the money. From now on you do what I say. Understand?'

'Sure, Gianni,' he said. 'You can trust me.'

But only as long as it suited him, I thought.

'Whereabouts is this holding camp?' I asked.

'In the Black Forest,' Natasha said. 'Near to a place called Freiberg. You can't miss it – it's surrounded by high fences.'

'Scout,' I said, 'I'm going to need you to take Natasha back to Amsterdam. She doesn't have a passport so she can't come with us. It will be safer too.' It also guaranteed that Carlo couldn't make a run for it without abandoning his loved one. 'Stay at the hotel and keep a low profile. It will give you the chance to keep a watch on your father.' I glanced round the table. 'OK, everyone. Till tomorrow then.'

We started to get up from our chairs and go to our rooms. Pieter held back.

'You know,' he said, 'it feels kind of good to be back in action again. It's like I've just been marking time for the last few years. When we stand together, who can stand against us?'

Almas for one. And a pretty formidable enemy we would be taking on. Hell, if life was easy we wouldn't value it so much.

21

It would be a long drive. We would need to follow the whole of the western border of Germany to the extreme south-west where the Black Forest dwelt under the mountains. Our journey would be speeded by the autobahns and would take us past Cologne and Bonn from where we would follow the Rhine to Heidelberg and then due south to Freiberg. I reckoned the 250-mile trip would take around four hours with stops, or three hours if Red was driving. Strangely, no one volunteered to travel with him.

It was Stan who would have the most dangerous journey. In the boot of his Volkswagen people carrier was an arsenal of guns. He couldn't afford to be stopped by the police for some minor traffic offence and have the car searched. He said he would go alone – no one else should be put at risk.

Pieter was to drive one of the hire cars with Carlo as a passenger and Bull as a minder. I took another hire car and left first so that I could get some cash and find us all some accommodation within striking distance of the forest, or better still, deep inside it.

I was lucky to find a hunting lodge with four bedrooms just inside the forest outside Freiberg. Carlo and I would share one room, the others could take their pick of the other bedrooms and the sofa bed in the central large living room. The hunting lodge was basic, no more than a glorified log cabin, but we'd known much worse. It would be just like old times.

Whilst in Freiberg I also stopped at a supermarket and bought some basic supplies – sugar, salt, rice, potatoes, ketchup, eggs, canned stuff and so on – as well as enough meat and beers to last a few days. We would need to be self-sufficient, as keeping a low profile was a priority.

When we were all assembled I started to allocate tasks. Red was to organise rotas for cooking and for watches during the night. Stan was to sort out defences for the lodge, Pieter and Bull to begin the reconnaissance of the area. By seven o'clock the September sun was starting to set and Pieter and Bull arrived back. Red set some beers on the big oak table and we lit a fire. It felt like home, or at least the sort of home we were used to during our mercenary days.

'Time for reports,' I said.

Bull started. 'The holding station is about five miles from here, deep in the heart of the forest. Natasha was right, you can't miss it. There's a well-made track, solid enough to take one of the trucks from the transport company run by Almas. It leads to a big compound surrounded by a high barbed-wire fence and watch-towers at each corner. The sign outside says it's a facility for war games, presumably so that if anyone hears shooting or anything untoward they'd think it was nothing to be bothered about. I don't think the watch-towers are as much of a problem as they seem at first sight. I reckon the guards are more likely to be looking into the compound to make sure that no one escapes rather than looking outside for potential threats. Inside the compound is a collection of huts to house the people and a large central building that I suppose is for admin, although it seems too big. I can't see what other purpose it would have.'

'Anna told me,' I said, 'that everyone has extensive medical checks before they are taken from the compound for their journey to Amsterdam or wherever. That could be it – some kind of medical facility with all the equipment they need. I doubt that Almas spares any expense. Be good to get another look earlier in the day when there might be more activity.'

'We need some binoculars,' Bull said.

'Can you take a trip into Freiberg in the morning and buy some and anything else we might need?'

'No problem,' Bull said.

141

We then looked at Stan.

'Firing positions,' he said. 'I've laid them out with gaffer tape – a big X for each one. We're very close to the trees, so we won't see any attackers until the last minute. The lodge provides all-round cover from the windows so you'll see the firing positions there. There's another inside by the door – you'll have to keep low there because the door will need to be open in order to utilize it. The biggest problem will be the roof. It's vulnerable to smoking us out by dropping fire or a smoke grenade, if they have one, down the chimney. They could also chop a hole in the roof pretty easily, so I've marked out a position in the corner of this room.' He pointed it out. 'But, on the whole, we can put up a fair defence from inside. If we get warning of an attack, I've also laid out positions in the forest, one at each quadrant.'

'You're not expecting them to attack us, are you?' said Carlo, sounding worried.

'No,' I said, 'but in our business you try to allow for any eventuality. They don't know we're here, or what we are intending, but it's better to play safe.' I turned back to Stan. 'Have you got everything on the shopping list?' I asked.

'Everything and a bit more,' he said. 'Playing safe again,' he said for Carlo's benefit. 'Do you want them now?'

'Let's eat first. What have we got, Red?'

'My special recipe chilli con carne. Hot stuff, like Pieter,' he said with a laugh. 'Man's food. You can't fight on an empty stomach.'

He left the table and brought in plates and cutlery for us to pass around and then returned with a big bowl of rice and another of his chilli. It smelt good.

The bowls circulated and we helped ourselves. I raised my can of beer and said, 'To the success of our operation.'

Cans were raised around the table. Then we dug in to the chilli. There was silence.

'Interesting,' I said. I had another mouthful to make sure. Remembered back to Scout's glass of water. 'We need to talk, Red. And you have to be honest with us. You've used sugar instead of salt. You can't see without glasses, can you? That's why you've been wearing sunglasses so much. They're prescription lenses, aren't they?'

Red looked down at the table, avoiding our eyes. 'My sight's been worsening for the last three years. I have to wear glasses all the time now. I thought if I told you about it you wouldn't want me.'

'Wearing glasses isn't a problem unless they get broken or something happens to them during the cut and thrust of battle. Then you're blind and a hazard to us as well as yourself.'

'I've got just the thing,' Stan said.

He got up from the table and went outside. Came back with a gym bag in each hand. Placed them on the sofa and began to unpack them. One by one he laid out the contents.

'Four Colt M16 assault rifles,' he said. 'I went for this instead of the Kalashnikov AK-74 because it's more reliable, less likely to jam. Lighter and a greater maximum range too. That was one for each of us. Your favourite Uzi, Johnny. Silencer already fitted. Five Browning High Powers 9mm with silencers, one each, leather shoulder holsters. Barrett M82A1 monster sniper rifle – you never know when one will come in handy. And for Red, this.' He reached inside the bag, pulled something out and passed it to Red. 'Pump-action shotgun. You don't need to see much with one of these – just aim at a shape and fire. You can't miss.' Stan paused. 'One thing to remember. Just make sure we're behind you. We don't want any collateral damage.'

Red nodded and got up from the table. He went into his room and came back wearing a pair of steel-rim glasses. He pointed at the chilli and said, 'What do you want me to do?'

'Two things,' Pieter said. 'Pass the ketchup, and pray that we're not still here when it's my turn to cook.'

Pieter was on breakfast duty – cereals and toast – which was good since he couldn't really mess it up. He managed to burn the toast though.

There was a chill to the autumn air and we all had on jackets over our sweatshirts and jeans. The jackets helped conceal the bulge of the holstered handguns too. It was a further reconnaissance mission so we left the assault rifles back at the lodge. We also left Carlo, whose laboured breathing and heavy footsteps would have been a liability when moving silently through the forest. He couldn't go anywhere because we had taken all the keys to the hire cars and wouldn't get far on foot. I still didn't trust him not to do something impulsive that would endanger us all.

The holding camp was about five miles away and we approached on foot rather than taking the people carrier and having to find somewhere to hide it. We set off at a jog and it was good to be doing some physical exercise again. Red had his glasses on and was leading with Bull close behind. Pieter and I took positions on the left and right and Stan watched the back door.

The forest was mainly pines and firs and provided good cover. Occasionally we would come across an open space where the trees had been cut down by mass logging. While in these clearings we could see the surrounding mountains, some already with snow on their peaks. It was easy going, the soft carpet of decaying needles from the trees cushioning our feet. Pieter was struggling – he was out of condition – and we had to slacken our pace from time to time for him to catch up.

When we reached the holding station we lay on our fronts and surveyed the scene. Stan produced a pair of binoculars and passed them to me. It was exactly as Bull had described it last night at dinner. It was like a scene from a prisoner-of-war movie with the watch-towers at each corner of a square. People were shuffling around in that aimless manner of the captive. It reminded me of the animals at the zoo.

'Entry won't be a problem,' Stan said. 'I've got some bolt-cutters so we can cut the wire easily.'

'Tell me, Stan,' I said, 'is there anything you didn't bring?'

'Only female company.'

'Spoilsport,' said Pieter.

'The best place to cut,' Bull said, 'would be at the base of one of the watch-towers. We'd be concealed from view there. The trickiest bit is covering the open ground of the square to get to the huts. Always presuming that Irina is in one of the huts.'

'Good enough place to start,' I said.

'We could use your silenced Uzi to take out the guards,' said Stan.

'I'd rather not start shooting yet,' I said. 'We don't know who are the good guys and who are the bad. Some may just be obeying orders.'

'That conscience of yours is going to get you in trouble one day,' said Red.

'But not today, hopefully,' I said, knowing that he might be right.

'Indian brave can take out a guard silently,' Red said. 'Bringum heap big rope to tie up and something to use as a gag.'

'It's a good idea,' I said, 'but we need to take out all four guards at the same time. Anyone not up for it?' No one spoke. 'Red, are you sure you can manage it?'

'No problem. I'm better close up.'

'OK, we cut holes in the wire one watch-tower at a time. When they're all done we move through simultaneously and take out the guards. Pieter, you stay on the outside in case there's trouble and move to any point that needs help.'

We carried on watching for a while. At intervals of around a half-hour one of the people walking around the square was singled out and taken to the central facility. At twelve o'clock the guards changed. At one, large tureens of food were taken into the huts and the inmates moved inside for a meal. It was as riveting as watching paint dry, but it was a necessary part of the preparations. After a further hour Bull volunteered to stay behind to continue the watch and the rest of us headed back to the lodge. As we were leaving, Stan turned to Bull and said, 'Dinner will be at nine. Don't be late. I wouldn't want it to spoil.'

'Are you doing something special? I don't have to wear black tie, do I?'

'Special Polish recipe.'

'So, it's stew then,' Bull said.

*

Bull was back on the dot of nine. He had jogged back and was breathing heavily when he walked through the door. The sight that greeted him must have taken him aback. The table had been laid and Stan had even managed to find some napkins. There were water glasses for each of us and he was just setting down a cold beer by each place.

'What's this in aid of?' asked Bull.

'If a job's worth doing,' Stan said, 'it's worth doing properly.'

'I'll go and clean up,' Bull said. 'I suppose that's all right?'

Stan sighed. 'Make it quick,' he said.

The stew was good. Some kind of cut of pork with paprika. To go with it were potatoes and a mixture of carrots, green beans and peas. There was a loaf of bread that Stan sliced into large chunks and placed in a wooden bowl for passing around. We fell silent for a while. Finally Red broke ranks.

'This is good,' he said. 'Where did you learn to cook like this?'

'It's what I do now,' Stan said. 'I'm a sous chef at a restaurant in Warsaw.'

'I suppose you can still kill people by cooking,' Pieter said. 'We could keep you in reserve in case we want anyone poisoned.'

'If you go on like that, you could be the first,' Stan said.

I turned to Bull. 'Did you learn anything new?' I said.

'They changed the guards at eight o'clock so it looks like they work eight-hour shifts. I'm going back there later to see what they do during the night. If it was me I'd make it four-hour shifts at night – hard to maintain concentration when it's dark. That would put the guard count to sixteen minimum. Be best if we could pen them in so they don't get in our way.'

'We hit them tomorrow when we know their movements. Do it some time in the hours of dark. Take out the guards and move to the huts. Find Irina and out.'

'You talk about it so casually,' said Carlo. 'Aren't you afraid?'

'Of course,' said Bull. 'Be stupid not to be. But you deal with it. Use the adrenaline to drive you on. And we try to plan for all eventualities. That's why we're not hitting them tonight – don't know enough about the set up.'

146

Carlo shook his head. The idea of actually waiting before doing something was foreign to him. Go with your instincts was his philosophy, even if past experience proved that the strategy was flawed.

'I'm not sure I'll ever fully understand you people. Why do you do it?'

'It's a living,' said Pieter. 'And we're good at it. Since we broke up as a group I've not felt really good at anything. I drifted, couldn't hold down a job. I missed the action. I missed the comradeship. I feel better than I have done for years, even if I'm now putting myself in danger.'

'Maybe the danger is part of it,' Red said. 'Testing oneself, overcoming the fear and the danger. The buzz when the plan comes together and we execute it perfectly.'

'We're a good team,' I said. 'And that's rare. When we go into action we each know our role. We depend on each other – and that's good. Being able to trust people is a good feeling.'

'I let you down badly, didn't I?' said Carlo.

'Yes,' I said. 'Don't do it again.'

'Or you'll have five of us after your hide,' said Bull.

22

Bull and I lay on our stomachs, keeping watch on the compound of the holding station. Running a stake-out is lonely work and since there's always a risk of falling asleep I had decided to accompany Bull. We needed to see if the guards stuck to eight-hour shifts or whether the timing was different during the night.

All was quiet and still. The only activity was the regular beam of light coming from the searchlight on the top of each watch-tower. As we had reasoned the lights only shone inwards and didn't scan for entry from the outside. The plan we had worked out looked good.

'Do you think we'll get thanked at the end of this job?' Bull said.

'Doubt it. Never got much thanks in the past.'

'We're like the wind,' Bull said. 'We breeze into town, blow away all the bad stuff and move on. Everyone's happy when we arrive and no one's sorry to see us go.'

'What brought on this burst of philosophy?' I said.

'Just thinking of the five of us. We don't really know any other kind of living. Pieter's been drifting around and is out of shape. Red told me he'd been doing the rodeo circuit and that the horses had started to beat him rather than the other way round. Stan is Stan and always will be, but one day his meticulous planning will miss out a vital element or he won't be able to think quick enough on his feet. We're all getting older. Should be wiser too. But this is all we know and we can't break out.'

'Wow,' I said. 'Some speech.'

'Just nervous, I guess. Makes me think more about failure and its consequences. In the old days we didn't have any ties. That made everything easier. But now, well, I wouldn't want to leave Mai Ling without a husband and Michael without a father. If things go wrong, promise me you'll look after them.'

'I promise,' I said.

He gave a sigh of relief.

The lights stopped their motion. Four figures appeared from the largest of the huts and walked across the compound to their respective posts. It was midnight – looked like they were working on four-hour shifts during the night. The best time for us to strike would be around two o'clock when tiredness was starting to get a hold.

Suddenly a lone figure ran from one of the huts and headed for the wire fence. He must have thought that the guards would be distracted at the changeover. They were, but not enough. A shout in a language I couldn't understand came from one of the guards. The figure kept running and then leapt at the fence. He started to climb, but there wasn't anything to give him sufficient hold. One of the guards turned to face him and shouted again. A gun was raised and pointed at him. The guard shouted again. The figure kept up his pointless climb up the fence. A burst of bullets rang out and the figure fell to the ground. It didn't move.

'Least we now know who the bad guys are,' said Bull.

'And what they'll do when challenged,' I said. 'Tomorrow night we take no prisoners.'

We slept late and had a large brunch which Carlo – turning over a new leaf, perhaps – cooked. The bacon was so crisp it shattered into a thousand pieces when you put your fork in it. The eggs were so hard that they had the look and the texture of a discus. Luckily none of us was hungry. Nerves were beginning to gnaw at our insides.

We spent the day packing all our things for an instant getaway that night and, when that was done, in various types of displacement activity. We cleaned all the weapons and then Stan, in sergeant-major mode, sucked air through his teeth and got us to clean them again. We checked out the firing positions marked by branches that Stan had laid out around the perimeter of the cabin and left spare clips of ammunition by the internal firing positions. Finally we adjusted the straps on the shoulder holsters and started to pack the cars.

'Where are the rest of the bearer bonds and the money?' I asked Carlo.

'Packed securely in my case,' he answered.

'Give them to me,' I said.

'I told you they're safe,' he said.

'Just look at it as insurance. Our insurance that you'll be here when we get back. Hand them over.'

He went into his room and came back with a bundle of paper. I checked the bearer bonds and counted the money. He didn't seem to be holding back on me. I put it all in my rucksack and locked it in the boot of one of the hire cars. I checked my watch.

'Hell,' I said. 'We might as well go as sit here twiddling our thumbs.'

'What do I do when you're gone?' Carlo asked.

'Pray that we come back alive,' I said.

'And that they don't follow us,' Bull added. 'Especially that they don't follow us.'

'I think I need the toilet,' Carlo said. 'Frequently, I suspect.'

23

We buddied up and smeared each other's faces with mud from the forest. Picked up our rifles and left the cabin. Red was to take point with the pump-action shotgun, Stan was to watch the back door, not that we expected any danger from there, but, as Stan says, you can't be too careful. It felt good to be on the move at last.

'We could well have some language problems,' I said to Stan. 'Do you speak Russian?'

'What accent do you want?' he said nonchalantly.

Ever reliable.

We tooled up.

Each of us carried an assault rifle, the 9mm Browning in a shoulder holster and a knife in a sheath on our belt, although none of us would want to use the knife – it was too messy and unreliable. Contrary to what you see in the movies, the victim doesn't necessarily die instantly and without sound when his throat's cut. We also carried a length of rope and some gaffer tape to make up for not using the knife. In addition, Pieter carried the bolt cutters, long handled and sharp, well fit for purpose.

The going was slow, the carpet of needles on the forest floor absorbing our tread and making it seem like we were walking on wet sand. On top of that there was cloud cover over the moon and there were times when we had to feel our way through the trees.

We had debated long and hard about the best approach – cutting the wire at four places and coming in from different directions or just one cut and spreading out from there. In the end, judging that one entry was less likely to attract attention than four, we carved a six-foot high length of wire from the south-east quadrant, bent it back, let ourselves through and spread out from there.

Red was to remain at the entry point with the pump-action shotgun and I was to take the diagonal tower at the north-west sector: Bull and Pieter fanned out, the former to the north-east and the latter to the south-west, Stan stayed with the south-east. A pause to check each others' positions and then the moment came – the game was on.

I climbed the steps slowly, concentrating on silence rather than speed. Halfway up I was able to peer over the top step. The guard was standing at the wooden rail that enclosed the tower, staring into the middle of the compound. His rifle was propped against a high stool that the guard could use to rest his weary legs during the course of his stint on duty.

I crept up the remaining steps and behind the guard. I lifted the Uzi and hit him on the back of the neck with the butt. He was propelled forward such that I had to grab hold of his collar and pull him back before he could go over the edge. I heaved a sigh of relief and lowered him to the ground. I put a length of gaffer tape across his mouth and, now that the danger of him crying out was past, took my time so that his hands and feet were tied securely. Lastly I picked up his rifle – the omnipresent Kalashnikov – and ejected the bullets from the magazine. Time to meet the others.

We left the administration building till later and converged on the largest of the huts – this was where the rest of the guards would be, sleeping peacefully, hopefully. I gestured to Bull to kick down the door and to Red to stand by to go in first. Bull duly obliged and Red was inside in an instant. As the rest of us went through he aimed the shotgun in the air and fired. The noise was like thunder. The guards had a rude awakening. When they opened their eyes all they could see was dust falling from the ceiling and five guys covering them.

'No one moves,' Stan said in Russian. 'Put your hands on your heads and face the wall.'

There was an air of reluctance from some of the guards, after all they had the numerical advantage. But we had the fire power.

There's always one. One man who thinks he's invincible or is just plain stupid. A guy at the back made a dive for what must have been a pistol under his pillow. I pulled the Browning from its holster and fired off a shot. The bullet went straight through his hand. He stood motionless, looking down at the hole in his hand in disbelief.

'You're getting soft,' said Stan. 'You should have used the Uzi.'

'At this range if I'd used the Uzi I would have blown his hand off.'

'Like I said, you're getting soft.'

Bull sprayed an arc from his rifle in front of the feet of the guards. Hands now went on heads without delay.

We patted them down, not expecting anyone to be carrying a gun in his pyjamas, but it pays to be thorough, to leave nothing to chance – that's what makes us professionals. We trussed them up and made a pile of their rifles, emptying the magazines as we did so.

Bull and I went to the admin block, leaving Red, Stan and Pieter to explore the other huts. The door to the admin block was unlocked – why bother when there's plenty of guards around? Inside was a long corridor with doors off to the right and left. Bull and I followed standard procedure – one flinging a door wide, the other leaping through ready to fire if there was any danger. The first door on the left was set up as an office for two people – two desks, two chairs, two computers and so on, just like the ark. There were even two mugs waiting to be washed up. We searched the desk drawers and found what we were looking for – passports, all Russian, about twenty of them. We put them in our jacket pockets and moved on.

The first door on the right opened into a large room with a desk and two chairs, a computer terminal and a long leather couch of the type you see in a doctor's surgery. If that wasn't enough of a giveaway, there was a machine to test blood pressure, another to run an ECG to check out someone's heart, and a lot more that I had no idea of their function. One thing was for sure – a lot of money had been spent on kitting out this place. In one corner was a locked cabinet. Naturally, we broke the lock. Inside was a variety of drugs: we examined the labels and apart from some tranquillizers the rest didn't make much sense to us.

Bull went to keep watch in the corridor, I moved the mouse on the computer. I was hoping that it might provide some clue as to why Almas had invested so heavily in an enterprise involving a group of people who would simply be sold into some form of slavery.

A program was minimized and I called it up to full-screen. It was some kind of medical database. Against the name were the sex and age of each person and what looked like full details of their health: medical history, blood group, HIV test results and a lot more that didn't enlighten me much. I flicked through some more names and there was nothing unusual. Except perhaps. . . .

Bull called my name and pointed down the corridor. I went to join him and saw what he was pointing at – the door handle of the next room was turning. I signalled him to go down the corridor past the door. We raised our rifles and waited, breath held, fingers on triggers.

The door opened and out stepped two women in night clothes. They saw us, rifles pointed at them, and screamed.

'Raise your hands,' I shouted above the noise of the screaming. 'Face the wall.'

Bull patted them down, which only caused them to scream louder. Satisfied they weren't armed, he nodded at me.

'OK,' I said. 'Hands down and tell me who you are. And for God's sake, stop screaming. We're not going to hurt you.'

They were a doctor and a nurse. The doctor had a hard face, greying hair and legs that would have benefitted from a longer nightdress. The nurse had brown hair, eyes to match, full lips and a figure that didn't deserve to be hidden by the folds of some long nightshirt in an artificial fabric that probably caused sparks to come off Bull's hands as he patted her down. I motioned them into the office and asked them to sit down.

'What do you do here?' I said.

They relaxed a little in the familiar surroundings of the room.

The doctor spoke. If Stan had been here, he probably could have told me exactly where she came from by just listening to the accent. I guessed at Russian by the slow, low tones.

'We work for Almas,' she said. 'You know what we do here, I assume by your presence and the guns you carry.'

'Your business is selling people into slavery of some kind – prostitution, menial jobs that others aren't willing to do, housework for rich people. . . .'

'We are here to look after the people – check that they are in good health and then keep them that way before they move on.'

'Why so much interest in their health?'

'It's simple,' she said, regaining her composure. 'Almas gets more money for those in good health and won't let their employers down. And no one wants a prostitute who is infected by HIV AIDS. It makes commercial sense, that's all.'

I could tell she was hiding something and I was beginning to get an idea of what it was.

'Put some clothes on,' I said. 'We're going for a walk.'

We joined Red, Pieter and Stan outside one of the huts. People were formed around them in a circle. Some looked nervous, some relieved. All looked stunned. Not surprising, I suppose. It's not every day that a bunch of guys carrying assault rifles wakes you up in the middle of the night.

'Have you found Irina?' I asked Stan.

He called over to a young girl on the edge of the group, gestured that she should come to him.

'How much English do they speak?' I said.

'Enough to get by in their intended position, I imagine. The girls can groan OK. Some of the boys too, by the look of them.'

I shook my head. What a life had been planned for them. Down to the last detail.

I took the passports from my pocket. Bull followed suit. We handed them to Stan who could read the Cyrillic script.

'Dish these out,' I said. 'Then translate for me.'

I waited while the passports were returned to their owners. There was one left over. The man from last night, I guessed, who had finished his life dangling from the barbed wire of the fence.

I spoke slowly and with plenty of pauses so that Stan could translate.

'You have a choice,' I said. 'You can stay here until someone from Almas shows up or the guards manage to untie themselves. If you choose that option, Almas will own you for life. You will have to do what they say until your dying day – which may be soon. Or you can take a walk through the woods and hand yourself over to the police. Throw yourselves on their mercy. The worst that can happen is that you will be sent back to your own lands. Make your choice, now that you are free to choose.'

The circle around us split into groups as they debated what we had said. They all looked so young and vulnerable. Irina, taken with Stan, stuck close to him like a besotted little sister.

'Tie up these two,' I said to Pieter and Red, indicating the doctor and the nurse. 'Anything else you would like to tell me?' I asked them.

'I was only doing my job,' the doctor said.

'Isn't that depressing?' I said.

I turned to Bull. 'Tie them up and put them with the rest,' I said. 'Then let's get out of here. We need to put some distance between ourselves and this place before morning comes.'

'We did it,' said Bull.

'Maybe,' I replied.

We were close to the lodge when we saw the lights. They were coming for us. Someone must have untied the guards. Someone who we were trying to help had betrayed us. There was no point in dwelling on it now, there was another battle to fight.

The five of us ran fast and were in the clearing around the lodge when I heard a cry from Red.

'Shit,' he shouted, 'my glasses have come off.'

I grabbed hold of him and led him to the left-hand firing position that Stan had marked out. We hit the ground. I motioned

Bull to the right-hand firing position and Pieter and Stan to go inside the lodge. We were ready for them.

I lined Red up so that his shotgun was pointing straight to the entrance to the clearing.

'Hell,' he said. 'I'm sorry about this. Damn stupid thing to do. Now I'm no use to you.'

'Bullshit,' I said. 'I'm going to call out instructions, right? Just aim where I tell you and fire.'

'Shoot low at first,' I shouted to everyone. 'Try to cripple them. Only kill if you have to.'

It was an unwelcome restriction to place on the others, but something told me not to get blood on our hands. There had been too much killing in the past. I did not want to go back to those ways.

The trees were obstacles to them and they came at us in a column rather than a line. That was their first mistake. The second was to carry on using their torches – they stood out against the darkness of the forest like they were actors under a spotlight. They might as well have had florescent targets tattooed on their foreheads.

We let them enter the clearing around the hunting lodge and, before they could spread out, opened fire.

'Two o'clock,' I said to Red and he fired off a volley. Straight and true.

Arcs of bullets came from our assault rifles as we swept right to left. The shotgun boomed again and again as I called out directions. The first rank of the column was down and out.

'Just keep firing,' I said to Red. 'The noise is turning them into jelly.'

I signalled to Bull that we should leave our positions and circle round them. We ran, keeping low and came up behind the guards. Then we opened fire. Now from front and back they were being attacked. They had nowhere to run. Caught in the crossfire their will was being sapped, their resistance wavering. Bull and I kept changing our positions so that it appeared that there was a lot more of us. Stan and Pieter came out of the lodge, spraying bullets as they ran to take up the positions that Bull and I had vacated. The constant movement was disorientating them. They whirled around trying to find a target only to find themselves shooting at nothing.

The guards dropped like flies, their legs riddled with bullets or pellets from the shotgun. They threw their rifles aside and put their hands in the air. They had been sensible – they had surrendered.

We took it in turns to guard our prisoners while the rest of us searched for Red's glasses – luckily they reflected in the torchlight – and then went inside the lodge to wash the mud from our faces and change into some less conspicuous clothes. Then we packed the guns into the people carrier, split up into our individual cars and headed towards the border. Stan was taking the biggest risk, but I had a feeling that we might need the guns again.

By the time we were across the border all hell was breaking loose in the area around Freiberg. Almas was going to have a lot of explaining to do. I wondered how they would try to wriggle out of this. I smiled and carried on driving.

24

We arrived back in Amsterdam around lunchtime, tired and hungry. Red, naturally, was the first to get back. Lucky not to be picked up by the police, I reckoned. Lucky to get back alive even.

I phoned Gus and arranged for him to come over for a meeting. Scout and Natasha were off seeing Scout's father so I thought the best plan was to grab a couple of hours' sleep and a snack and then all meet up. I hoped that the sleep would help clear my mind. There were some big decisions to make.

Stan had arranged for the matron who ran the hotel to provide us with a snack – various smoked fish, bread of all sizes, shapes and colours, and a plateful of Polish pickled cucumbers. 'You can't eat smoked fish without a pickled cucumber,' he said. 'And no one makes a better pickled cucumber than a Pole.' In addition to the food there were beers, a bottle of vodka, a bucket of ice and some soft drinks. Everything we needed.

When the matron brought the first tray of food she came up to me.

'Advance,' she said.

I noticed that she had had her hair done. No longer lank and shapeless, it was shorter and styled into short curls. I could guess who'd paid for that.

The dining-room was getting cramped. There were the five of

us mercenaries, Carlo and Irina, and still Scout, Natasha and Gus were to arrive. We spread ourselves around the two tables and dug into the food. I poured myself a vodka and waited.

Gus was the next to arrive. He was brimming with happiness when he saw Carlo, then walked across to me and gave me a big hug.

'You did it,' he said.

'Sort of,' I replied. 'I'll explain later.'

When Scout and Natasha came into the room, Carlo rushed to Natasha and kissed her with embarrassing fervour. I made introductions, took a slug of my vodka and prepared to put the cat among the pigeons.

'We have fulfilled our contract,' I said. 'Do you agree, Gus?'

'You have found Carlo. That was your mission. You've carried out your side of the bargain. I'll arrange with Roberto to settle the account.'

'We found Carlo and now we're going to let him go. He and Natasha – and Irina too – are going to ride off into the sunset and start a new life.'

Carlo smiled.

'You can keep what's left of the million-euro bearer bond. The other eight million stays with me for the moment.'

'But how am I going to live?' he protested.

'I imagine Natasha can show you a few tricks on how to save money. You're going to have to draw your horns in and budget for the future. Time to ride on, Carlo, and consider yourself lucky. I could hand you over to Roberto and he'd probably arrange for someone to break every bone in your body, if that's what you prefer.'

He thought for a moment, looked at Natasha and squeezed her hand. 'Riding off into the sunset sounds fine by us.'

I turned to Scout. 'How's your father getting on?'

'He's mending. It took a while to get the drugs out of his system and for the burn on his back to start healing, but he'll be all right. Be out in a day or so.'

'Get him out tonight,' I said.

'But why?' she asked.

'Bear with me for a minute and I'll give you the answer,' I said.

I got up from the table, walked across to the table where the drinks were and refreshed my vodka. I took a sip and realized I was just playing for time.

'As I said earlier, we fulfilled our contract. But there's one big problem. We poked a stick in a hornet's nest which leaves some unfinished business. What I'm going to ask is a lot. I won't blame anybody who wants to get out.'

'I'm with you,' Bull said.

'You don't know what I'm going to ask yet.'

'I'm not as stupid as I look. I saw the people at the holding station too. I think I know what the situation is.'

I looked at Gus. 'Let's go through it from the top. Carlo, in his normal impetuous way, basically signed over the bank to Almas. And Almas has fingers in many pies. Drugs, gambling, prostitution to name just three. And there's worse to come. When I looked at the medical records and at the people at the holding station, one thought struck me.'

'They're all young and fit,' Bull said.

'Perfect transplant material,' I said.

Scout looked at me and started to get the picture.

'Yes, they are sold into slavery, but they're also being prepared for their young and fit organs to be donated to the highest bidder. That's where the hospital fits into the Almas portfolio. When someone needs a transplant – you remember the old lady you met at the hospital, Bull? – a suitable donor is located and shipped there.'

'Never felt better, she'd said. Liver of a twenty-year-old. Ties in.'

'So the people – the illegal immigrants – take up some position for which Almas gets paid. Then when someone comes along needing a transplant, they pick the most suitable person from their human stock.' I turned to Natasha now. 'When I spoke to Anna last time she said that girls had left the casino before, but she'd never heard anything from them. I wonder why. I even reckon that it wasn't only Carlo they were searching for: Natasha might have been singled out as a donor – if you use that word when it's not voluntary. She could have been valuable to them. That's why Almas has gone to such trouble.'

'Oh, God,' Scout said, going white.

'What is it?' I asked.

'When Natasha and I were at the hospital today we bumped into Anna. She said she was being admitted for a full medical before being allowed to leave to take up a new life. You don't think—'

'It's precisely what I think,' I said. 'I want to stop this trade in human organs, release those inside the hospital and put the fear of God into the staff there. This has to stop now before another innocent person gets killed for the greater good of the rich and wealthy.'

'So that's what you want us to do?' asked Red. 'Raid the hospital? Hell, it'll be like shooting fish in a barrel. Count me in.'

'There's more,' I said.

I fell silent for a moment, contemplating what had to be done to put things right.

'Spit it out, Johnny,' said Gus. 'Or would you like me to take a guess.'

I nodded. Couldn't bring myself to say the words.

'We know that Almas,' Gus said, 'has its claws in the European operation – pardon the pun – of Silvers. Using the bank to launder its filthy lucre. You're afraid that the same sort of thing has happened in America. Am I right?'

'Having Ms Oakley – Bellini as is – as your compliance officer is like putting the fox in charge of the henhouse. I think they control the New York operation and have their eyes on Europe. Carlo's disappearance presented them with a golden opportunity to get involved in the Amsterdam operation.'

'So what are you going to do?' Scout asked.

'I'm working on a plan,' I said. 'But first I'm going to hit the hospital. If anyone wants out, now's the time.'

'Hell,' said Red, 'I haven't had such fun for years. I'm with you all the way.'

'I hate to admit it in front of the lovely ladies,' Pieter said, 'but

I wish I was fitter. I'm not the man I was.'

'None of us is,' said Bull, 'but that doesn't mean they can write us off.'

'I'm in if you'll have me,' said Pieter.

I looked at Stan. His face was the usual solemn picture, betraying no emotion.

'Where would you be without me?' he said. 'You're the sort of guy who would forget the pickled cucumbers. I'm in.'

'Bull,' I said, 'I wouldn't blame you if you had mixed emotions about this. If you weren't tempted to take the opposite route. The odds are probably good that the hospital could find a match for Michael. Would scour this continent and all others to find the right donor.'

'And how would I live with that?' he said. 'Every time I looked at Michael I would be thinking of the poor innocent kid who'd died for him. One thing I've learnt from you over the years is that you have to do the right thing – a man's gotta do what a man's gotta do. If you don't have standards, you're no better than the guy you're trying to kill for the evil he's doing. You have to be able to look at yourself in the mirror when you're shaving and feel proud of what you see, otherwise how can you live with yourself? I'm in.'

'OK,' I said. 'I didn't want to mention this until I had your answer. Money.'

'Who gives a damn about the money,' said Red, 'when you're having so much fun?'

'Scout,' I said. 'You and your father can keep the million euros from the bearer bond he cashed. That's for your contribution to helping to find Carlo. We'll split the remaining eight million between us. I don't see why Roberto should get a cent of it back. And, if I have my way, it wouldn't do him any good if I handed it over.'

'Sounds like you have a plan,' said Gus.

'It's nearly there,' I said. 'But first I have to meet my mother. There's a question she has to answer and I'd rather like her approval for what I intend to do. It needs to be soon, Gus. Can you arrange it?'

'I'll pull in a favour,' he said.

'OK,' I said. 'Let's meet again in an hour. We have a hospital to visit.'

25

We went *en masse* to the hospital. It wasn't that I expected to need all of us to achieve the task in hand, but a show of strength never does any harm. Scout went directly to her father to get him out as quickly as possible. I positioned Stan at the left-most H block, Red at the right and Bull at the rectangular building. Pieter came with me to the rotunda.

The same receptionist was on duty, as immaculately made up as before. She gave us her practised sincere smile and asked how she could help.

'I'd like to speak to the person in charge,' I said.

'Do you have a complaint?' she asked. What a question to ask in a hospital. 'Because,' she continued, 'we have a special form for that.'

'Complaint?' I said. 'I suppose you might call it that.'

She handed me a form and I wrote the following words on it – *I want to talk transplants. Do you want me to go to the media with what I know, or will you see me?*

I handed her the form and asked her to get it immediately to the person in charge. She picked up the phone and dialled a number. Little Miss Clipboard appeared. She took the form and went away. It was maybe five minutes before she reappeared – five minutes when the mind of the person in charge must have been in turmoil.

'If you'd like to follow me,' she said.

I turned to Pieter. 'You speak Dutch, don't you?'

165

'*Ja.*' he said.

I hoped that wasn't the limit of his knowledge.

'In South Africa many people still speak Dutch – a legacy of the old Boer days.'

'Stick close to the receptionist,' I said. 'Make sure she doesn't make any calls she shouldn't.'

He nodded and went to the other side of the counter, sat on the desk and looked the receptionist in the eye. 'Now,' he said, 'let's get to know each other better, Brown Eyes.'

I was led to a large office at the back of the rotunda. There was a sign on the door that said DR VAKANTIE, CHIEF ADMINISTRATOR, in bold capital letters to show the importance of the owner of the title. The office had a panoramic view of the manicured lawn through its round window, a further signal of the status of the occupant. There was a long black rectangular table with eight chairs, black with chrome arms and legs, around which meetings could be held. In the middle of the table was a vase of flowers whose delicate perfume filled the air. Behind a mahogany table sat a man in his late fifties with thin greying hair. He had on a dark-blue suit, light-blue shirt, striped tie and half-moon spectacles. He peered over the glasses at me, trying to make some sort of judgement which would help him to bullshit me.

I walked over to the desk, sat down on a chair opposite him, undid the jacket of my suit and looked him in the eye.

'How long has it been going on?' I said.

'I don't know what you're talking about,' he said.

'In that case why are you seeing me?'

There was a pause, followed by a cagey question. 'So what is it you think you know?' he said.

'You're running a special deal on transplants. No waiting, perfect match, fit, young organs that will last a lifetime. But not for those you get them from.'

'I suppose it's money that you want?'

'An admission would be good for a start. Although the offer of money implies an admission.'

166

'You really should be talking to our owners, Almas. I'm sure Mr Garanov would be pleased to deal with you.'

'We've met already. And the feeling would be mutual. But right now I can't wait for Garanov and his goons to show up. I'll tell you the deal.'

He leaned forward in his chair.

'I want every person here who is due to be a donor released straight away. In return, I'm willing to take your word that this practice will cease.'

'I can't make any such deal. Even if I knew what you are talking about.'

I sighed. Took the Browning from the shoulder holster inside my jacket. Turned round and fired at the vase of flowers. There was a short phut from the silencer and the vase shattered. The flowers dropped and water spread over the tabletop. I turned back to Dr Vakantie. His face was white and his hands were shaking.

'Look into my eyes, Dr Vakantie. What do you see there? Do you think I'll show you any mercy for what you've done? The next shot I fire will be through your elbow. The one after that will be through your knee. You're a medical man. You know what damage that will do. And if you don't do what I want after that, the final shot will be through your heart. What's your decision?'

'You can't come in here waving a gun and threatening to kill people. Where do you think you are – the Wild West? This is a civilized country.'

I shot him through the elbow.

He gave a whimper, stared at me incredulously and grabbed his elbow. Blood ran down his fingertips.

I stood up, walked around the desk and spun him round in his chair. I put the gun on top of his kneecap and let him feel the pressure.

'OK,' I said. 'Let's get this over with one way or the other. I'll give you a count of three.'

'No,' he said, shaking his head rapidly. Panic had replaced the earlier calm. 'Don't shoot. You can have what you want. Anything.

Just don't shoot.'

'Make a call,' I said. 'Someone who will take me round the rooms and point out any that are due to be operated on. I'm taking them with us.'

He picked up the phone and punched a button, his hands still shaking. Relayed my instructions to the person on the other end of the line.

'Now call reception,' I said. 'Tell the woman to come up here and to bring my friend Pieter. She'll know who you're talking about. For all I know they could even be engaged by now.'

He did as he was told. I never doubted it. I went and stood by the door. Let in the receptionist and Pieter. The receptionist knew there was a problem, but didn't know what it was. She didn't have anything to worry about, just as long as she didn't start screaming.

'Keep Dr Vakantie company,' I said to Pieter. 'Make sure he doesn't feel the need to talk to anyone outside this room. I'm off on ward rounds. I'll call you when it's time to go.'

Miss Clipboard came along the corridor and I intercepted her.

'You have your instructions,' I said. 'Lead the way.'

As we left the rotunda I saw Scout. Her father was sitting on a bench. He looked better than when I had last seen him, but that wasn't saying much. His face was still pale and he seemed to be staring into the middle distance. Scout started to come towards me.

'How many people are we talking about?' I asked Miss Clipboard.

'Nine,' she said.

Nine! The scale of the operation was frightening.

'Can you order cabs?' I asked Scout. 'Enough for us and nine people. We go back to the hotel and the rest to the airport. We'll be ready in about ten minutes.'

'OK,' she said. 'How did it go?'

'He was stupid,' I said. 'I had to shoot him in the elbow. Came close to losing his kneecap too. Can you mastermind the transport while I collect the people?'

'Leave it with me,' she said.

I turned to Miss Clipboard. 'One of them is called Anna – don't know her second name. I want to see her first.'

She consulted her board and nodded. 'This way,' she said.

We went into the left-most H-shaped building. Stan was on door duty.

'All quiet,' he said.

'Not for long,' I answered. 'You'd best join me. I think I might need an interpreter. There's a hell of a lot of explaining to do.'

Anna's room was a replica of the one that Scout's father had occupied. Same hotel-style furniture, same missing trouser-press. Anna was in bed, sitting up reading a book and leaning back against about four pillows. She had less make-up on than usual, but still looked a million dollars. She smiled as we entered.

'Johnny,' she said. 'What are you doing here?'

I explained the con that had been played on her and the others. She shivered at the thought of her internal organs being plundered and at the death that would surely follow.

'Have you got your passport?' I asked.

'Yes, they gave it back to me before I came here.'

'Get it, Anna,' I said. 'Then get dressed. We're leaving in five minutes. Meet us out front.'

Anna and the eight other people were all in the same quadrant of the building. At first we started to explain, but it was taking too long and we had to resort to telling them to get dressed, grab their passport and meet us outside. When the whole nine were assembled, we explained the situation fully, Stan translating for those whose English wasn't up to it.

I walked round the group. 'Here's a thousand euros each,' I said. 'That will get you on a plane home. When you get back, tell everyone what's happening here. We have to stop this trafficking.'

I handed out the money. Anna took hers and shook her head.

'Can I stay with you?' she asked. She blushed. 'I meant just for a while, till I get myself sorted out and know what I'm going to do.'

'I'd be honoured,' I said.

A tear came to her eye.

'No one's ever said anything like that to me before.'

'Then you've only ever known fools.' I took her hand. 'Come on, let's go. It's time to start a new life.'

26

We had hurt Almas twice now. Once more would finish them. I only hoped that it wouldn't be the finish of us instead. My plan was a big gamble, but before I put it into effect I had to talk to my mother. Apprise her of the situation and get her approval for the actions that had to be taken. She was flying over from London this morning and I was already getting nervous. It wasn't just that there were inherent dangers in my plan and consequences to pay, but she would need to fulfil the final part of the bargain struck – naming my father. Would I be ecstatic or disappointed? Proud or ashamed? Would it have been better to leave well alone, let the sleeping dog lie? I would know soon enough.

The hotel was now full. What had started out as a safe house for the six of us, now included as well Scout's father, Carlo, Natasha and Irina, and of course Anna. The woman who ran the hotel must have thought that she'd won the lottery. The old shabby dress had gone, replaced by a pin-stripe blouse and a dark-blue skirt. The shoes were new too. Nothing was now too much trouble for her – the breakfast had improved, the ice in the bucket was constantly replaced. But she still had her eccentric ways. When we asked for coffee when we got back from the hospital she had shaken her head and insisted that we have caffeine-free hot chocolate instead. A big jug arrived and we sat around in the shabby lounge and thought of what had been done.

Scout's father sat in one of the armchairs and sipped his chocolate. He still had that seen-it-all-before look of an ex-cop.

He was still pale from his trauma and this accentuated his heavy five o'clock shadow. His greying hair was cut short and was practical if not stylish. He looked me in the eye with a raised eyebrow.

'Scout says that you don't want the money back,' he said. 'Is that true? We can keep it?'

'I'm sure you'll put it to better use than Roberto and won't squander it like Carlo.'

'I'm a changed man,' said Carlo indignantly.

'But for how long?' I asked.

He grinned at me. 'You could be right. It'll take time to change the habits of a lifetime, but I'll have Natasha to keep me on the straight and narrow.'

He looked at her with dreamy eyes and I saw there was someone who might be able to change him. It was a strange match, but one that might work. And who was I to talk? Anna was sitting beside me, her hand on mine and it felt right. It would be good to get to know her better and to see if the feelings we felt grew or withered with familiarity.

'What will you do with the money?' I asked Scout's father.

'Start the biggest detective agency in the Netherlands,' he said. 'Put some aside for my old age and some for Scout's wedding. How is Arnie by the way?' he said to her.

Scout blushed. 'Dad,' she said. 'Really!'

So it wasn't an act. The dressing up, the little incidents of body contact, the kisses, were all for real, not just to extract information. It seemed a case of odd matches all round.

'If there's to be a wedding, I want an invite,' I said. 'At last I would find out your real name.'

She blushed again.

'That makes me want to hear it even more.'

Scout's father yawned and it became infectious. It was a signal that we had done enough talking for one evening and it was time for bed. I escorted Anna to her room and watched her open the door and look up at me.

'You can come in, you know,' she said. 'I'd like that.'

'Best not to get too close too soon. There's one more dangerous act to do. I don't want you getting attached if I get killed in a couple of days' time.'

'If that happens, think what we would have missed out on.'

'Are all Russian girls as sensible as you?'

'Yes,' she said, 'but not as in love as I am.'

'Hell,' I said. 'Then the damage is already done.'

I put my arm around her, drew her close to me and kissed her tenderly. Together we walked into her room.

My mother was due in ten minutes. I went around the lounge plumping up the cushions on the chairs, emptying ashtrays and generally tidying up.

'What are you doing?' Carlo said. 'Do you really think any of that will make any difference. It's a shabby room. You're not going to change that. And, anyway, it isn't what Mother has come here for: she's come to see you, not to write an article for *Ideal Home* magazine.'

'Leave him alone,' Natasha said. 'Right now he needs to be busy. You could even help him.'

Carlo sighed, saw that resistance was useless and started to gather up the hot chocolate mugs from the night before. When he had as many as he could carry he left the room to take them to the kitchen.

'How do you feel about meeting Mother?' I said to Natasha.

'Scared,' she said. 'I doubt whether I'm anything close to her ideal daughter-in law.'

'She's always spoilt Carlo,' I said. 'This time won't be any different. She may even be relieved that he's settling down at last.'

'Maybe,' she said, unconvinced. 'Anna likes you a lot, loves you even. She's a strong woman – you have to be to cope with the life she's been forced to live – but she has a heart like the rest of us. Don't hurt her.'

'I don't intend to,' I said.

The door opened and in stepped Gus and my mother.

She had aged, her black hair, streaked in places with grey, still in her preferred bun, her skin a little saggy around the neck, deeper lines under her eyes, but she was still a beautiful woman. Something about the bone structure perhaps. Whatever it was, it was undeniable – a classic Jewish woman; how Rebecca in *Ivanhoe* would have looked twenty years after meeting the knight.

She came across to me and a tear came to her eye. She wrapped her arms around me.

'Gianni,' she said, 'it's been too long.' She stepped back a pace to get a better look at me. 'How you've changed. You are a handsome man now. And the muscles and the tan. Life must have treated you well over the last ten years.'

'I can't complain,' I said.

'No,' she said. 'You never did.'

Carlo entered the room and rushed across to Mother. He put his arms on her shoulders and kissed her on both cheeks.

'Carlo,' she said. 'You are safe. We were all worried about you, but Gianni found you, just as I thought he would. He always keeps his promises.'

'Mother,' he said, 'you must meet Natasha. We are going to be married.'

She didn't show any shock – maybe Gus had already broken the news to her.

'Delighted to meet you, Natasha,' she said. 'You must have great courage to marry someone like Carlo. Not to mention fortitude too. You will be welcome in my house.'

She sat down in one of the better armchairs and motioned to us to do the same.

'Carlo,' she said, 'Gus tells me you've been a naughty boy. What do you have to say for yourself?'

'I'm in love, Mother.'

'And love is supposed to cover a multitude of sins?'

He looked at her blankly. Wasn't that what always happened?

'Carlo has agreed that he will step down from Silvers,' I said. 'There's still some of the stolen money outstanding. I've said he could keep that to get him started in a new life.'

'You're a strange one, Gianni. From what I've heard of your

exploits over the last ten years there must be a hardness within you and yet there is still the soft streak. I'm glad of it. I am proud of you, Gianni. You're a good man.' She paused and turned to Carlo. 'Now you and Natasha run along. I need to talk with Gianni alone.'

Carlo and Natasha got up from their chairs and began to walk to the door. Carlo turned back.

'I've got an admission to make,' he said.

'If it is about that business with the loan and shares in the computer company and the loss Silvers suffered, I know all about it. Have done all along. I read the folder that Roberto threw in the bin. I think we can say that I have indulged you enough for one lifetime. From now on, Carlo, I expect more of you, especially if you have a wife to look after. Now go, the pair of you. We will celebrate your engagement another time.'

Carlo and Natasha left the room. Gus looked settled in his chair – it seemed he would be privy to our discussions. I was glad of it. Any advice that Gus could give would be valuable.

'You knew?' I said to my mother. 'All this time you've known?'

'I'm sorry,' she said. 'I knew that as soon as Alfredo was better he would get rid of you. I didn't want to lose Carlo, too. As I said, I've indulged him too much. I thought it might make a man of him and that he would learn by his mistakes. But it was you, Gianni, who was the responsible one.'

I looked at Gus and shrugged.

'Best to move on from the past,' he said. 'I have contacted Roberto and he has agreed that the balance of your fee should be paid.'

'Through gritted teeth, I imagine.' I turned to look at my mother. 'That still leaves one part of the bargain to be settled – the question of my father.'

'Like you, I do not break my promises. Gus will tell you what you want to know as soon as this business is finished. Now tell me what you plan to do and what is my part in it.'

27

Almas had a different receptionist this time. Presumably the last one thought the handling of guns was beyond the call of duty. Still, what can you expect if you share office space with a bunch of gorillas? Free bananas? No, trouble.

The new woman was younger, thirty at the most, and had chestnut hair. She was pretty in that heavily made-up beautician way, but looked like one large grin would cause an avalanche of foundation to break off and fall to the desk. She didn't like it when we said we didn't have an appointment.

'Mr Garanov doesn't see anyone without an appointment,' she said, hoping we'd turn on our heels and meekly exit the offices.

'Tell him Mr Glock is here,' I said.

'And Mr Browning,' Bull added.

She picked up the phone and swivelled round in her chair so that her back was towards us in the mistaken supposition that we wouldn't be able to hear the conversation.

'Are you sure yet?' I said to Bull. 'Is this Garanov the same Russian as in Angola?'

'I need another look,' he said. 'My view was pretty restricted last time, remember.'

One of the gorillas poked his head round the door and motioned us inside Garanov's office. Garanov was seated at his black desk, running his hand through the stubble on his head. He looked up as we walked in and from the furrowed expression on his face wasn't exactly delighted to see us. The gorillas took up pre-prepared positions either side of their boss and the third had his back to the door.

'You're back,' Garanov said.

'Reckon so,' I replied.

'What do you want this time? To offer your apologies for what you've been doing to my organization? It was you, wasn't it? The compound, the hospital?'

'Reckon so,' I repeated.

'Reckon so? Is that all you're going to say?'

I resisted the temptation to say 'reckon so' again and instead said, 'I bring greetings from Mr Bellini. You do know who Mr Bellini is, I take it?'

'Of course,' he said. Then he looked at Bull. 'Why do I get the feeling I've seen you before?'

'Maybe you've seen me hanging around someplace,' Bull said. Then he turned his back and concentrated on the gorilla by the door.

Garanov shook his head as if trying to dislodge the memory from his unconscious mind and send it up to Brain Central.

'What has Mr Bellini got to do with anything?' he asked, giving up on trying to place Bull.

'Mr Bellini feels that you have been disrespectful,' I said. 'You have stepped on his toes, invaded his territory. Mr Bellini regards Silvers as his domain and you have encroached. He has shown his power, what he can do to your organization. He hopes you are impressed and will give him the respect he deserves.'

'So Bellini—' he started.

'*Mister* Bellini,' I corrected. 'Respect, remember?'

'OK. So Mr Bellini is trying to put me out of business, is that what all this is about?'

'Mr Bellini feels that it would do neither side any good to fight over control of Silvers,' I said. 'He is willing to make an accommodation. Come to some agreement on how to divide control of the European operation. This is a big gesture on Mr Bellini's part and you would do well to listen to what he has to say.'

'Or else? Is that what you are saying?'

I shrugged. 'Do you need another demonstration of what he can do?'

'And what does Mr Bellini propose?'

'What is good for Silvers could be good for both sides. Mr Bellini is willing to recognize your interests by apportioning your involvement.'

'Giving me a share of Europe when I already have a hundred per cent?' Garanov laughed. 'I don't think so.'

'Mr Bellini has asked me to point out to you that operating a casino can be a very high-risk venture. He could provide some insurance for you.'

'Is that a threat?'

'Reckon so,' I said.

Garanov paused to think. We'd hurt him badly twice and he would be assessing the likelihood of further damage. The casino would be an easy target – it wouldn't take much to give the clients reason to take their custom elsewhere. A brawl breaking out maybe. An accusation of cheating. Revelations about the prostitution business.

'And what does Mr Bellini have in mind?'

Wise man.

'He proposes that there should be talks held between the two of you to reach an amicable agreement – one where the hatchet could be buried and business return to normal. I am to issue you with an invitation. A meeting is to be held in three days' time at the zoo. You know it?'

'Of course.'

'Good. Nine o'clock on Friday evening. You may bring ten men only. Mr Bellini will bring the same number. You and your men may be armed, as will Mr Bellini and his men. You should also bring a gift to cement the new relationship – something appropriate for Almas. To the value of one million dollars. Mr Bellini will do likewise. He will extend his hospitality to you and your men – canapés and vodka for your side, Italian red wine and antipasto for his side. He advises you to accept his hospitality and to be prepared to discuss the future. He asks me to inform you that a hundred per cent of nothing is still nothing.'

'And if I don't agree?'

'You will be out of business within a week,' I said. 'Oh, and dead within two.'

Garanov frowned as he considered his options. None, would be a good summary.

'I agree,' he said. 'Nine o'clock on Friday then. And no tricks.'

As if we would.

Stan came with me to Silvers. I needed someone who would pass as a Russian to add a texture of reality and I was banking on Ms Oakley not being able to tell the difference between a Pole and a Russian.

We walked past Arnie with no hint of recognition and into Carlo's ex-office. Ms Oakley was sitting at the head of the conference table and indicated that we should sit at the side. I sat at the other end opposite her so that I could stare her straight in the face.

'Coffee would be good,' I said.

'*Da,*' Stan said in agreement.

Ms Oakley frowned, but went to the partner's desk, pressed a button and issued instructions. I was after all the son of a Silver – it had to count for something.

'I don't think you've been totally honest with me,' I said to Ms Oakley.

She was wearing a light-grey power suit of straight-cut jacket and a skirt that reached just above the knee. Her heels were high and she had obviously given up on the deception of the last time we had met. Or maybe I'd just caught her on a good day.

'In what way?' she said with feigned innocence.

'You're either an inept compliance officer, or a bad liar. What is it to be?'

The coffee arrived, giving her time to think. Stan and I sipped. Stan said something that was supposed to be Russian and I said, 'Yes, it is good', as if I understood.

'You've found Carlo, I understand,' she said.

'And he spilled the beans,' I said. 'We could save a lot of time if you admit to what you know. You've been through the books. You've seen the involvement Silvers has in Almas. You've heard the alarm bells ring. And presumably have reached the only possible conclusion. Silvers here in Amsterdam is up to its neck in drug-running, prostitution, people smuggling and carving people up for organ donations.'

'And what do you want me to do about it?' she said, adding a sweetener to her coffee and stirring it round. Got to watch that figure.

'Turn a blind eye,' I said.

'That wasn't the answer I was expecting from a member of the Silvers dynasty.'

'I have a message for Mr Bellini,' I said.

She nearly choked on her coffee.

'Bellini?' she spluttered.

'As a member of that family I want you to make sure that the message gets straight to Mr Bellini. I bring greetings from Garanov at Almas.'

'I don't know what you mean,' she said.

I said the only Russian phrase I know to Stan – I love you.

He got up from his chair, walked across to the desk, picked up Ms Oakley's handbag, rummaged inside, took out her passport and threw it across the room to me. I caught it skilfully. I hoped Ms Oakley was impressed.

I flicked through the passport, examining it.

'The picture doesn't do you justice, Mrs Bellini,' I said. 'Now about this message. I have been asked by Almas to open up a dialogue with Mr Bellini. It does no one any good to squabble over Silvers. Mr Garanov is willing to make some accommodation – an arrangement with Mr Bellini – so that the profits of our endeavours can be shared in some fashion. In that way everyone can go about their business unhampered by the other side.'

'And what is Garanov proposing?'

'A meeting to discuss how the cake can be cut so that both sides

180

are happy with their slice. The meeting will be at nine o'clock on Friday evening at the zoo. Garanov will lay on some refreshments so that the atmosphere can be conducive to talks. Mr Bellini must attend personally and may bring ten men.'

'Armed?'

'If it makes him feel safer, which I assume it would. And you should bring a gift – something appropriate – for Garanov. To the value of one million dollars. Garanov will be doing the same.'

'And what if Mr Bellini does not want to come?'

'Then Garanov will assume that there can be no deal and that he will be free to move on Silvers in New York. The gloves will be off.' I let the threat hang in the air for a moment. 'But why should Bellini turn the offer down? If he comes and reaches an agreement with Garanov, he can have a slice of the Amsterdam pie. He'll be better off than he is now and his future will be secure.'

Stan said something to me in Russian, or whatever language he was speaking. Could have been Swahili for all I knew. Then he patted his coat where a gun would have been.

'Garanov's representative here wants to know what you would recommend Mr Bellini to do. And whether he will listen to you. Something about monkeys and organ grinders, too.'

'Tell him,' she said, leaning forward in her chair and staring at Stan while she spoke. 'Tell him Mr Bellini will listen to his daughter-in-law who has the ear of his favourite son. He will be there on Friday.'

I made a sort of grunting noise at Stan and he nodded his head. He got up from his chair and extended his hand towards Mrs Bellini. She took it and he smiled. She didn't. I got up and we left her sitting there with her fingers steepled and touching her lips. She had a lot of persuading to do.

And we had a party to arrange.

28

'Make a list, Stan,' I said.

'Already started,' he replied.

We were gathered again in the sitting-room. Carlo and Natasha were perched on a battered sofa, Anna was on a cushion on the floor with her long legs tucked under her and Scout sat watching the rest of us in our armchairs as we stripped down the guns, cleaned them and reassembled them with practised dexterity. Irina we'd sent home that morning – our crew was getting passenger heavy.

'We pick up the uniforms in the morning,' Stan said.

'Flat shoes,' I said to the girls.

Natasha and Anna looked at me as if I had suggested they wear mail bags. There was no support from Scout either.

'I was looking forward to wearing some high heels with the outfit,' Scout said. 'Short black dress, white pinafore, frilly cap – you need the heels or it won't look right.'

'We don't want the Russians recognizing Natasha or Anna. And these are waitresses' costumes, not French maids.'

'Spoilsport,' she said.

I imagined that Arnie would have a treat in store if we got out of this alive.

'You have to be able to run,' I reminded them. 'The three of you go out shopping this afternoon and buy something you can sprint in.' A thought occurred to me. 'We'll need gloves,' I said to Stan.

He gave me a withering look. Was there nothing he hadn't thought of?

'What about one of those elasticated things to hold Red's glasses in place.

He uttered what I took as a swear word in Polish.

'Dammit,' he said, for the benefit of all of us, before reluctantly picking up his pen and adding the item to his list.

I didn't know if I felt good or bad about catching him out. Good, as long as that was the only thing he had overlooked. Bad didn't warrant thinking about.

'How many people from the zoo will be there?' I asked Scout. She'd been the one to book the venue and sort out all the details.

'Just two,' she said. 'The manager and the night keeper in case one of the animals gets sick.'

'We'll need somewhere we can lock them away and keep them safe. Once the shooting starts all hell will break loose. I don't want any innocent bystanders hurt.'

'The reptile house is tucked away in the far corner,' Scout said. 'The manager will have all the keys, until we take them, that is.'

She was used to thinking like one of us now.

'You know where the exit route is?' I said to Scout. She was the one I was relying on to look after Natasha and Anna.

'You must have told us three times by now,' she said with a sigh.

'And I'll probably tell you three times more. There's going to be a lot of bullets flying around. Plus it will be dark. When we start firing you have to be able to find the exit route by instinct.'

She nodded. 'We'll be fine. You stick to your task and I'll get the three of us out to safety.'

'Don't forget to give us the signal when the main gate is locked so that we're sure everyone is shut in. And no silencers,' I reminded everyone. 'I want as much noise as possible.'

We sat there for a while, listening to the clicking of the parts of the guns as they snapped back into place. There was something therapeutic about the exercise as if everything would fit into place and that would be an omen for Friday.

'We can get access from six o'clock,' Scout said. 'That should give us plenty of time to set up the tables and load them with the drinks and food.'

'Make sure the tables are far apart and directly opposite each other. I don't want Garanov and the Bellinis mingling. Eye contact, yes, but only that close.'

'I'm sure now,' Bull said. 'Garanov is the one from Angola.'

The weapon cleaning stopped for a moment. All eyes fell on Bull.

'No doubt in my mind,' he said.

'Then we need some special treatment for him,' I said. 'It's payback time.'

I walked for about half a mile from the hotel until I found an internet café. Most of the people sitting at the terminals were young men and women who looked like they were students on gap years and this month it was the turn of Amsterdam. I booked a two-hour session. What I had to do had to be very precise, the wording exactly right.

I'd been writing the Cyclops column for nearly four years now and this was the first time I had missed a copy date. It had started off as a bit of light-hearted fun. Even the name was a bit of a joke – the quotation, 'In the land of the blind the one-eyed man is king'. It was just a game, a challenge – could I beat the full-time professionals in the prediction of shares to sell or buy? It gave me something to do when there were no customers at the bar. I could sit in the shade and trawl through all the company news on the internet. I had to sift out all the fluff – the PR releases that were more about image than information – and concentrate on the detail of the balance sheets of companies and the way their share prices would be affected by seemingly unrelated events – raw material prices, the vagaries of the weather and so on. Then I found I was good at it. Unfortunately I was playing the game with other people's money – I never had enough myself to invest in the stock market. Maybe when all this was over I could play on my own account, handle the others' money even. Turn over a profit that could act like a pension: that much was certain, this job would really be our last in the mercenary business. Pieter getting flabby, Red with his dwindling eyesight, Bull with a family: none of us was getting any younger and this was a young man's game.

It took me the full two hours to get the column exactly right and I emailed it to Gus with explicit instructions to forward it on to the editor at nine o'clock in the evening on Friday. Allowing for the time difference it would arrive on time to make the Saturday issue and give a lot of people time to sweat over the weekend.

On the way back I stopped off at the market and bought three large watermelons and one small cantaloupe and a tube of glue from the stationers. I went back to the hotel, collected the Barrett monster sniper rifle and a pair of binoculars and placed them, the melons and the glue in one of Stan's gym bags. I picked up the hire car and drove to the woods to the south of Amsterdam. I was going to use the rifle on Friday and would need a direct hit. The Barrett had been credited with a kill at 1800 metres during the Iraq war. The manufacturers claim was for 1000 metres and that it could pierce body armour and do a lot of damage to an armoured vehicle at that distance. I was going to shoot from a hundred metres – the Barrett could hit a pinhead from there. I had to set the telescopic sight for the precise distance between rifle and target at the zoo.

I found an old tree stump lying on the ground covered in moss. I dragged it in front of a tree. I put the four melons on top of the horizontal stump, the cantaloupe being the last on the left. I paced out the distance, around a hundred yards, and got down on the ground. I took the sniper rifle from the gym bag and checked the magazine. Plenty enough bullets for the test run.

I lay and tucked the rifle firmly into my shoulder – one of the drawbacks of the Barrett was that it has a mighty kick and could break a man's shoulder if it wasn't tucked in properly. I got the first watermelon in the sight and let off one round. Through the greater magnification of the binoculars I could see that the shot had hit at the seven o'clock position on the outer edge of the melon. I adjusted the sight and moved on to the second. Closer this time, but still to the left and down of the centre. Another adjustment, another shot. Very close to the centre this time. I made the slightest adjustment and moved on from the big watermelons to the small cantaloupe. Dead centre and the melon blown apart. Perfect. As long as I could keep my cool on Friday I should be able to replicate the shot as many times as were possible in the time limit. If I could get in four, then I would be very happy. Anything else would be a bonus. I put a large blob of glue over the adjusting screw of the sight – when hard it would mean that it wouldn't get changed accidentally.

I trudged back through the woods to the car and drove back to the hotel. There were still days to kill, days to go over and over the plan, to do a further recce on the zoo and then just sit and wait. None of us was good at waiting. Those guns would be the cleanest in history by the time Friday night came around. And nothing wrong with that. None of us wanted to take a bullet just because our gun was dirty. None of us wanted to take a bullet full stop. If I had been a religious man I would have prayed. I settled for crossing my fingers and hoping for good luck.

Anna sensed that I had a lot on my mind. When I arrived back at the hotel she immediately poured me a large vodka with lots of ice and settled down next to me on the sofa. She put her head on my shoulder and wrapped one arm around my waist. I took a big slug of my vodka and the frown I was wearing turned into a smile.

'Will it be all right, Johnny?' she asked.

'If it goes wrong, it won't be for lack of planning. Stan and I have pretty much covered all the angles. But you never know with these things – a random event can happen that destroys all your planning.' I took a sip of the vodka this time and thought for a while. 'If things do go wrong, I want you to go to Gus. He'll give you money and set you up somewhere.'

'And what if you do come back? What about us?'

'Let's not think of that for the moment. Best not to count your chickens.'

She managed a laugh. 'You talk funny,' she said. 'Counting chickens. What does that mean?'

'It means that it's best not to tempt fate. If we all get out of this alive, then that will be the time to talk about the future.'

'Then let's talk about the present. Do you want another vodka, or to come upstairs with me?'

I got up from the sofa, walked across the room and picked up the vodka bottle. Then I opened the door and stood by it.

'Greedy boy,' she said. 'Let's live each day as if it were our last.'

'Amen to that,' I said.

29

I met Arnie after work at the botanical gardens. It was just across a couple of streets from the zoo and I wanted to be around at nine o'clock to check out the light exactly as it would be on Friday evening, weather permitting. And that was one big hole in the plan – if it rained we'd be sunk.

We found a secluded spot on a bench surrounded by giant palms – it reminded me a bit of my home on the island, except about ten degrees chillier. Arnie was wearing sand-coloured chinos and a navy-blue bomber jacket; he still wore the steel-framed glasses, but out of his suit he looked less like a geek and more like Clark Kent. I didn't need him to have super powers, but there were a couple of things I wanted him to do.

'Ms Oakley has left,' he said.

'I was hoping she would,' I replied. 'So no one to supervise you, what with Oakley gone and Carlo out of the picture?'

'With Ms Oakley it wasn't supervising, it was breathing down your neck. I'm not used to that. Carlo let me get on with running the day-to-day business.'

'That's good,' I said. 'How would you like to do some overtime on Friday night? There's some things I need you to do.'

'I suppose you're as near to a boss that I've got now. What is it you want me to do?'

'There are three tasks,' I said. 'The first is the missing bearer bonds. I want you to go back and change the entries regarding them so that they came from Almas and not Silvers. Almas must be the loser from the theft.'

'Is that strictly legal?'

'Not in terms of the letter of the law,' I said, 'but when you've heard what I have to tell you, you'll come down on the side of the spirit of the law.'

I told him all that we had learned about Almas and their operations, medical and otherwise. At the end he gave a big whistle.

'Should we be messing around with these guys?' he asked.

'After what we've been doing to them in the last week, and what we have in store, a few book entries is hardly on their radar.'

'If you say so,' he said, sounding unconvinced. 'You said three things?'

'The second task is to create a suspense account.'

He let out a groan. A suspense account is usually a pain in the neck. It is used when there are items you can't reconcile in the accounts – a temporary hiding place until you find out what is happening and what to do with the money. A suspense account involves a lot of back-checking and time-consuming detective work.

'Don't worry,' I said. 'I know exactly what is going to happen to the money in this suspense account. I want you to parcel together all the accounts that Almas have for their individual businesses and their holding company and put them in a new suspense account. We'll sort out on Monday where it is going.'

'Why do I have to wait till Friday? It's going to take some time. Why can't I do it now?'

'Because if you do it now Almas may spot it. Carlo gave them remote access to their accounts so they could see what the position was day by day. It has to be Friday after closing hours.'

'OK, boss,' he said. 'What's the third thing?'

'Helping Scout,' I said.

'Scout?' he said, a wistful tone in his voice. Then it changed to concern. 'What have you got her involved in? Is she in some sort of danger? If she is, I'll . . . I'll . . . I don't know what, but I'll do something to you that you won't like.'

189

'Relax, Arnie. We've got all the bases covered. We're very thorough when we plan an operation, and that's what we have on Friday night. Scout and two Russian girls are going to act as waitresses at a gathering we're holding at the zoo. At nine o'clock the guests will arrive. Scout and her friends will make sure they have something to drink and something to nibble on. As soon as they've done that they are going to make a quick exit. I want you nearby with a car so that you can ferry them back to the safety of our hotel.'

'I haven't got a car,' he said.

That was a base we didn't have covered. Did no one in this city drive a car?

'OK,' I said. 'We'll park a dark-blue people carrier outside the Portuguese synagogue. We'll put the keys in the exhaust pipe. When Scout and the girls come out of the zoo, you get them as quick as you can to the car and away.'

'I don't drive,' he said.

'Arnie,' I said. 'What are you doing to me? It seemed like a simple enough task when I'd thought of it. You're just going to have to get Scout to drive and you sit in the back with your eyes closed. That's the biggest danger you'll be in.'

'Are you saying Scout is a bad driver?' he said threateningly.

'No,' I said. Atrocious was the word I was thinking of. Time to change the subject. 'You and Scout – how long have you been going out together?'

'Around a year now. Strange really. She was doing what she called a "fishing expedition". Trying to get a contact within Silvers who would feed her information if ever it was needed. Apparently, she'd watched some of the staff and settled for me. We met first over dinner and it developed from there. She's a great woman. I know she comes across sometimes as, well—'

'Feisty?' I said.

'I was thinking more of single-minded.'

'Ah, stubborn,' I said.

'I won't hear a word said against her.'

'Calm down, Arnie, I'm only teasing. Let's take a walk. I need to show you where Scout and the girls will be coming out of the zoo.'

'But I know where the exit is.'

'But they won't be coming out of the exit,' I said with a sigh. 'What would a bunch of jittery guys think if they see their waitresses heading for the exit. Trouble, that's what they'd think. No, they'll be coming through the fence and over the wall behind the camel enclosure – I'll mark it with a chalk cross so that you know the exact spot.'

'I should have asked before. Who is coming to this gathering?'

'Almas and the Bellinis.'

'Shit,' he said.

He had destroyed my illusions with the swear word, but summed up pretty accurately what the position was.

'Yeah, Arnie,' I said. 'Shit. And we don't want it to hit us.'

I waited till nine to check the light and the number of people still on the street at that time, then went back to the hotel. Bull was alone in the lounge. He had a beer in his hand and a sad look on his face. I poured myself a vodka and joined him.

'A penny for them,' I said.

'What?' he said.

'Seems like you're in another world. I reckon you're having second thoughts as to what side to be on. Would you be better off with us, or a bunch of crooks who could get you a donor for Michael?'

'Hell,' he said. 'I talked to Mai Ling and there's still no news. They're just sitting around waiting and hoping someone will die. Ain't that terrible?'

I nodded. He didn't need me to talk; he needed to get it all off his chest.

'It don't seem right, hoping someone will die. But it would be worse with Almas. I've killed people before. Plenty, you know that. But never have I let someone die who didn't need it to make the world a better place.'

'It's a good philosophy,' I said.

'It's the only way you can justify the actions of the past and live

191

with what you've done.'

'And then there's maybe more killing on Friday.'

He nodded his head and took a long pull from the beer bottle.

'Jeez, Johnny, there's a lot that can go wrong.'

'We'll cope,' I said. 'We're good at thinking on our feet.'

'We're older and probably no wiser.'

'But still good enough to take on Almas and the Bellinis.'

He looked at me sideways and shook his head. 'Yeah,' he said. 'They won't know what hit them.'

'That's what I'm hoping,' I said.

'You've hardly touched your food,' Gus said.

We were sitting in Gus's favourite restaurant, a small family-run place on the Leidseplein, all wooden tables, pink tablecloths and subdued lighting. We had a window seat and could see El Dorado across the way. But it wasn't that which was putting me off my food. I pushed the half-full plate of steak and *frites* to one side and toyed with my wine glass.

'Tomorrow's the big day,' I said.

'Having regrets?' Gus asked. 'Wished you'd stayed on that island in the sun?'

'Yes and no,' I said.

'Good to be decisive,' he said.

I managed a passable smile.

'When I think back over that story about the baby at the airport I know that these people have to be stopped and if it falls to me, then so be it. It's just that about now the nerves start to kick in. Hands sweat, mouth dry, belly churns. I've been here before many times and yet it still happens.'

I took a sip at my glass of red wine.

'Will it work?' he asked. 'Your plan?'

'Unless something unexpected happens, yes, it will work.'

'And what are the chances of something unexpected happening?'

'We know that both sides won't trust each other. So they'll both do a reconnaissance of the zoo – see the places where they might get ambushed, sort out the best firing positions for an ambush of their own. We just have to hope that they're not as good as we are, otherwise they'll work out where we'll be and be there waiting for us. There will be twenty armed men milling about and we don't want to get caught in the crossfire. I'm not too worried about Bellini – it's Garanov who's the problem. We've hurt Garanov twice. He knows our fire power and will plan for us getting involved. He'll be more watchful than Bellini.'

'What about the police? When the shooting starts, someone will alert the police. How are you going to avoid getting arrested.'

'By being quick on our feet. We have an exit route planned and we just have to make it there before the police arrive.' I pondered, then frowned. 'To be honest, it's going to be tight.'

'Anything I can do?'

I took out a slip of paper from my pocket and passed it across the table to him.

'That's the number of an account I opened. I cashed the rest of the bearer bonds and paid the money into that account – eight million euros. I've made you a signatory. If anything happens to me, look after everyone.'

He nodded and tucked the slip of paper in the top pocket of his jacket.

'You can count on me,' he said.

'That means a lot,' I said. 'If it all goes well, let's meet back here on Saturday night – all of us.'

All of us who are still alive.

30

We cleaned the guns one last time. This time we had done it with latex gloves on. No fingerprints, nothing to link us to what would happen. Stan checked and rechecked all the equipment while we watched him and filled ashtrays. Scout, Anna and Natasha were fussing about with hair that was already perfect and applying another coat of lipstick to the three that they had put on at intervals earlier. Every minute or so one of us would look at our watches. Finally it was time to leave.

The girls, neatly dressed in their black outfits with the white aprons and the flat shoes, sat in the middle seats of the people carrier. The glasses, booze and snacks were loaded into the back compartment with the seats folded down. Red drove and Pieter sat beside him – they were the only two of us that either the Bellinis or Garanov hadn't so far seen. Bull, Stan and I took one of the hire cars, the boot stuffed with all the rest of the equipment – the assault rifles, the sniper rifle, the pump gun, bolt cutters, a rope ladder with grappling hook and two fat reels of gaffer tape, all packed into two long gym bags. We each had a Browning in a shoulder holster. While the people carrier headed for the front entrance to the zoo, our destination was one of the little-used side streets backing on to the perimeter wall.

We had to make the assumption that both sides would be watching the front entrance – it was what we would have done – so the plan was for Red and Pieter to help with the unpacking and setting up and then exit. That way, as far as anyone watching was concerned, only the three girls would be inside the zoo. No threat from that direction. Meanwhile, the rest of us had some climbing to do.

The zoo was surrounded on all sides by a brick wall around ten feet tall, its main purpose to stop anyone getting a free look at the animals or pestering them. Inside this outer perimeter wall was a narrow track for the keepers to use and then the wire fences enclosing the animals. Stan threw the grappling hook over the wall, tugged it to test that it was firmly in place, spread out the rope ladder and, when the coast was clear, we climbed over. The tricky part was manhandling the heavy gym bags over the top of the wall and then dragging back the ladder and engaging the grappling iron so that the ladder was ready for the girls to exit. Once we were all over – Pieter puffing a bit – we regrouped at the wire fence outside the camel enclosure. The camels were sound asleep – but wouldn't remain so – on beds of straw in their indoor area. We started cutting a hole big enough for Bull to get through – if Bull could get through, the rest of us would have no problem. Then we repeated the procedure with the inner fence – from there we had access to the whole zoo. But first we had to deal with the manager and the keeper.

I picked up the Barrett monster sniper rifle, checked the blob of glue on the sights – still in tact – and slung it over my shoulder. I couldn't handle two rifles so I left the Uzi in one of the gym bags, just in case I needed it later. The others picked up their guns and we made our way to the reptile house and waited for Scout to do her spiel – oh, how she adored snakes and could she just have a peep.

I heard the sound of the keeper's heavy boots and pressed myself into the wall. The others took their lead from me and did the same. When they came round the corner they faced five Brownings.

'Do as I say and you won't be harmed.' I motioned with the Browning. 'Unlock the door.' I turned to Scout. 'Best be back to the restaurant before someone wonders where you've been.'

'Good luck,' she said.

The manager, a short, thin man in a dark-grey suit, stared at me, unmoving through shock. The keeper was a big man with muscles honed from lifting bales of straw. He stepped in front of the manager – a hero in the making.

'Don't do anything foolish. There's five of us and we're all crack shots. Now, step aside and let your friend unlock the door.'

The keeper took one last defiant look at me and wisely did as he was told. The manager took a bunch of keys on a large ring from a loop on his belt and unlocked the door. I opened it and waved them inside with the Browning. Bull and Stan followed them and then I stepped inside. The heat hit me like a sledgehammer. The air was so humid you could have grabbed a handful and squeezed out water.

Bull and Stan, out of habit, frisked the keeper and the manager. Bull found another bunch of keys in the keeper's green dungarees and handed them to me – I now had both sets. We stood the manager and keeper with their noses pressed on the glass of one of the display cases.

'Hands behind your backs,' I said.

Bull unwound some gaffer tape and wrapped it around the keeper's hands. Stan did the same with the manager.

'Now sit down,' I said.

Bull and Stan bound their feet and then put a large strip of tape around their mouths.

'In an hour you'll both be free. Just sit tight and ignore any loud bangs – they're not for you.'

We came outside and I locked the door. I left the key in the lock and placed the other set of keys on the floor.

'Stage one over,' I said.

We took up our guns and made our separate ways to our assigned positions. Mine was at the centre of the restaurant roof with Bull at one corner and Stan at the other. Red and Pieter took the other two sides of the square opposite the restaurant. Then it was time to keep low and wait.

There were arc lights shining down from the restaurant so that anyone looking up would be blinded and we would effectively be invisible. I looked down and could see Scout and Anna. Natasha was hidden from view from where I lay. Tables from inside the restaurant had been dragged outside and set up in lines facing each other so that both sides could have a staring contest before their leaders came into the middle to meet, exchange gifts and parlay. On the tables were being placed wine and shot glasses, bottles of red wine and vodka and trays of canapés that our housekeeper at the hotel had prepared. Anybody we missed with bullets would probably die a slow death from food poisoning.

I checked my watch. Ten minutes to go before the guests would turn up. I wondered which group would arrive first. Was there some etiquette among the mafia and Russian mafiya that dictated that, like the bride, one should always be late.

The girls had finished setting everything up as per the plan. Scout moved towards the entry gate to greet the arrivals, while Natasha and Anna took up their stations by each set of tables. Anna was to be serving Garanov and his mob, while Natasha looked after the Bellinis.

Garanov and his gorillas showed up first. They were wrapped in long overcoats and raincoats, concealing, I presumed, assault rifles. It was important that Garanov should take the far station, otherwise he wouldn't be in line with my sight. He cast his eyes round, weighing up the ground. Would he be a good boy and do as he was told?

Scout went up to Garanov and did the little curtsy that she had practised at the hotel and waved her hand in the direction of the far table. He looked her over, assessing any risk as well as her figure. They stepped across the courtyard and went to where Anna was pouring vodka into shot glasses. Thank God for the Russians love of vodka.

Garanov was suspicious of the vodka and I could see him take Anna by the arm and lead her to the table. He picked up a shot glass and made her drink it. When she hadn't protested he reckoned they were safe. He took a glass and his men did the same. I'd never seen so many people drinking with their left hand before. One swig and it was gone. Anna refilled the glasses. Garanov nodded to his men and they spread out, taking up what I assumed were positions decided upon after their reconnoitre. They formed an arc with Garanov in the middle.

In came the Bellinis. They favoured drovers' coats to hide their weapons and looked like they had just stepped out of the Wild West, a lawless posse after lawless men. Old Man Bellini, pushing seventy and still holding the reins tightly in his bony hands, walked across to one of tables and examined the bottle of wine. Apparently our Barolo wasn't good enough since he pushed it away like it was a smelly sock from a teenager's laundry basket. He walked to the middle of the area outside the restaurant and let his men take a similar formation to Garanov's. The two crescents waited for someone to do something. I was about to oblige them.

The plan was that the girls would now retreat and, after giving them a minute to get to safety, I would start firing. My sights would be on Garanov, but I didn't want to kill him unless absolutely necessary. Others would do that job for me. I was going to shoot him in the shoulder to pay back for the bullets in mine, in the thigh for Bull's hamstring, the back in the place where the iron had been held, and anywhere else for Stan. Once my bullets started sounding and Garanov was reeling around, the others would open fire. All we had to do was keep everyone penned into the area of the restaurant. Both sides would assume it was the other who was shooting and they'd massacre each other. St Valentine's Day all over again. That was the plan and the first part was getting the girls to safety. That was the problem I faced now.

Scout and Natasha had moved to the outside of the square, but Garanov was still talking to Anna. He had hold of her arm and wasn't letting go. Maybe he recognized her from the casino, or he might just have wanted to progress things with her – she was extremely attractive after all. And then I got it. I felt it in the pit of my stomach. He wasn't merely talking to her, he was using her as a human shield, placing her in direct line of sight with the Bellinis.

Shit. If I couldn't start the shooting, then none of the others would know what to do and when. We could all end up lying there watching the Bellinis and Garanov make peace and carve up Silvers, not to mention take a stronghold of organized crime – the drug-running, prostitution and people trafficking. We would only have made matters worse.

If Anna had been wearing heels I would have had no option. As it was, her flat shoes meant that she stood about four inches shorter than Garanov. From my vantage point it gave me a target, albeit a pretty small one. But could I take the risk?

I'd practised with the gun, set the sight, knew it was deadly accurate, but melons are a little different from real people. I saw in my mind's eye the way that last melon had disintegrated, blown apart from the impact of the huge 12.7mm bullet from that range.

I lined Garanov up in the sights, then leant upwards. A bead of perspiration was running down my forehead. I wiped it away with my sleeve. Before I lost my conviction, I lined him up again. Took a deep breath, exhaled slowly, squeezed the trigger gently. And fired.

I saw Garanov's head explode and his body fall back with the momentum of the bullet. Then Anna looked at what was left of him, clutched her head and screamed. She was covered in blood and bits of brain and wouldn't stop screaming. The whole scene was like a tableau, no one moved. It wouldn't last long.

Scout ran in and grabbed Anna's hand, pulled her sharply away and ran for the edges of the space around the restaurant and away from the arc lights. It was our signal. We started to open fire, bullets raining down around the perimeter and in front of the two opposing forces. I heard the boom of Red's pump gun and the thunderous noise woke everyone from their moment's inactivity. The drovers' coats and overcoats were swept aside and the guns were pointed in the direction of the opposing side. They opened fire.

We continued to hem them in with firepower and one by one we began to climb down from our positions on the roofs. With nowhere to go, Garanov's men and the Bellinis were involved in a bloodbath. We left them to it and made our way back to the camel enclosure and our exit. And all the way there I could hear Anna screaming.

Before we climbed the wall we put all our guns on the ground. We would need them no more.

31

'How is Anna?' I asked Scout.

It was the only question that had come into my mind since the sound of the gunfire had receded. We'd travelled back to the hotel as quickly as we could without drawing attention to ourselves. The sitting-room was now full of people – the five of us mercenaries, Scout, Arnie and Carlo – all high on adrenaline, yet there was no sign of Anna or Natasha.

'Natasha is with her,' said Scout. 'She's giving Anna a shower – she was covered in stuff I don't even want to think about.'

I let out a sigh of relief which Scout was quick to stifle.

'I have to warn you, Johnny,' Scout said, more serious than I'd ever seen her before, 'Anna's in shock. She doesn't know what she's doing at the moment, and she might not know what she's saying. We may need to give her time to get over what happened tonight.'

I nodded and thought again about what she must be going through. To be that close to death, as I knew from past experience, does something to a person: elation at having survived comes way down a list that begins with the knowledge that you could just as well have been lying on some cold slab someplace dead with a bullet in your heart.

'What a shot!' Red said, pouring himself a Scotch.

His hands were shaking and I looked down at mine to see what shape they were in. Not trembling yet, but that could well set in as the magnitude as what we had done sank in.

Pieter took the bottle from Red and turned his back to us – I guessed that his hands were shaking too and he didn't want anyone to see it.

'What a shot,' Red said again and shook his head in disbelief. 'You are one lucky bastard, Johnny Silver.'

'Luck?' I snapped back at him. 'Do you think I would have relied on luck before pulling that trigger with Anna slap bang in the firing line.'

'Easy, Johnny,' Bull said. 'Red don't mean nothing.'

Bull filled a glass with ice, picked up a bottle of vodka and passed both to me. I poured a very large measure and took a gulp. The fire hit my belly and brought me round.

'Yeah,' said Red. 'Sorry, Johnny. Comanche warrior put heap big foot in mouth.'

'No, I'm the one who should say sorry. I'd forgotten just what it was like to complete a mission and come out the other side still in one piece. It takes a while before the nerves stop jangling and your brain returns to functioning properly.'

'Vodka always helps,' said Stan, raising his glass to me. 'And this is Polish. Cures all ills.'

I drained my glass and poured another.

'Reckon so,' I said, recovering my composure and sense of humour at the same time. I looked at my watch. 'What's taking Anna and Natasha so long?'

'Give her time, I said, Johnny,' Scout said.

She turned on the television ready for the news. Muted the sound and we all waited expectantly. Bottles were passed around and glasses refilled.

'Tell me all about it,' said Carlo. 'What happened, what was it like, what did you feel?'

'You don't feel nothing,' Bull said. 'You function by instinct. There's no time for it to be any other way.'

'But don't you get a buzz?' Carlo asked.

'If we got a buzz from it,' I said, 'we'd be no better than cold-bloodied killers like Garanov. We do it because it's a job that has to be done. That's all.'

'A man's gotta do what a man's gotta do, eh?' said Carlo.

'Something like that,' I said, too drained to argue.

'Quiet,' said Scout. 'There's a newsflash coming.'

She turned up the sound and we all stared expectantly at the TV. A male newsreader with glasses and a serious look started to speak. It was in Dutch.

'Hell,' said Red. 'What's he saying?'

'Shush,' said Scout. 'I'll tell you when he's finished.'

The camera cut away from the newsreader and he was replaced by an external shot of the zoo that filled the screen. It was more circus than zoo. There were people held back by barriers, trying to get a glimpse of whatever was happening, police massing around and four ambulances that we could see. Stretchers were being wheeled from the gates of the zoo towards the waiting ambulances – most had their faces covered. A different camera took over and there was a red-haired presenter talking to the zoo manager and the keeper. When she had her sound bites from them, the camera zoomed in for a close-up of her. She spoke with a grave expression.

'Seventeen dead and three critically injured,' said Scout. 'Police say that it was likely to be some kind of gang warfare. They found a "considerable quantity of weapons".'

'I bet they did,' said Stan. 'Shame we had to dump them. It felt good to have a gun in my hand again.'

'Plus a bagful of diamonds and a kilo of heroin,' Scout continued, brushing aside the interruption.

'The gifts to seal the deal,' I said. 'Something appropriate. Good for Garanov and Bellini.'

'They won't miss them,' said Bull. 'Ain't no pockets in a shroud.'

'Police are appealing for witnesses,' Arnie said, looking worried. 'What if someone saw the cars?'

'They would hardly have registered,' I said. 'We were just guys going about our business. Off for the weekend, maybe, or to a restaurant, perhaps even the casino. No sweat, Arnie. Keep cool. If someone had reported something they would have given out details of make and models of the cars, asked people to keep a look out.'

Scout moved from in front of the TV and went across to where Arnie was sitting. She took his hand and squeezed it. Young love. Lucky people.

'Seems like the plan worked perfectly,' Stan said.

'Except for the Anna bit,' I said. 'Thank God that Scout had the presence of mind to grab her and make a run for it. I'm in your debt, Scout.'

'Seems to me,' she said, 'that we're all in your debt. My dad has the money to start a big business, Arnie and I have enough money to get married. . . .'

'And Natasha and I,' said Carlo, 'can lead the easy life.'

'Not to mention the rest of us,' said Bull.

'Any more news of the transplant?' asked Pieter.

'Still waiting for a donor.'

'It'll work out,' Scout said. 'I've got a feeling that God smiles on you guys.'

'Maybe this should be the last time we push our luck,' said Pieter.

'Trouble is,' said Red, 'I don't know how to do anything else. Beats the rodeo any day. Better paid by far. And I don't know when I last had such fun.'

'Fun?' said Scout incredulously.

'Maybe not fun, I suppose,' said Red. 'But there's a helluva kick from a job well done.'

The door opened and in came Natasha. She was leading Anna by the arm. Anna was as white as a ghost and was visibly shaking. Natasha helped her into a chair where Anna sat staring into space. I went across to her and settled down on my haunches so that I was at her eye level. I took her hand – it was as cold as ice as if all her blood had drained away. Anna pulled it away quickly. Then she turned her head and looked at me as if I were a stranger.

'You killed a man,' she said, shaking her head in apparent disbelief. 'You actually killed a man.'

'He was a bad man,' I said. 'Deserved to die. And anyway, you knew the plan. You knew that people would die. The only difference between the plan and the actuality was that I happened to kill him instead of one of the Bellinis. Garanov was using you as a human shield – that's how bad he was. He didn't care if you lived or died. I did, though.'

Natasha placed a glass of vodka in Anna's hand. Helped her raise it to her lips so that she could drink some without spilling it.

'More,' Natasha said. 'Drink the whole glass. It'll do you good.'

'Nothing will do me good ever again,' Anna said. She paused to take another mouthful of vodka. Then said, 'There was so much blood. And other stuff; brains, I suppose. I was covered in it. I could taste his blood on my lips. Feel it on my face and in my hair. I don't think I'll ever feel clean again.' She downed the vodka this time – she was past sips. 'I didn't think it would be like that.'

'Real life is not like the movies, Anna,' I said. 'People get killed, it's the end. They don't get up and start shooting another movie. And think of this. How much of other peoples' blood did Garanov have on his hands?'

'We were just settling the score,' Bull said. 'A lot of folks should be grateful to us.'

'By the morning it will all look different,' I said. 'It will be easier to see everything in perspective.'

'Do you really think it will be as easy as that?' Anna said sharply.

'A good night's sleep always helps,' said Scout.

'Sleep?' said Anna. 'Sleep? How do you think I will be able to sleep tonight, or ever again for that matter? It happened before my very eyes. I felt the life force go from him, just as much as I felt his blood and brains covering my face.'

'If it hadn't been him,' I said, 'it would have been you.'

'And if you had missed it could have been me, too. Did you think of that before you pulled the trigger?'

'I thought of nothing else,' I said. 'Then I cleared my head of those thoughts, aimed, took a deep breath and fired. Just like I had done in practice.'

'One of the greatest shots you'll ever see,' said Red.

'Probably aiming for the camel,' said Bull.

Anna didn't laugh. Would she ever laugh again? I didn't fancy the odds on that right now.

'Tomorrow night we're all invited to a celebration dinner with Gus,' I said. 'It will all look different then.' I turned to Red. 'They do a great steak and chips.'

'I'm gonna eat me a sixteen-ounce one,' he said.

'Count me out,' said Anna, rising from her chair. 'I'm going to bed.'

I made a move towards her. She backed away and raised her hands as if to ward me off.

'Alone,' she said.

'If that's what you want,' I said.

'I don't know what I want right now, Johnny. That's why it has to be alone. I need time to work out how I feel. About me, you and the blood that's got in between. The blood that's on your hands.'

She gave a shiver and walked out of the room.

And out of my life?

32

I slept fitfully that night, my mind filled with a dream where I knew that I was going to miss Garanov and trying in vain to catch the fatal bullet in mid-air before it hit Anna. I woke in a sweat and with a hangover when my alarm went off at 5.30 – I felt lousy. This was not, however, one of those days for trying to sleep off the effects of the night before. I had managed to agree an embargo on the Cyclops story until midnight New York time last night and I wanted to be in front of the television when the proverbial hit the fan. I was showered and shaved and in front of CNN by six. The hotel keeper, alerted by the noise of the TV – or perhaps by me groaning – shrugged at me as if after the happenings of the last week nothing would surprise her, but she came into the sitting-room ten minutes later with a jug of coffee and a bacon sandwich. How she had changed since our arrival.

The word *Newsflash* came up on the screen and there was an immediate cut from the current story to a pretty brunette presenter. Unprepared for the change in running order, but able to read the autocue, she started to give some details. The words sounded like the producer was stalling for time and I guessed the reason – they were trying to line up footage of the zoo.

The woman, immaculately dressed and made-up, especially given the hour, started to read the gist of the story from the Cyclops column – how mafia gangs had infiltrated the Silvers Bank in both New York and Amsterdam. Then she read the pre-prepared statement that my mother and I had agreed upon – how Silvers had initiated a sting operation to flush out the illegal funds as soon as they had been made aware of accounts owned by criminal organizations. Both bank branches had isolated and frozen all suspect assets. Silvers in both countries would be giving full assistance and co-operation to the police investigation. Next came the hastily assembled footage from the zoo – the ambulances, the police, the flashing blue lights, the stretchers and a statement from the head of the Amsterdam Police Force stating that the body count had now reached eighteen, with two seriously wounded. He didn't look particularly bothered and who could blame him. The only explanation that the police could come up with was a gang war over disputed territory in Amsterdam. The head policeman thanked God that no civilians had been involved in the carnage. So did I.

I wondered what was going through Roberto's mind and how much warning my mother had given him of the way events would unfold. Had he been warned at all? Had Mother gone straight to someone reliable and trustworthy in New York to parcel up the Bellini accounts and freeze them as Arnie had done so well with the suspense account in Amsterdam? Whatever, he could hardly have thought that he would have a conclusion like this when he stepped off that helicopter back in St Jude. It would cost him his job, no doubt about it. Give it a while for the dust to settle and so that no one would jump to the right conclusion, but Roberto was a dead man walking. Just as Carlo had to go – willingly in his case – so must Roberto. Time to clear Silvers of the rotten apples.

My thoughts turned to Anna. How would she be feeling this morning? Probably not good, if she had slept as badly as I. Might not even have slept at all. Might not have wanted to in case she had nightmares of Garanov's brains showering her. That vision might not ever leave her. That was a lot of mights, none of them making me feel any better.

Bull came in. He was carrying a fresh pot of coffee and a mug. He poured himself some and topped me up. He looked at the plate where the bacon sandwich had recently been.

'Blue-eyed boy,' he said.

'I shall be sorry to leave this place,' I said.

'It ain't much, but it's home, eh?'

I nodded.

'Not your usual self this morning,' he said. 'Didn't say reckon so.'

'Reckon so,' I said.

'It's too late now.' He drank some coffee. 'Anna?'

I nodded.

'You did it again,' he said. 'You're beating yourself up, aren't you? About what happened last night? You had no choice, Johnny. Who knows what would have happened to Anna with Garanov using her as a shield. Or if Bellini and Garanov actually got together. Don't bear thinking about. You had to kill him. Sooner or later she'll understand that.'

'It's the later bit that worries me.'

'Have patience, my friend. Sometimes you just have to believe it will all come right in the end. Trust me. I should know. Been there. Still there, in fact.'

'It's not just Anna,' I said. 'There's something else bothering me.'

'Which is?'

'What if Bellini tries to take revenge.'

'Bellini's dead, as far as we know. And why should he come for us. Nobody outside our group knows we set Bellini and Garanov up. Gus and your mother won't tell. Who's left?'

'Roberto,' I said. 'Roberto who's had the red carpet dragged from under his feet. Is he smart enough to work it all out? That's the question.'

'And the answer?'

'Hell knows, I sure don't.'

We were gathered in the sitting-room waiting for a fleet of taxis to take us to Gus's favourite restaurant in the Leidseplein. No Bull, Natasha or Anna, though.

Everyone had smartened up. We guys were wearing, for some, recently purchased suits and Scout had on a skinny dress in red with high heels to match – Arnie couldn't keep his eyes off her and I didn't blame him. It would have been hard to believe that last night five of us had been crawling through a camel enclosure and across roofs with guns in our hands. Butter wouldn't melt.

Bull came in with a grin as big as Texas. He punched his fist in the air and excitedly shouted, 'They did it. They've found a donor. The operation's tomorrow.'

I gave him a bear hug and stepped back to take a look at the happiest man alive.

'Seems like this will be our last supper, pilgrim,' I said. 'Let's make it a good one.'

'If you can wait another ten minutes, I'll book a morning flight.'

'No problem. We're still waiting on Natasha and Anna.'

'Just me,' Natasha said, coming into the room. 'Anna's packing her bag. She's leaving tomorrow.'

The tight-knit group we had been for the last couple of weeks was beginning to break up. This could be the last supper for us. A celebration and a farewell rolled into one. They didn't fit together in my book.

Bull returned, still grinning from ear to ear.

'We might as well start to go,' I said. 'No point waiting anymore, it seems.'

We drifted down the stairs and on to the pavement. I squeezed into the first taxi with Carlo, Natasha and Red and headed due north to the Leidseplein. The pretty, young waitress – tall, slim, sparkling eyes – recognized me from the previous visit and showed us to 'Mr Gordini's table for eleven'. Didn't seem worth correcting her and removing one of the chairs and place settings from the table. The atmosphere was relaxed with each table secluded from the others. From our table it was hard to see across the room for the shadows cast by the wall lights and the candles on the table. They flickered each time the door opened.

Gus stood to greet us and sat Carlo on one side of him and me on the other – family gathering. There was champagne in two large buckets placed at each end of the table. The waitress popped a cork and we started what I assumed was going to be a heavy night's drinking – toasting successes and drowning sorrows. The others entered and soon the table was buzzing.

'I'm off tomorrow,' said Red. 'Time for Comanche warrior to move wigwam. Can wear feathers with pride again. Thanks, Johnny.'

'Give your bank details to Gus and he'll sort out the split and the transfer. That goes for the rest of you, too.'

'A toast,' said Gus. 'Here's to the Magnificent Ten.'

We raised our glasses and drank.

'And to a job well done,' Gus added.

We drank again. Like the job it was almost perfect.

'What about you, Pieter. What will you do?'

'I thought I might hang around a day or so, depending on how I get on with the waitress.' He grinned at her across the room. She looked down to hide a blush. 'Then back to South Africa. Set up a safari business, I reckon.'

We ordered. I hoped they had enough steaks.

'Stan,' I said. 'Any plans?'

'Retire,' he said. 'Get a little place by the sea. Maybe open a restaurant, if I can be bothered. Meet a nice girl and have me a family. Something to hold on to and keep me from being tempted to do stupid things like this again.' He gave me a smile. 'No matter how much I enjoy them.'

'And you, Johnny?' Bull asked. 'What's in store for you?'

'Maybe go back to St Jude. Rebuild the bar and enjoy the sand, sun and sea.'

'Why the maybe?' said Bull.

'Depends on Roberto.'

'Huh?' said Bull.

'The Bellinis might be out for revenge. Roberto has a big mouth and a small conscience. He could rat on me. I might have to move on someplace else.'

'With Garanov dead I thought we might be able to stop hiding,' Bull said.

'Would be good,' I said.

'I'll have a word tomorrow with your mother,' said Gus. 'He

wouldn't dare to go against her. It would be his inheritance down the drain. Roberto will see sense.'

The first courses started to arrive and the conversation dipped for a while as ten hungry people concentrated on food. I had a platter of smoked fish with a horseradish sauce that would have blown Garanov's head off more effectively than my bullet.

'I think Natasha and I will go to Italy,' Carlo said, finishing his plate of pâté and laying down his knife. 'Explore my roots. Then off to see Natasha's parents and ask her father for her hand in marriage. You're all invited to the wedding. You must be my best man, Johnny. I won't take no for an answer.'

'I'd be honoured,' I said. 'But you're entitled to think about it. No more impulsive decisions, OK?'

'All in the past,' he said. 'And Natasha will keep me on the straight and narrow.'

'You bet,' she said. 'I will be holding – how do you say – the purse strings. Is that right?'

'Very,' I said. I had a feeling that Carlo would be looked after without my intervention in the future. He had finally grown up.

Plates of steaks arrived for the men and some fish and chicken for the girls. Gus, against character, joined us in a steak.

'I'm sure your mother would get you a job in the bank,' he said to me. 'What about running the European business? Would be nice to have you based here in Amsterdam. We've been out of touch for too long. I don't want that to happen again.'

'Neither do I. But let's see what the situation is when the dust settles. It would be good to have the Bellinis off my back and not to be looking over my shoulder all the time.'

'You'd be bored,' he said. 'Going back to running the beach bar after all this. Admit it. You've loved it, haven't you?'

'Reckon so,' I said. 'How does it feel to be right all the time, Gus?'

'Not all the time,' he said. 'But I have no regrets for how my life has turned out.'

'Don't you get lonely, Uncle Gus?' said Carlo.

'Don't we all sometimes?' he said.

I looked across the table to the empty chair and nodded my agreement.

'More wine,' Gus said to the waitress, sensing the change of mood and trying to move on.

Stan, ever vigilant, sensed the mood, too.

'Did you here about the Russian who had a paper shop?' he said. 'It blew away.'

There was a chorus of groans. And the sound of a crash. The waitress, carrying desserts on a tray, saw it fly out of her hand and on to the floor. A figure behind her, unrepentant and unsteady on his feet, appeared out of the shadows and approached our table.

'Well, if it isn't little Gianni,' Roberto said. 'You're not a hard guy to track down. If you want to stay alive, you've got to be less predictable. Gus's favourite restaurant. Where else would you go for your triumphal procession?'

He was red-faced – through anger and booze, I suspected – unshaven as if he'd jumped on the first plane east. He was out of his depth here and didn't realize it. Or didn't care. He'd been too long bossing everyone around that it was hard to break the habit.

'You're drunk, Roberto,' I said. 'Let me get you a cab and take you to a hotel. Sleep it off. Go home.'

'Go home?' he said. 'What for? I've been sacked. No job, no prospects. And all because of you. It took me a while to figure out, then it came to me. You arrive in Amsterdam and all hell breaks loose. Why couldn't you leave well enough alone?'

'Because it's a bad world out there and someone has to do something about it.'

'Even if it means ruining your brother?'

'Stop exaggerating,' I said, 'and show some sense. You stick to the prepared story – Silvers ran a sting operation on the Bellinis – and none of the blame will be put down to you.' I thought about it some more. 'And what are you doing being so sanctimonious about everything? It was all your fault. You were the one who succumbed to the Bellinis. Took the profit out of greed. Now you've got to live with the consequences.'

'You had to stick your nose in, didn't you?' he said, swaying a little. 'All you had to do was find Carlo and get our money back. But you had to go another step further. And look where you've landed up. A crap little place for crap little people.'

Bull go up from the table and faced Roberto.

'Time to move on, friend. This is a private party and you weren't invited.'

The restaurant was quiet now. The other diners were conscious that something was going to happen and didn't want to be involved. It wasn't just our evening that Roberto was spoiling.

'We had a good operation,' Roberto said, 'and you had to spoil it.'

Pieter was the next to stand up. There was both him and Bull in front of Roberto now. Still he didn't take the hint.

'Come and face me, Johnny' he said. 'Don't hide behind the Neanderthals.'

How to win friends and influence people.

'I have you know that I am a Comanche brave, not a Neanderthal,' Red said. 'May Manitou rain his wrath on you.'

'You're not just facing one man,' Stan said, standing up. 'All for one and one for all.'

The candles flickered.

'Back off, Roberto,' I said. 'This is a fight you can't win. You can't bully your way through life anymore.'

'I'll second that,' said Carlo, standing up.

'*Et tu, Brute*,' he said. 'Mummy's little boy found some courage at last? You don't frighten me. None of you.'

'How about me, then?' a voice said.

Someone tapped Roberto on the shoulder. Whoever it was I couldn't see because the figure was blocked from my view by Roberto's bulk.

As he turned around a right hook hit him on the nose and he was sent reeling backwards. Bull caught him and laid him down on the floor. There was a round of applause from the other diners.

'Drinks for everyone,' shouted Gus.

'Sorry I'm late,' Anna said. 'But it seems I was just in time.'

'Now we are eleven,' I said.

I got up from my seat, walked around the table, stepping over Roberto in the process, and wrapped her in my arms. She hugged me tight.

'Sorry I was such a fool,' she said.

'Come and sit down,' I said. 'Have some champagne.'

I took a hundred euro note from my wallet and handed it to Bull.

'See if you can get Roberto a cab to the airport,' I said.

Bull took his feet and Red took his shoulders and together they carried him outside and laid him on to the pavement while waiting for a passing cab.

'What changed your mind?' I said to Anna.

'I got to thinking,' she said. 'I've done some bad things in my time. Most men would treat me like dirt, and maybe they'd be right. But it didn't matter to you. It was the Anna inside that you saw. If you can forgive, then it seemed like I should too. It's the Johnny inside that I love. I can see that now.'

'How do you fancy being a waitress at a beach bar in the Caribbean?'

'My previous job as a waitress didn't go too well.'

'Make that manageress then.'

'I'd do anything for you.'

'Maybe not anything,' I said.

'Maybe you're right.'

Gus blew his nose loudly and wiped his eyes.

'Must be the mustard,' he said.

33

I slept soundly that night. We slept soundly.

I was tempted to roll over when the alarm went off – I wasn't looking forward to saying the goodbyes.

Bull was the first to leave.

'See you in St Jude,' he said. 'And thanks for everything you've done. We'll have a party when we all get back from the States. You'll have given Michael a new life. Deserves a celebration.'

'Reckon so,' I said.

'Yeah,' he said, turning his back and walking out of the hotel. 'Reckon so.'

Red and Stan were sharing a cab to the airport.

'Let's all get together for a pow wow every year,' Red said.

'It's a date,' I said. 'And no more rodeos, eh?'

'Time for Comanche warrior to put on a new pair of moccasins and settle down with a squaw.'

He shook my hand and turned to Stan. 'Let's get out of here,' he said.

'Remember,' said Stan to me, 'expect the unexpected.'

He grinned.

That made two jokes in one day. One lifetime, maybe.

'Look after yourself,' I said. 'And I'll want an invite to that house by the sea.'

He nodded and followed Red out the door. They felt as I did about goodbyes. Get them over quickly and don't look back.

Carlo and Natasha left next. They were going to pick up his Lamborghini and head to Italy, first stop Rome.

'Thanks, Brother,' he said. 'Don't forget that promise about the wedding. I'll invite everyone and we can talk about old times.'

'You sound like you're married already,' I said.

Anna kissed Natasha on the cheek and so did I.

'Look after Carlo,' I said. 'He's your responsibility now. Keep him on a tight rein.'

'You can trust me,' she said.

'And me too,' Carlo added. 'The Carlo of old has gone for good.'

'Keep it that way,' I said. 'Now, get going before I forget I'm a grown man.'

Arnie and Scout had their bags in their hands.

'You'll get an invite to our wedding too,' Arnie said. 'I don't know what we'll do for excitement from now on.'

'I'll handle the excitement,' Scout said. 'Thanks, Johnny,' she said, kissing me.

'One question,' I said to her. 'What's your proper name?'

'You won't believe it,' she said, blushing, 'but it is actually Scout. My dad was a fan of the Lone Ranger. Was drunk when he registered my birth. If I'd been a boy I would have been called Tonto. Instead I was named after his horse.'

'Nothing wrong with that,' I said.

'Reckon so,' she replied.

That left only Pieter. He wasn't carrying a bag.

'I think I'll stick around for a while,' he said. 'Get to know the place better.'

'And the waitress,' I said.

'Good to know the old magic still works,' he said.

'Stay away from married women,' I said. 'Don't push your luck.'

I looked at my watch and saw it was time for my meeting with my mother. I kissed Anna goodbye and walked out on to the street. I was having second thoughts – was this a good move or not? Ignorance is bliss, they say. I'd soon see.

*

Mother had booked herself a suite at the Hilton. She'd spend today in Amsterdam dealing with the police, fly to New York in the morning and do the same and then back to London. Remarkable woman. She should never have passed the reins of the business to Roberto and Carlo – neither had her temperament nor her ability. Doomed to fail from the start.

The lounge area of the suite was decorated in neutral – nothing stood out, nor would offend. There was a dining table big enough for four and Mother, Gus and I sat around it drinking coffee.

'Went to plan then,' my mother said.

'A last-minute hitch, but we overcame it.'

'Gus told me Roberto turned up. Made a fool of himself.'

'He did that a long time ago,' I said.

She nodded. 'He and Carlo came close to ruining the business. Someone was bound to find out that the bank was being used to launder money. Then we would have lost everything. Once you lose your reputation you're finished in this business. I'm grateful to you, Gianni.'

'Glad to be of service.'

'There'll be a bit of a hiatus,' she said, 'while we bed in new staff. But Silvers will go on, although God knows what will happen when I go.'

'That'll be a while yet, Mother. Plenty of time to work out long-term solutions. And Gus will help. Lean on him and you won't go far wrong.'

She finished her coffee. 'Down to business,' she said.

My stomach churned.

'Tell me the truth,' I said. 'Don't hold anything back. I can take it.'

'Yes,' she said. 'I believe you can. Ironic that you should have turned out to be the best of my three sons. The only one who grew up without a father.'

'It made me independent and strong,' I said. 'Screwed up, but independent and strong.'

'Like some mythological figure from ancient Greece. Abandoned by the gods, but still becomes a hero and shames them.' She paused. Stared at the ceiling as if seeing past events projected there. 'Where to start? It took me a while,' she said, shaking her head, 'before I realized I married the wrong man. Roberto takes after Alfredo – they are both bullies and used to getting their own way. Maybe I was looking for someone who would relieve me of some of the pressure, someone who would take some of the burden from my shoulders. It wasn't easy running the business, especially when you want a normal life – a husband, home and a family.'

'Nothing wrong with that,' I said.

'Alfredo and me. Maybe doomed to fail from the start. Then there was no way out. The Catholic side disapproved of divorce and the Jewish side dreaded the slur on their family. The sham that the marriage had become had to continue. No way out.'

'So you found a diversion,' I said.

'No. I found a true love. Someone to bring some joy into my life.'

'Nothing wrong with that either,' I said. 'But then you became pregnant with me and something had to give. None of you could ignore the situation any longer.'

'I confessed to Alfredo and told him that I was having the baby, even though there would be complications. He thought he could cope with it, but every time he looked at you he saw the father and the shame. All we could do was keep packing you away to another boarding-school. Hide the shame, hide the blame.'

Much of this I had guessed already. It was the revelation of the father's name that I was interested in. But Mother had to tell the story her way and I had to be patient.

'It was agreed that I would break off the relationship and that we would try for another baby to seal our new commitment to each other. That baby was Carlo. That's why he was always spoilt – like we were spoiling ourselves, telling each other that everything was all right when in reality nothing much had changed.'

'Tell him,' Gus said. 'He's waited long enough.'

'So are you finally going to tell me the name of my father?'

'Better than that. I'm going to let you speak to him.'

She took out her mobile phone, pressed a couple of buttons and passed it to me.

'Press send,' she said.

'And that will be my father?'

'That will be your father.'

I took the phone from her and hesitated. Did I really want to go through with this? Would the voice on the other end of the phone coincide with my fantasy or would it lead to a whole new disappointment in the cards that life had dealt me?

'What do I say?' I asked.

'How about "Hi Dad"?' Mother said. 'He's waiting for your call.

Strange that I had been prepared on more occasions than I dared to remember to throw myself into the lion's den and here was I showing cowardice in the face of a mobile phone. Didn't make sense, but sometimes that's the way of life. I pressed the send button.

There was a silence in the room. I could hear my heart beating. Then that silence was shattered by a strange sound. A tinny ringtone. Gus took a mobile from his pocket.

'Hi, Son,' he said.

I sat there stunned, speechless, unmoving. Finally I recovered enough to walk round the table and give Gus – Father now – a big bear hug. Now I could feel his heart beat. I brushed away a tear.

'Excuse my sense of humour,' Mother said.

'Nice to know that someone in this family has one,' I said.

I stopped hugging Gus. Pushed him away, stepped back and looked at him deeply.

'But you can't be,' I said. 'You're—'

'My penance,' he interrupted. 'Bad enough for Alfredo to be cuckolded, but to be cuckolded by his brother. . . .'

'I didn't just marry the wrong man,' Mother said. 'I married the wrong brother.'

'I don't understand,' I said. 'Do you mean to say all this time I've been trying to find out who my father was and there he was right in front of me?'

'There was an agreement with Alfredo,' Mother said. 'Because of the state of our marriage he knew the baby couldn't have been his – we'd been sleeping in separate rooms for a while back then. I owned up as to who your father was, we had a family meeting and Gus agreed to go into exile – just as you would do years later. He left Silvers, was given a generous payoff and told to keep his distance. He was, however, allowed to see you from time to time. That was to be the closest he would come to being a father.'

Gus broke in. 'So as to be especially sure that if the truth came out that you were illegitimate no one would suspect me of being your father, I agreed to play the gay role.'

'What about Carlo?' I asked. I felt like history was being rewritten before my very eyes. 'He is Alfredo's son, isn't he?'

'After you were born,' Mother said, 'Alfredo and I tried to make the marriage work. We conceived Carlo as a sealing of our differences and our problems. Carlo was to be our new start. That's why he's always been spoilt.'

'I need a drink,' I said.

Funny that when I was aiming that bullet at Garanov my hands were steady: now they were shaking. I walked over to the minibar and took out a small bottle of vodka and drank it straight down.

'Should be champagne,' Gus said. 'Or are you disappointed?'

'God, no,' I said. 'I couldn't have wished for more. It's just there's now a void. Something I have thought about for so many years has gone. I need to readjust my thinking. What are we going to do?'

'See more of each other for one,' said Gus.

'But you mustn't tell anybody,' said Mother. 'I promised Alfredo that I would never reveal the truth. I've broken that vow and you must now take it up. None outside us three must know.'

'The secret is safe with me. I'm going back to St Jude with Anna. You must both come and visit. We've been too long apart.'

'I'll come when the mess at Silvers is sorted out,' said Mother. 'I'll need a holiday by then.'

'And I'll come in a month or so,' said Gus, 'stay at the hotel. You and Anna need some time together first. And some space. But I promise you we'll get to know each other properly at last.'

'Reckon so,' I said, smiling.

34

St Jude – six months later

'Sit down,' I said to Anna.

'It's a baby,' she said. 'Not an unexploded bomb. I don't need to be kept in cotton wool. Now sit down, the pair of you, and I'll bring you some coffee and water.'

Bull and I had just finished our daily run and swim. We sat down outside the rebuilt bar, drying ourselves in the sun. It was twice the size of the old one and had the works – big espresso coffee-maker, machine for squeezing oranges and other fruits into juice, gigantic ice maker, a separate kitchen for a more adventurous menu and a big generator to run it all. We had a house now too. Single-storey, two bedrooms and right by the sea. Views to die for. And on top of all that we were ecstatically happy. There was nothing more I could wish for.

'Kinda quiet,' Bull said as we sipped our coffee.

'Like going cold turkey from a drug addiction, only in our case the drug is adrenalin.'

'Amsterdam certainly spiced up our lives.'

'Would you do the same sort of thing again?' I asked.

'Hell, no,' he said. 'Leave here, island paradise, Mai Ling and Michael for some cheap hotel and chance to be shot at? What do you think?'

Something in his tone told me he wasn't convinced by his own argument.

'Me neither,' I said. 'Time to settle down and enjoy the fruits of our labour.'

'Still, is kinda quiet though.'

I looked at Anna, bronzed and hair bleached a golden blonde by the sun. Her long legs were tanned and accentuated by what you could see through the slit of the sarong. The T-shirt couldn't hide her curves either. I'm sure some of the customers only came here to gaze wistfully at her. Still, good for business. She was three months' pregnant now. Seemed like a long time to go.

My mobile rang. I'd left it behind the bar while we went for our exercise. Anna answered it. Frowned, walked across the sand and handed it to me.

'It's Red,' she said.

I said hello and listened intently while the words tumbled out. He sounded serious, none of the Comanche-warrior stuff intruding into his speech.

'I'll get back to you,' I said.

Anna sat down between me and Bull.

'What did he want?' she asked.

'Something about running into some bad men. I wasn't really paying attention.'

'I noticed,' she said.

'Talked about needing some help.'

'And he did come when you called,' she said.

'He said Stan had agreed to go – yet to contact Pieter. Maybe the two or three of them can sort it out.'

'Maybe,' she said.

'So what do you think? Should I go?'

She looked at me a gave a big grin.

'Reckon so,' she said.